All rig
associa

The moral right of the author has been asserted (vigorously).

No part or parts of this publication may be reproduced in whole or in part, stored in a retrieval systems, or transmitted in any form or by means, electronic, mechanical, photocopying, recording, or otherwise (including via carrier pigeon), without written permission of the author and publisher.

Author: **Crumley**, M.M.
Title: THE IMMORTAL DOC HOLLIDAY, ROGUES
ISBN:9798764302225
Target Audience: Adult
Also available in this series
THE IMMORTAL DOC HOLLIDAY: HIDDEN (Book 1)
THE IMMORTAL DOC HOLLIDAY: COUP D'ÉTAT (Book 2)
THE IMMORTAL DOC HOLLIDAY: RUTHLESS (Book 3)
THE IMMORTAL DOC HOLLIDAY: INSTINCT (Book 4)

Subjects:
Urban Fantasy/ Horror Comedy

This is a work of fiction, which means it's made up. Names, characters, peoples, locales, and incidents (stuff that happens in the story) are either gifts of the ether, products of the author's resplendent imagination or are used fictitiously, and any resemblance to actual persons, living or dead or dying, businesses or companies in operation or defunct, events, or locales is entirely coincidental.

Also by **M.M. Crumley**
Urban Fantasy

THE IMMORTAL DOC HOLLIDAY SERIES

BOOK 1: HIDDEN
BOOK 2: COUP D'ÉTAT
BOOK 3: RUTHLESS
BOOK 4: INSTINCT
BOOK 5: ROGUES
BOOK 6: EMPIRE
BOOK 7: OMENS
BOOK 8: CHASM
BOOK 9: FERAL
BOOK 10: OBLIVION
BOOK 11: RELENTLESS
BOOK 12: REQUIEM
BOOK 13: HELLION
BOOK 14: SHADOWS

THE LEGEND OF ANDREW RUFUS SERIES

BOOK 1: DARK AWAKENING
BOOK 2: BONE DEEP
BOOK 3: BLOOD STAINED
BOOK 4: BURIAL GROUND
BOOK 5: DEATH SONG
BOOK 6: FUNERAL MARCH
BOOK 7: WARPATH

THE HOUSE OF GRAVES SERIES

BOOK 1: THREE LITTLE GRAVES & THE BIG BAD WOLF
BOOK 2: OVER THE RIVER & THROUGH THE WOOD
BOOK 3: FIRE BURN & CAULDRON BUBBLE

Writing as **M.M. Boulder**
Psych Thrillers

THE LAST DOOR
MY BETTER HALF
THE HOUSE THAT JACK BUILT
MY ONE AND ONLY
WE ALL FALL DOWN

www.facebook.com/m.m.crumley
www.mmcrumley.com

Book 5:
ROGUES

M.M. Crumley

For my readers...

For your support, your encouraging comments, your time, and for saying "more, more, give us more"!

No you; no me.

Thank you.

Character List

Doc Holliday: our intrepid hero

Thomas Jury (witch): Doc's friend

Jervis (vampire): Doc's friend & Dulcis's manager

Señora Teodora / Tozi: the shaman who "turned" Doc

Thaddeus or Thaddy Whythe: Doc's talking plant

Ahanu/Grey Shaman (shaman): Meli's brother, Doc owes him a favor

Aine (banshee): Bree's daughter & owner of the House of Banshee

Ana & Ina Zaitsev (vampires): sisters from Russia

Andrew Rufus (norm): Doc's friend from the past

Apollo: Bluegrass's sentient house

Baker Children—Johnny, Jules, Addison (witches)

Bennie (Worm): go-to guy

Bluegrass Goodhunt (shaman): Doc's friend

Boudica (witch hound)

Bree (banshee): Doc's adopted daughter

Cynric Jury (witch): Drustan Jury's brother, was just a head in book 3

Doyle (norm): Andrew's friend

Dublin O'Connell (wolf shifter): Doc's friend, owner of Wolf Club

Edgar Achaean (norm): Appointed One, Doc killed in book 3

Eloise (ogre): Doc gave Brad and Tami to her in book 2

Emily (Myhanava): works for Dulcis

Francisco (norm): Doc's real-life adopted brother

Frankie (norm) Baker children's babysitter

Graven Birch (Takaheni): leader of the United States Council

James (vampire): works for Dulcis

Janey Falke (norm): Doc's friend from the past, also Andrew's wife

Julian LaRoche (Roma): Sydney's son

Kaylee, Kylie, Kinsey (witches): triplets

Lydia (norm): girl Doc took from bar in book 4
Meli/Black Shaman (shaman): Andrew's nemesis
Phillip and Abigail Jury (witches): Jury's parents
Pierre (norm): chef at Dulcis
Sagena Redgrove (Takaheni): Simon's sister
Sami Caruso (norm): Jury's manager
Simon Redgrove (Takaheni): Hidden businessman
Sydney LaRoche (Roma): owns charm store in Hidden
Tetrarch Mitcham (Zeniu): tetrarch of the Hidden
Winks (gargoyle): tiny gargoyle of Jury's

1

Doc Holliday tapped his fingers irritably on the hood of his borrowed car. He was so sick of waiting. Granted, he'd only been standing here for an hour, but an hour was much too long. If he leaned on the car very much longer he might dent it, and that wouldn't be very considerate. He had every intention of returning the car when he was done with it.

He sighed and restrained his desire to pull out his cards and start shuffling. If Andrew caught sight of the pin-up girls on the cards, it would be a dead giveaway. And Ahanu, sneaky shaman that he was, had specifically warned Doc that if he screwed this up, he screwed up everything.

I should just go, he thought, glancing at the house one last time and jerking slightly when the door cracked open. Doc had to fight not to lean forward anxiously; instead he forced his body to maintain its casual pose.

A young man stepped out onto the porch and closed the door behind him. He wasn't as tall or as broad as he would be when Doc met him, but he was definitely Andrew. Same alert movements, same air of thrumming power.

Doc pulled out his phone and pretended to look at it, but he was really watching Andrew walk past from the corner of his eye. How he wished they were in a different time. How he wished he could greet Andrew, listen to one of his ridiculous jokes, ride into battle with him.

He felt a surge of sorrow, knowing this was the last time. The final goodbye. The end. He'd never see Andrew ever again. He was already dead.

"Hey, kid," Doc said, moving away from his car and pretending to pick something up off the sidewalk. "You dropped this."

Andrew turned slowly, cautious eyes searching Doc's face. Doc grinned blandly, and Andrew's eyes dropped to the twenty dollar bill Doc was offering him. "It's not mine," Andrew said, eyes narrow.

"Pretty sure it is," Doc shrugged. "I saw it fall out of your pocket. Anyway, I don't need it, so you can have it."

Doc practically held his breath, waiting for Andrew to take it, hoping he would. He'd written "I owe you, Doc" on it, and someday he imagined Andrew might read it.

With a shrug, Andrew took the bill and slipped it into his pocket. He turned to leave, but paused by Doc's car. "Is that a Ferrari?" he asked.

"It surely is," Doc chuckled.

"It's pretty cool." Andrew said with a crooked grin, and somehow Doc knew what he was thinking. He was thinking, "My horse can beat it."

"You're right," Doc said with a laugh, slipping into the driver's seat. "He absolutely could." Doc revved the engine and was gone before Andrew could say another word.

"Did not exactly toe the line, did you?"

"I don't know what you're talking about," Doc replied.

"And it's a terrible idea to zap into people's cars when they're driving."

"You are still on the road," Ahanu said evenly.

"I nearly ran into that mailbox," Doc countered.

"You did not even twitch."

"But I wanted to," Doc retorted. "Only years of self-control kept us from dying."

Ahanu snorted and began to light his pipe.

"No!" Doc snapped. "Not in my car."

"I can make it smokeless," Ahanu offered. "And furthermore, it is not your car."

"It is right now; put it away."

Ahanu sighed, "Fine. I allowed you to see him. What now?"

"How the hell should I know?" Doc growled. "This whole thing is insane, and your timing could literally not be worse." Ahanu chuckled at that, and Doc fought the urge to punch him. "Unless, of course," Doc ground out, "you know something I don't."

"There are many futures," Ahanu said vaguely. "You just have to pick one."

"But I have to pick the right one?"

"Naturally."

"And how am I supposed to do that if you don't steer me in the right direction?" Doc questioned.

"I suppose we will just have to hope that your quintessential nature will guide you," Ahanu replied.

Doc sighed and pondered the upcoming onramp. He could plow the car into a semi-truck, cause a pileup, and maybe kill them both. Except Ahanu was invincible, so he'd just walk away, and Doc would have destroyed a perfectly good Ferrari for no reason.

Doc zipped between two cars, pulled into the left lane, and pressed the gas pedal all the way to the floor.

"The speed limit is not merely a suggestion, you know," Ahanu said thinly.

"Sure it is," Doc replied, pleased to see that Ahanu's jaw was tight. "And anyway, you could just zap us there."

"'Zap' is a truly derogatory term," Ahanu retorted. "What I do requires—"

He broke off as Doc squeezed between a semi-truck and a van, slammed his brakes, pulled back into the left lane, tailgated the car in front of him until it moved, then shifted into sixth, and zoomed past several cars.

"Enough," Ahanu ground out.

For once Doc was unable to control his outright shock as both the car and the interstate completely disappeared.

"My car!" he gasped.

"It is fine," Ahanu said dismissively. "I returned it to its owner."

"You mean you zapped it," Doc mocked.

"I am about to 'zap' you," Ahanu said irritably.

The ground solidified beneath Doc's feet, and he sighed. They were back at the cabin. The one room cabin. With no running water, no silk sheets, and no way to escape. The same cabin he and Jury had been sitting in for the last two days. A grey cabin in the middle of a grey forest, surrounded by grey mists.

"If I could do it again," Doc muttered as he sat beside Jury and yanked the whiskey bottle from Jury's hand. "I would kill everyone Mitcham asked me to."

"No, you wouldn't," Jury sighed. "I've run through it a million times in my mind, and every time we end up here."

"I hate here," Doc grumbled.

"It is a tad... wearing," Jury agreed, glancing around the cabin with a caged expression.

"I thought you liked the woods," Doc retorted as he drank the rest of the bottle, then took Jury's coffee as well.

"Yeah." Jury glanced nervously at the door. "Where's Ahanu?"

"How the hell should I know?"

Jury's eyes darted around the room, and then he whispered "These woods aren't... right."

"Right how?"

"I don't know. They're... frozen?"

Doc raised an eyebrow. "Exactly how much whiskey did you drink before I got here?"

"No, seriously," Jury hissed. "It's not dead or living. It's neither. There aren't any... I can't... I'm like human," he said, tone a little desperate.

"That's not possible," Doc snorted. "Is it?"

"I don't know." Jury got up to pour them more coffee. "I think... God, I feel crazy just saying it," he said as he sat back down. "I think we're out of time."

"I think we knew that," Doc said. "By now there are probably wanted posters all over the Hidden."

"No, no," Jury interrupted. "I mean out of time! Outside of time. Not in time!"

"What?" Unfortunately, Doc knew exactly what Jury was trying to say; he just wished he didn't.

"Like we were in time, and now we're out. We're not in the past or the future; we're like... time adjacent." Jury met Doc's eyes and said, "That makes no sense. Even I know that doesn't make sense."

"If only," Doc muttered.

"If only what?" Ahanu asked from the doorway.

"If only I'd never met you," Doc smirked.

"That truly hurts," Ahanu said with a short chuckle. His pipe was already smoking, and a large grey smoke ring drifted lazily towards the ceiling. "This is not the first time I have gotten you out of trouble, hence why you owe me."

Doc sighed. "You haven't gotten me out of anything; all you did was move me. The trouble is still there; in fact, you've probably made it worse."

"Definitely made it worse," Jury chipped in.

"These things happen," Ahanu said dismissively.

"Goddamn, just tell me what you want from me, and I'll do it!" Doc exclaimed.

"I already did."

"Fine. You want me to wake the Black Shaman. How? Where is she? When?"

"You will figure something out. You will have to find her. Anytime within the next three months."

Doc's eyebrow twitched. Which made him absolutely furious. His eyebrows never twitched without his express permission.

"If I didn't know that Andrew still needs you, I'd kill you right this minute," Doc snarled.

"I'm invincible," Ahanu laughed.

"I would find a way. Are you seriously not going to give me anything more than that?"

"I suppose not."

Doc clenched the coffee cup and felt it crack in his hand.

"I just filled that," Jury muttered.

"If you're not going to help us, why exactly are we here?" Doc demanded.

"I thought you might like some time to regroup," Ahanu replied, lips turned up in a sly smile.

"If I agree to do this," Doc said sharply, "are we square? I will never see you again?"

"Most likely."

"I can't do it," Doc muttered. "I have to kill him. It's the only way."

"Just remember," Ahanu said cheerfully. "Three months."

Ahanu was gone before Doc could strangle him, and then Doc and Jury were standing in the middle of a sidewalk, just a stone's throw from Union Station.

"I absolutely hate him," Doc ground out.

Jury didn't respond, and when Doc glanced at him, he had a goofy smile on his face and his hands were glowing.

"Put that away!" Doc snapped. "We're in the middle of the goddamn street."

"I don't care," Jury responded happily. "You have no idea what it felt like. I don't ever want to feel that way again." The blue glow around his hands flared, and Jury laughed out loud, drawing several people's attention.

Doc smiled widely and announced, "Sorry, folks. He's testing out a new invention. Rave hands." Doc wiggled his hands in the air and winked at them.

They all stared at Doc for a brief second before dropping their eyes to the sidewalk once more and hurrying past.

"I love humanity," Doc murmured. "We better get out of here." He headed down the street toward Dulcis, pausing when his phone beeped. And beeped. And beeped.

Doc pulled out his phone and stared at the screen. He had thirteen hundred and twelve messages. Which was really strange. He tapped on Jervis's name.

The first message read, "You had better be dead, because if you're just ignoring me, I'm going to kill you."

That's a little unlike Jervis, Doc thought as he scrolled

through the messages, frowning when he saw there were hundreds of messages just from Jervis, spanning...

"Oh hell," Doc whispered.

"What?"

"I hate Ahanu."

"You said that," Jury replied.

"But I hate him more than I did a minute ago."

"Okay?"

"You know how we've only been gone two days?" Doc asked.

"Yeah?"

"Turns out we've actually been gone eight months."

"No way..." Jury breathed.

"Yes, and by now... Well, I don't really know what will have happened, but one thing I can say for sure is that Jervis is going to flay me alive."

"Well, that's... Goddamn," Jury stuttered. "Mitcham's going to... I don't... Oh hell. We're totally fucked."

2

"You really think Mitcham's still watching the hotel?" Jury asked as they walked casually towards Dulcis's revolving front door.

"He strikes me as the kind of man who carries a grudge," Doc replied.

"So yes?"

"Yes."

"I wish Ahanu had fed me something other than jerky and dried fruit," Jury grumbled. "You know, if we'd taken a taxi instead of walking I wouldn't have had to hold these damn glamours for so long."

"Quit complaining," Doc replied. "We're almost there."

Doc caught sight of Jervis as soon as they were inside the lobby, and he immediately noticed the tension in Jervis's frame. A tension that wasn't generally there.

When Jervis's eyes met his, Doc nodded his head slightly, then said with a slow drawl, "Perhaps you can help me, sir. I have a standing reservation under the name Eric Young."

Jervis's eyes lit with immediate recognition, but he

controlled all his mannerisms, gave a short bow, and said, "Of course, sir. Please follow me."

They stepped into the elevator, and Jervis pressed the button for the sub-subbasement. They didn't speak as they rode the elevator down or as they walked through the short hallway. They didn't speak until they were inside the room.

"What is this place?" Jury asked, only letting the glamours drop as the door closed behind them.

"Just bits and pieces of the past," Jervis replied before turning to Doc and demanding, "And where exactly have you been?"

"Before you kill me, let me explain," Doc said, holding up his hands in surrender. "You remember me telling you about Ahanu, right? The Grey Shaman, timey wimey? Anyway, he took us, and we were only gone two days. I swear it was just two days. But it appears as if Ahanu returned us to a slightly different time," Doc finished tentatively.

"Slightly different?" Jervis replied coldly. "It's been eight months."

"But I didn't know that," Doc insisted.

"You would not believe what I've gone through," Jervis stated. "Between dealing with Mitcham and searching for you. I can't believe..." He trailed off and breathed deeply, controlling his anger.

"Sorry?" Doc said.

"I hate it when he does that," Jury said from his position on the fainting couch. "The least he could do is say it with a straight face. I mean, he lies all the time."

"Shut up," Doc said wearily.

"I'm hungry," Jury complained.

"Get some food then."

"I'm a wanted man in a basement," Jury pointed out.

"Use one of your hole thingys."

"Hole thingys? It's a... Well... It's a... Never mind," Jury muttered.

Doc turned back to Jervis and said, "Look, I'm sorry. I didn't mean... Anyway..."

Jervis shrugged stiffly, and Doc figured that was the most he was going to get in the way of forgiveness.

"So where are we at?" Doc asked.

"Three million merlin bounty."

"Goddamn," Doc hissed. "That's a little higher than usual. Mitcham's pretty upset then?"

Jervis's lips turned up fractionally. "Indeed. He attempted to seize all your assets and was very disappointed when he found you don't have any."

"He obviously has no idea how long I've been at this," Doc chuckled. "Did he cause you any trouble?"

"Of course not," Jervis said dismissively. "Since Dulcis isn't part of the Hidden, there really wasn't much they could do. They acquired a norm search warrant, which allowed them to comb through our records and search your suite, but that was all they managed."

"Did they find anything of importance?" Doc asked, thinking of his safes.

"No."

"Good." Doc paced for a minute, then asked, "Did you find a home for Lydia?"

Jervis snorted. "Yes; and I gave myself a raise."

"You deserve it. Is she alright?"

"She's actually adjusting quite well. The LaRoches took her."

"What?!" Doc exclaimed.

"Apparently Mrs. LaRoche always wanted a girl."

"And you just let them have her?! They're con artists!"

"Technically," Jervis argued, "since their artifacts are genuine, they aren't. They just exploit situations for their own personal gain."

"Exactly! Not the kind of people I want raising Lydia!"

"She seems quite happy," Jervis said softly. "And you know I would have never let them have her if I thought they would hurt her."

Doc glared at Jervis, but it was true. Most of the time he trusted Jervis more than he trusted himself.

"I need whiskey," Doc mumbled, rubbing his head.

"Catch!" Jury called out.

Doc glanced up, caught the whiskey bottle sailing through the air, pulled out the cork, and took a swig. "If I can't kill him, maybe I can tie him to a rock or something."

"Mitcham?" Jervis asked.

"No," Doc sighed. "Ahanu."

"Based on what you've told me," Jervis mused, "I'm quite certain that wouldn't work."

"Fine, whatever. Forget Ahanu. What am I going to do about Mitcham?"

"What you always do."

"And that is?"

"Figure it out."

"Thank you, Jervis," Doc drawled. "I cannot tell you how absolutely helpful that was."

"You're quite welcome."

Doc rubbed his head again. He needed a nap. And a shaman-killing artifact. And a dead tetrarch. But since he couldn't have any of that...

"Could you just tell me what's happened since we left?" Doc asked.

"Certainly," Jervis replied. "Mitcham put out a warrant for your arrest. Any Hidden citizen with any information regarding your whereabouts will be rewarded with ten thousand merlins; anyone who brings you in will be rewarded with three million merlins."

"Just me? Or both of us?"

"Mr. Jury's bounty is set at one million."

"That's it?" Jury exclaimed. "Why?"

"I couldn't possibly say," Jervis replied.

"Never mind that," Doc said. "What else?"

"It appears that you were in league with Bosch," Jervis went on. "However, the official story is that you had a falling out and you brought the Acolytes back to life and Achaean was your puppet. You kidnapped the Jurys for nefarious means, but they defeated you. And your hatred of all cryptids is leading you to try to utterly destroy the Hidden. Anyone caught aiding you will be imprisoned, tried, and executed if found guilty."

"Ah. Is that all?" Doc asked witheringly.

"No," Jervis said. "They interviewed all your known associates, including Dublin and his family, Bree, Ana, Aine, Bennie... Well, it's a rather long list."

Doc stopped himself from demanding to know if Bree and Aine were all right; Jervis would have told him immediately if they weren't.

All in all, it was nothing less than he'd expected, but he still wanted to kill Mitcham really, really slowly for messing with both his reputation and his family. He hated politicians.

"I guess I better figure out a plan," Doc said, sitting beside Jury. "In the meantime, do you have any ideas on how to track down a dead shaman?"

"Fully dead or mostly dead?" Jervis inquired.

"Um... Mostly?"

"No."

"Fully?"

"No."

"Then why did it matter?" Doc snapped.

"I was just working it out."

"Go away," Doc sighed. "I need to think."

"Certainly," Jervis said tightly, turning and heading towards the door.

"Jervis?"

"Yes?"

"I really am sorry. I should've made Ahanu contact you right away. He just... Well, what he wants me to do..." Doc sighed. "I just wasn't thinking."

"I'm just glad to see you alive," Jervis said without turning around.

As soon as Jervis was gone, Jury snapped, "I never get a real apology."

"We've been friends a hundred years now," Doc chuckled. "I'm sure I've apologized to you at least once or twice."

"Not without a question mark."

Doc rolled his eyes. "We have bigger things to deal with right now."

"You could at least say you're sorry for never saying you're sorry," Jury grumbled.

"Sorry?"

"Goddamn it, Doc!"

"Sorry? I mean, sorry."

"You're such an ass," Jury mumbled. "This is all your fault."

"That is... true. And I am sorry," Doc said slowly.

Jury didn't lift his eyes from his sandwich, but he grinned. "Thanks."

"Don't mention it. Ever. Now we have two problems. Mitcham and the Black Shaman."

"No," Jury said around a bite. "I only have one problem. You have two problems."

"Really?" Doc demanded.

"Really."

Doc took a deep breath and ground out, "Fine. But you will at least help me with Mitcham?"

"I guess. I really don't understand why your bounty is so much higher than mine."

"You don't get that at all?" Doc asked flatly.

"No. I'm a witch!" Jury snapped. "I'm much more dangerous than you."

"Is that so?"

Jury threw his sandwich onto his plate with a disgusted hiss. "Why can't you ever let me have it? Just once I'd like to be the one listed first on the wanted poster!"

"You cannot be serious right now!" Doc snapped.

Jury shrugged.

"I don't believe you," Doc said. "It's not like I set the damn bounty. Next time, you do the talking and maybe you'll be first."

"That's what you always say," Jury grumbled.

"Just shut the hell up!" Doc commanded. "I need to think, and I can't do it with all your whining."

"Whining?!"

"Yes, whining!"

"Fuck you!" Jury yelled, jumping to his feet. "Every single time, it's all about you! I never get any credit or any glory. It's always 'Doc Holliday this', 'Doc Holliday that'. And I'm fucking sick of it!"

He picked up one of Doc's unopened whiskey bottles and

hurled it against the wall. Doc flinched as it burst and golden liquid ran down onto the floor.

"I'm surprised Ahanu didn't just leave me standing on Mitcham's doorstep," Jury snarled. "He didn't want me; he only wanted you. 'The infamous Doc Holliday'. 'Always honors his favors Holliday'. He didn't say a word to me. Not ONE WORD!!!"

"I—"

"No! I don't want another one of your half-ass apologies! I mean, what can't Doc Holliday do? He saved the Hidden from Bosch, from Achaean; he saves orphans and widows; he even managed to save me from my own family! You're a fucking paragon of heroism!" Doc opened his mouth to argue, but Jury cut him off once more. "Shut up! I'm not interested in a goddamn thing you have to say right now."

Doc stared at Jury in shock as he turned and stormed towards the door. "Where're you going?" Doc demanded.

"Anywhere but here!" Jury threw back.

"Fine! Just don't expect me to break you out of jail!" Doc snapped.

"As if I need you!"

The door slammed behind Jury, and Doc glared at it irritably. "Good riddance," he muttered.

He waited for a moment, curious to see if Jury would come back, and when he didn't, he sighed. "Now I have three problems. Mitcham, a crazy devil shaman, and how to make Jury feel needed. No big deal. I captured and humiliated eighteen of the most powerful witches in the world. This should be easy."

He didn't believe himself for a moment, and that wasn't good. When you started lying to yourself, you were in big trouble.

Doc sat there for hours, just staring at the wall and wondering what to do next. He devised and promptly discarded a hundred different scenarios. The problems were too big; and he honestly had no idea where to start.

Furthermore, Boudica was making it very hard to focus because she was sulking in a corner casting pouty glares at him every few seconds.

"It wasn't my fault," Doc sighed for the seventeenth time. "Ahanu doesn't exactly ask me before he does things. He's annoying like that."

She turned away with a snort.

"You're not even my dog," he tried to point out. "You belong to Jury; you should be mad at him."

The look she gave him was so filled with hurt he had to look away.

"Goddamn it," he muttered. "Now I have four problems. If you count dogs, which I don't."

Boudica snarled.

"Fine. I count dogs, but first things first," he said. "I need to build a case against Mitcham to present to the council because otherwise when I kill him I'll still be wanted."

He emptied another whiskey bottle and tossed it over his shoulder. If he was honest, he was feeling a tad apathetic about the whole thing. He didn't even belong in the Hidden. Why should he be the one to dethrone Mitcham?

"Jury's a witch," he mumbled. "He belongs to the Hidden. He should take care of it. His family should take care of it." But they wouldn't, and he knew they wouldn't. And if no one else would do it, why should he care?

Doc hadn't even met Mitcham, or had any opinion about him whatsoever, until the day he and Jury had saved him from Bosch. Which brought him back to point one. If everyone in the Hidden hated Mitcham so much, why didn't they just revolt or, better yet, elect someone else? Why did they just freeze when Mitcham was mentioned and get that strange, terrified look in their eyes?

He suddenly remembered Emily's stilted words when they'd been in the car together and he'd asked her about Mitcham. Instead of speaking a single word about the tetrarch, she'd merely said, "I like my job, sir, and I'm paid very well."

And Simon's words about Mitcham. "I can say nothing against him." A very carefully phrased statement.

Sydney's horror at realizing he'd implied Mitcham was a difficult customer.

Thane's outright disgust at the mere mention of Mitcham.

Doc closed his eyes and replayed his first real conversation with Simon. "Each country has its own version of the Hidden, with its own governmental system," Simon had explained. "But all of the Hiddens are under Tetrarch Mitcham's leadership."

That didn't make much sense because the Hiddens were all very different. One man couldn't possibly rule them all, at least not well or fairly. And how had Mitcham even gained that control in the first place?

In his mind, Doc flipped through Julian's folder on the Baudelaires. The Baudelaires were deeply entrenched with Mitcham. Perhaps Mitcham had used their unscrupulous magic to somehow gain control. But to what end? What was his ultimate purpose? Did Mitcham have a plan besides ruling the Hiddens?

He suddenly remembered Mitcham's strange front door, and those disturbing scenes that were engraved in the wood swirled in his mind. He still couldn't figure them out, just knew they bothered him. The Zeniu had a violent and bloody history, but as far as Doc understood, they had left those ways behind hundreds of years ago when they'd realized they could use their persuasive power in more civilized ways.

It was rather difficult for them to blend in, this was true, but they had had their ways. Sometimes the priest behind the curtain in confession. Sometimes the face behind the speakeasy door. Sometimes just a shadow in the dark convincing a passing pedestrian to leave behind his wallet.

Their persuasive skills were legendary, which was half of the reason Doc had never cared for Zenius in the first place. As far as he was concerned, persuasiveness and compulsion were just two different shirts cut from the exact same cloth.

Doc tapped his fingers on the empty bottle in his hand. He wasn't going to solve anything from the basement. He needed information, but no one was willing to talk. He supposed he could take his dental tools along; that was sometimes encouraging. But he wasn't trying to make more enemies; he already had plenty of those.

He texted Jervis. "I'm going out, but Jury's not helping me right now, so I'm going to need the kit."

"I'll bring it right down, sir."

Doc stood and paced the room impatiently. He felt a bit like a rat in a cage, and he didn't like it. Mitcham had him backed into a corner because he wanted Doc to kill people at his bidding, and Ahanu had Doc backed into a different corner because he wanted Doc to wake up an evil, blood-drinking demon. That was two too many corners to be in.

The door swung open, and Jervis entered, rolling a large suitcase behind him. "Are you sure this is the best course of action?" he asked.

"No," Doc replied. "Do you have any better ideas?"

"None that you will listen to, I'm sure," Jervis said dryly.

"Try me."

"You could spend some time on that little island in the Caribbean; after all, it's not really your problem."

Doc considered that for a moment. "I could."

"But?"

"Goddamn it, Jervis! If I don't do it, who will?"

"Does anyone need to?" Jervis questioned.

"I don't know," Doc sighed. "I guess I'll find out, won't I? Somehow... I mean Mitcham... He bothers me. I don't know if it's just because he's a Zeniu. You know how I feel about compulsion."

"Technically..." Jervis began to say.

"Same difference," Doc interrupted. "He bothers me in a way very few people do, but if I discover everything's copacetic and that my gut is wrong, then I'll grab an umbrella and head to the beach."

"Good enough. Now it's been awhile since we've done this so I have quite a few more style options. Personally I think you should try punk. Or," Jervis mused, tilting his head thoughtfully, "goth. They'd never expect that."

"You have pictures?" Doc asked.

"Of course." Jervis handed him a folder, and Doc flipped through it.

"This one," Doc finally said.

"Grunge?"

"It looks... the least difficult."

"You'll need to shave," Jervis said. "While you do that, I'll find the appropriate clothes."

Doc walked to the mirror and stared at his angular face. This was one of those moments. One of those moments that would change his life forever; he could feel it. How it would change it, he couldn't say.

He laughed softly, remembering another world changing moment. The mirror blurred, and Doc drifted into a memory. He and Jury were in Mexico, doing nothing of importance, just gambling, drinking, and enjoying the company of fine women. To tell the truth, it wasn't very different from New Orleans except the bars served tequila instead of watered-down beer.

"You might want to go easy on those," Doc suggested as Jury tossed back another shot of tequila. "You're not much for hard liquor."

"Mother would die if she knew what I was doing," Jury laughed. "I mean, look! I'm sitting with commoners!"

"Do you listen to yourself?" Doc asked with a heavy sigh.

"What?"

"Commoners?"

"Well they are."

"So were all the people in New Orleans," Doc pointed out.

"Yes, but I was doing that to spite my parents. Now I'm just... living."

"I see," Doc drawled. "I think you've already had one too many. Let's get you back to the cabana."

"We should go down to the water," Jury said excitedly.

"You know what they say," Doc chuckled. "Never go swimming drunk."

"I'm not drunk!" Jury insisted. "I've never felt better. You want to see something amazing? Even more amazing than Andrew doing whatever it is he does." Jury's face twisted with resentment when he mentioned Andrew. "What is he anyway?" he asked irritably. "How does he do all that? I don't think there's a classification for him, but that doesn't make sense. Everything is classified. Witch, troll, sprite, Takaheni, Lutin, banshee..."

Jury kept talking, but Doc wasn't paying attention to him anymore. He was trying to decide how much notice the other patrons had taken of what Jury was saying. Unfortunately, it was a lot of notice.

"He's not used to tequila," Doc said casually to the man nearest them. "I should've cut him off sooner."

"Oh!" Jury exclaimed. "We can't forget about boglets. Of course, you've probably never seen a boglet; I'm not even sure you have them here."

Doc rolled his eyes and told the man confidentially, "He's a scholar, and when he gets drunk he tends to believe in fairy tales."

Jury rambled on, and Doc kicked him under the table. If Jury noticed, it didn't stop him. "There was this one time, in England, Father took us out onto the moors to meet with the Zeniu leader, and Margaret and I wandered off..."

"I should probably get him sobered up," Doc said with a cheerful laugh. "Next he'll be going on about the time he met the queen of fairies."

No one laughed with him, and Doc stood, trying to make his movements as casual as possible. He pulled Jury to his feet, wrapped his arm around Jury's back, and said, "Let's go get some coffee in you."

"I don't need coffee," Jury insisted as Doc towed him out the door.

"You really do. If you're not careful, you're going to get us lynched."

"Why?"

"You're talking about trolls and sprites and all kinds of fairy tale hokum like you actually believe in it. That makes people a little leery. And when people get leery, they like to lynch people."

"Wait... what?" Jury said, bleary eyes turning to focus on Doc. "What do you mean like I really believe in it?"

"You just told a story about having tea with a bog monster," Doc said with a sigh.

"Because I did," Jury insisted.

"I'm not sure we were drinking the same tequila," Doc chuckled. "Come on."

"No. Listen. I can prove it to you," Jury said firmly.

Doc briefly considered knocking Jury out and carrying him back to their cabana on the beach, but Jury didn't actually seem all that drunk. He wasn't slurring his words or stumbling; he was just talking crazy.

"Fine," Doc said. "Prove it to me."

"Come on," Jury said excitedly. "I saw a marking earlier when we were walking downtown."

Doc didn't know what that meant, but he followed Jury down the narrow street; and within the hour, Jury was pointing excitedly at a blank wall.

"It's right there," he said. "It's a mark to let people know this is a marketplace. You just can't see it because it's hidden."

Doc raised an eyebrow, but didn't say anything. It was possible Jury had just learned to walk drunk.

"There's a door right here," Jury said, pointing at a solid adobe wall. "Technically, I'm breaking about five laws right now..." Uncertainty crossed Jury's face, but then he grinned and said, "You want to go inside?"

"Sure," Doc said with a slight grin. It would be worth it to see Jury walk into the wall.

But Jury didn't. Instead he reached out his hand, turned an

invisible bit of air, and the wall opened up just like a door, revealing a bustling neighborhood within. A neighborhood with humans and... not-humans. Really not-humans. Maybe he and Jury had been drinking the same tequila after all.

"You are planning on shaving someday, aren't you?" Jervis asked, bringing Doc back to the present.

"What?"

"Shave."

"Right," Doc said. "I was getting to it."

He lathered his face and lifted the straight edge. "Did you always know about the Hidden?"

"There wasn't a Hidden when I was born," Jervis replied. "Not like there is now. We were careful to hide in plain sight, and those of us who couldn't hide, lived deep in the woods."

"There is a simplicity to that," Doc said.

"Yes. It was quite... different. There were many more wild places then. There were places that had never seen a human foot..." Jervis trailed off.

A moment later he said, "There wasn't an official Hidden established in Germany until the early eighteen hundreds. They got the idea from Napoleon, who had copied Jefferson."

"Seems like Jefferson would have kept that secret locked up tight," Doc commented as he removed the rest of his facial hair.

"He certainly tried, but he couldn't control the members of the Hidden, and many of them corresponded with family on the Continent."

Doc turned and surveyed the clothes Jervis had laid out for him. "Those jeans have holes in them," he pointed out.

"You did pick grunge."

"Fine. But when I finally get to kill Mitcham, I'm killing him extra hard for inflicting this on me."

"Naturally. Why did you ask about the Hidden?"

"I was just curious. Do you know how to kill a Zeniu?"

"No."

"Fantastic. I may as well give up then," Doc drawled. "Because if you don't know how to kill one, it can't be done."

"I've never had a reason to," Jervis replied. "You'll find a way."

"Your faith in me is overwhelming."

"I've never seen you fail," Jervis said sincerely.

"I believe you just jinxed me."

Jervis's lips twitched. "So I did."

"Tell me about Mitcham."

"I can't tell you anything."

"Why not?" Doc asked.

"No one will speak of him."

"No one?"

"No one."

"Why not?"

"I don't know," Jervis said.

"I don't like this," Doc admitted. "To be perfectly frank, Mitcham gives me the heebie-jeebies."

"One of Mr. Rufus's terms?"

"Obviously, but it fit the moment," Doc said.

"Perhaps," Jervis allowed.

"I won't be out long," Doc said as he pulled on the worn flannel jacket Jervis had laid out. "Probably. And I'm switching to burner phone number..." Doc opened the box sitting on the long ornate dining room table, took out a phone, and read the label on the back. "Twenty-seven."

"Noted," Jervis said.

"If Mitcham or his men keep poking around... I want you to be careful," Doc said, tone hard. "Don't do anything that will bring attention to you."

"I have everything completely under control," Jervis said. "No need to worry."

"I'm not worrying, Jervis, but I already have three pretty big problems to deal with right now, and I don't need a fourth one."

Boudica growled loudly.

"Apologies," Doc drawled. "I have four problems, and I don't need a fifth one."

"I'll be careful," Jervis said.

"Thank you. I guess I'll take the back door."

"Probably for the best," Jervis said before taking the large suitcase and leaving.

"I can't believe Jury picked today of all days to throw a fit," Doc grumbled as he filled one pocket with hundred dollar bills and the other pocket with merlins. "He's never happy. Why would he even want the bigger bounty? That's insane."

Doc continued to complain as he crawled through the never used heating ducts and out into the alley. He hated these clothes; he hated skulking; he hated wearing sneakers. He'd find a way to make Jury pay. After he'd soothed his ruffled feathers of course; and by then, Jury would never even see it coming.

3

It didn't take Doc long to wonder if perhaps he should have picked a different disguise. Grunge might be trendy on the streets of Denver, but the Hidden was a little more traditional. Things like intentional holes and deliberate tatters were not a fashion statement here.

Doc ignored several confused looks as he passed through the main plaza. It was probably best people took notice of him. After all, what kind of maniac actually tried to draw attention to himself when he was running from the law? Perhaps it was the perfect disguise.

He veered off onto a side street and wandered deeper into the neighborhood until he reached the LaRoches' shop. The sign on the door said closed, but Doc knocked anyway, and after a minute, Sydney cracked the door enough to say, "Oh, it's you."

"Yes, it's me."

"It's more effective than a glamour, really," Sydney went on, not opening the door any wider. "But you gotta work on your stance; you're still projectin' way too much confidence."

"Thanks for the tip," Doc said, slouching marginally.

"Better."

"Can I come in?" Doc asked.

"Are you kidding?!"

"Better than me just standing here banging on your door."

"You're a pest," Sydney grumbled, but he opened the door wide enough for Doc to come inside. As soon as the door was closed again, Sydney demanded, "Whadda you want?"

"I need to talk," Doc said. "Privately."

Sydney glanced around the empty store. "Don't get much more private than this."

"No, I mean, privately. In a way that you're assured no one will hear what you say."

"Oh. It's like that?"

"It's like that."

"I knew as soon as I met you you were gonna be trouble," Sydney grumped.

"That's a lie," Doc chuckled. "I saw the money symbols pop up in your eyes."

"Slander!" Sydney snapped.

"Not if it's true," Doc replied.

"Well it ain't, 'cause it's impossible to have money symbols in your eyes," Sydney growled. "So there. Now follow me."

He opened the basement hatch, but once they were inside the artifacts room, he kept walking towards the back. In a far corner, surrounded by crates was a tall black plastic box. Sydney walked inside, and Doc followed him.

"Can't have no light," Sydney said.

"Why not?" Doc asked, eyes trying to adjust to the absolute darkness.

"The only way to be sure."

"Sure of what?"

"That no one can hear."

"Is that why no one will talk about Mitcham?" Sydney snorted, and Doc wanted very much to see his expression. It just so happened that his ability to read people was somewhat hindered by the dark.

"Nobody talks 'bout him on account of what happens to people who do talk 'bout him," Sydney said.

"And that is?"

"Nobody knows," Sydney said mysteriously.

"Explain."

"Had a cousin who didn't like what Mitcham was doing to the tax rate. He said somethin' to his wife, and no one ever saw 'im again."

"You can't really be sure though that his disappearance had anything to do with Mitcham," Doc argued.

"Ha! No one has run against Mitcham in the last three elections," Sydney said.

"So?"

"The reason for that is that five different representatives of five different species ran against 'im in the first election, and they all mysteriously disappeared."

"Why wouldn't he just kill them?" Doc asked, thinking of Mitcham's request for him to kill Bosch's family.

"That ain't as frightenin', is it? No one knows where they've gone. Are they dead? Alive? Being tortured?"

"What about Bosch's family?" Doc asked.

"What 'bout them?"

"Are they still alive?"

"How the gods should I know?"

"What kind of things does Mitcham buy from you?" Doc asked, changing his approach.

Sydney was quiet for a moment. Finally he said, "Are you tryin' to get me killed?"

"You said they just disappear," Doc drawled.

"Same difference," Sydney snorted.

"Let me ask you this, is Mitcham a good ruler?"

"Gads, man. It's just a plastic box!"

"Here's the thing, I'm in a bad spot, and I have two choices," Doc said slowly. "Mitcham is out for blood, so I can either hide on a tropical island for the next fifty years or I can take Mitcham out. I like beaches, but that's a long time to shake sand out of your hair. You know?"

Sydney was silent for a very long time, and Doc fought the urge to push open the door so he could see the expression on his face. He also quietly palmed one of his knives as he belatedly realized that it was really rather foolish to step inside a dark void with someone he didn't completely trust.

"Are you sayin'... Do you mean to suggest..." Sydney paused, then said rapidly, "Do you actually mean to kill Mitcham?"

"That's sort of where I was going with this, yes."

"You ain't lying?"

"No."

"How do you plan to kill him?" Sydney demanded.

"Haven't quite figured that bit out yet."

"Hum," Sydney said softly. "Let me think on it."

Doc sighed, but said, "Alright. But just to make sure we're on the same page..."

"I ain't a stoolie, Holliday," Sydney said firmly.

"I never thought you were," Doc drawled.

The second he stepped out of the box, Doc breathed deeply and examined Sydney's face. He looked just as grouchy as usual, but there were slight concentration lines around his eyes as though he was thinking.

"How's Lydia?" Doc asked as they headed towards the shop proper.

"She don't like being called that. She prefers Selina. Means 'moon'."

"Selina," Doc murmured "I like it. Please give her my regards."

"She's a good girl," Sydney said defensively.

"Never said she wasn't."

"She says you owe her fifteen thousand dollars; don't know what that translates to in merlins, but there you have it."

Doc burst out laughing.

"Why's that funny?" Sydney demanded.

"No reason," Doc chuckled. "Did she earn it?"

"If you mean does she spew filth words every time she turns around, not unless she wants a mouthful of cod liver oil. My wife's very particular."

"Excellent. I'll have Jervis send it over," Doc promised. "Please let her know I'm impressed, and I feel she's turned over a new leaf, so I don't need to bribe her anymore."

"You mean pay her."

"Exactly."

"You should have set the terms up front," Sydney chastised. "Very sloppy."

"I'll remember that."

"Now get out of my shop! I've got work to do."

As Doc walked through the maze of streets back towards the Hidden exit, he was surprised to realize he was glad Lydia, now Selina, had found the LaRoches. In spite of Sydney's gruff manner and greedy ways, Doc rather liked him.

He turned a corner and felt a pair of eyes follow him. He didn't look back. Maybe they were just curious. Or maybe they didn't like grunge.

Another block passed before Doc heard several sets of footsteps following him. And then a voice. "I'm pretty sure you don't belong here, norm," the voice snarled.

Doc pretended not to hear and continued to walk sedately towards the exit.

"Didn't you hear me, norm? How did you get in here?"

Doc kept walking, listening carefully for the sounds of approach. He casually surveyed the courtyard in front of him, noting the distance to the exit and winking at Julian LaRoche when he saw him sitting on his bench, pen poised above his journal.

Something juicy splattered on Doc's back, and he paused. There was a limit to how much he could ignore. He may not care for flannel jackets, but it was still his flannel jacket.

He turned slowly, taking in the scene as he did. Most of the merchants and customers were quickly exiting the courtyard, stumbling into each other in their haste. Leaving only five angry-looking young men.

At a glance they appeared human, but that didn't mean anything; they could be any number of shapeshifters, not to mention vampires, witches, or a handful of other deadly cryptids.

"I'm just leaving," Doc said pleasantly.

"But I wanna know why you're here," the leader snarled.

"I came to see my cousin," Doc easily lied. "He lives two streets over."

"Who's your cousin?" the leader demanded. "What is he, because you're nothing but a filthy norm; I can smell it on you."

Smell, huh? That narrowed it down some. Most likely vampires or wolf shapeshifters.

"Look, man," Doc said, holding out his hands to the side. "I don't want any trouble."

"You shouldn't have come here then. This place isn't for you. The Hidden is for cryptids; and norms shouldn't be here spoiling what little land we have left."

The five men had stalked closer, eyes hard and intent. They were riled up, and Doc knew they weren't going to just let him walk out the door.

No one was on the street now except them and Doc. Even Julian was gone, although Doc was certain he was nearby, watching.

"I don't suppose it's ever occurred to you that just because someone is human, doesn't mean they're a norm?" Doc asked.

"Norms are humans," the leader snapped.

"Are they? All of them? Because I've known some humans who definitely weren't norms."

"I know your kind," the leader snarled angrily. "You use words to twist the truth until it can't even be recognized!"

"Look," Doc said with a sigh. "You're clearly very committed to your anti-norm cause, but the thing is I don't have time for this. I'm not interested in killing you, but if you attack me, I have to. It's the only way to communicate with others like you. Norms aren't bad; norms aren't good. Cryptids aren't bad; cryptids aren't good. Should the majority of norms be aware of the Hidden and the existence of cryptids? Absolutely not! Can we just agree on that and part ways?"

"No," the leader said with a wide, toothy smile. "We're going to kill you. Slowly. And then we're going to hang your body parts all over town to send a message to the weak cryptids out there, the ones who've turned their backs on their own kind."

Doc rolled his eyes and dropped his flannel jacket onto the ground, then peeled off his shirt. The grunge look didn't include blood spattered clothes, and this way he wouldn't have to work to reach his knife.

All five of the men uttered a strange guttural word, and with a sudden gleam of yellow magic they weren't young men anymore.

"Right," Doc said with a sigh. "I forgot about goddamn cyclopes."

They towered above him now, shoulders brushing the awnings of nearby buildings, strange long snouts snarling, single eyes glaring.

"Can we please not do this?" Doc asked, giving it one more try. "I'm sure each of you has family at home, waiting for you."

"Silly little man," the leader rumbled, "as if you could possibly hope to win."

"Let's squash him!" one of the others exclaimed.

"So be it," Doc muttered and started throwing knives with all the power he could muster.

One knife tore through the leader's chest, another through a cyclops' throat, another bounced off a skull, and yet another ripped a hole through a thigh the size of Dulcis's revolving door. But not one of them fell, because cyclopes were so damn big that it was nearly impossible to hit anything of importance.

They were laughing at his futile attempt to hurt them, great booming laughs that rattled the cobblestones; but Doc didn't bother to be annoyed. They were going to be difficult to kill, no doubt about it, but he WAS going to kill them.

He ran forward, circling behind the leader and slicing through the man's ankle with a large sweeping arc. Blood spewed out, flooding the street; and the cyclops' laughter turned into a shriek of pain. As the giant fell forward, Doc leaped onto his back and ran up it. When he reached the giant's shoulders, Doc stabbed his knife and entire hand through the man's neck, then turned the knife sideways and ripped it back out.

Blood spewed from the giant's neck, and his scream died just as abruptly as he did. His head flopped lifelessly to the street, and even though Doc's tattoo didn't draw in the cyclops' life force, Doc knew he was dead.

"You can still walk away," Doc advised the other cyclopes as he leaped from the dead cyclops' back. Letting them go broke a rule, but he had more important things to do right now and killing cyclopes wasn't on his list of favorite things.

"Never," one growled. "When we're done with you, we'll be able to drink you through a straw."

"Lovely image," Doc said, ducking a fist the size of a trash can lid.

They rushed him all at once, jostling into each other and knocking each other back as they did, and Doc watched them intently, keenly aware that if even one of their punches landed, he was dead.

He could make it to the exit now while they were struggling to reach him, but he wasn't going to do that. He'd offered to let them go, but they had been committed to the idea of killing him, and so they would die.

Doc leaped backwards as two fists smashed into the ground where he'd been standing, and then jumped forward and wrapped his legs around one of the cyclopes' wrist. The giant pulled back his hand, and Doc rode it into the air, then jumped from the wrist onto the man's shoulder. Doc grabbed the man's ear to keep from falling and shoved a knife deep into the cyclops' eye.

The giant's shriek of terror and pain tore through Doc, pounding into his skull so deeply that he felt his nose start to bleed, but he kept his hold and added a second knife to the first.

A hand wrapped around Doc's waist and ripped him from the sightless cyclops, but not before Doc managed to hurl three more knives into the giant's bleeding eye.

The hand holding him tightened, and Doc felt several ribs snap. He didn't waste his time attacking the hand because he knew his knife would be about as effective as a pin prick. Instead he leaned backward, then swung his body forward driving the cyclops' hand into the giant's own face.

The cyclops jerked in surprise, grip loosening just enough for Doc to push free from the giant's grasp and jump onto the startled man's shoulder. Once again, Doc grabbed hold of the ear to steady himself and then jabbed his knife repeatedly into the giant's cheek.

The cyclops screamed angrily and turned his snout towards Doc. Doc released the ear, struggled briefly for balance, then thrust his knife into the giant's eye, twisting it in a circle as he drew it back out. The cyclops howled in pain, and Doc took the opportunity to fling a knife into his open mouth.

Just as Doc was getting ready to hurl another knife down the gurgling cyclops' throat, the plaza erupted with noise.

"Cease fighting immediately and lay down your weapons!" a loud voice commanded.

Doc cast a glance over his shoulder. He and the cyclopes were surrounded by Magistratus officers, and they looked none too pleased.

The cyclops Doc was standing on began to wobble back and forth, and Doc raised his hands innocently and jumped from the man's shoulder just as the giant dropped heavily to the ground.

For a moment the Magistratus officers stared past Doc, seemingly mesmerized by the dead cyclopes lying in the street, but then several gun barrels leveled on Doc's chest.

Doc sighed heavily. He'd just wanted some answers. Was that really too much to ask for?

"What's going on here?" the Magistratus captain demanded.

"He's trespassing in the Hidden!" one of the remaining cyclopes accused. "Look! He murdered Thypon, Ryan, and Aegis, just as Johanns warned us would happen!"

"That's ridiculous!" the Magistratus captain scoffed. "How could a norm kill Thypon?" He studied Doc intently, taking an instinctive step backwards when he finally recognized him. "Mr. Holliday," he said with surprise. "Tetrarch Mitcham will be very pleased to see you."

"I'm sure he will," Doc drawled. "But I can't say I return the sentiment."

Just as the last word left Doc's mouth, the street in front of him exploded, hurling dust and debris in every direction. The captain yelled "Secure the prisoner!", but Doc was already running.

"Quick," someone hissed from the mouth of an alley. "This way."

Doc followed the voice and before long he was standing in front of an out-of-the-way Hidden exit.

"Here're your clothes," Julian whispered, shoving Doc's discarded shirts into his hands. "You'd better hurry; they'll have the witches out before long."

Doc smiled and drawled, "But thanks to your father, I don't need to worry about witches, do I?"

"I suppose not," Julian said flatly. "But they also use bloodhounds."

"I see your point," Doc laughed. "Thank you."

"Don't thank me. Thypon and his gang are out of control. I'm just disappointed someone alerted the Magistratus."

"There's always tomorrow," Doc chuckled as he slipped through the door and closed it behind him. And that's when he realized that he was standing on a somewhat busy Denver sidewalk, shirtless, and covered in blood.

He hugged the wall, hoping the glamour, or whatever it was, of the building would keep anyone from seeing him while he put on his shirt, but apparently that wasn't quite how it worked.

"Are you alright, dude?" a teenager asked, stopping his skateboard right in front of Doc.

"I'm fine," Doc replied. "But thanks for checking."

"You're covered in blood," the boy pointed out. "You sure you don't need me to call an ambulance?"

"Quite sure. I was just at my niece's birthday party, and her mom thought it would be a laugh to fill the water balloons with dye," Doc said with complete seriousness. "Turns out, it was not a laugh."

"What if you used glow-in-the-dark paint and did it at night?" the boy suggested excitedly.

"That might be a laugh," Doc agreed, buttoning his flannel jacket.

"I'm gonna try it."

"Let me know how it turns out," Doc chuckled as he stepped towards the curb and flagged down a taxi.

"For sure, dude."

The cab was already moving when Doc heard the boy cry out, "Hey, dude, you didn't give me your number!"

Doc laughed softly. This was turning out to be an absolutely ridiculous day.

4

"What I'd like to know," Doc said irritably around a mouthful of steak, "is how everyone and their dog can walk around looking like a human and then all of a sudden you find out they're a cyclops instead?"

"That's actually a rather interesting tale," Thaddeus began.

"Goddamn it, old boy! It was a rhetorical question!"

"But I have an answer," Thaddeus grumbled.

"I know but..." Doc paused and glanced around the basement. It wasn't as if he had anything else going on. "Oh, go ahead," he sighed.

"I would never dream of burdening you with facts you aren't interested in," Thaddeus sniffed.

"I am interested," Doc insisted.

"You made it quite clear that you aren't."

"I'm sorry; I shouldn't have snapped at you," Doc said. "Now will you tell me?"

"I've only had Rosa for company these last eight months," Thaddeus grumbled. "She also doesn't care about the finer details in life."

"I said I was sorry; and, furthermore, Jervis told me that Jules visited you every week."

"Ms. Baker did certainly lighten my sorrowful days."

"Goddamn it, Thaddy. Tell me about the shapeshifters or I'll shove you in the dumb waiter."

"There is no dumb waiter on this level," Thaddeus pointed out with an injured tone.

"I will walk you up a level," Doc growled, "and put you in that dumb waiter."

"No need to get snippy."

"I only have three bottles of whiskey down here; don't make me give one to you," Doc threatened.

"As I was going to say," Thaddeus began, "shapeshifters have a long and varied history. In some tribal lore the story goes like this. Wolves watched man for hundreds of years and began to envy their ability to walk on two legs and fashion weapons that could destroy. In their envy, they visited the mother and asked for legs like humans."

Doc propped up his feet and gave Thaddeus his full attention. He always liked stories about the mother. Perhaps because Andrew's wife, Jane, had been quite convinced that the mother had birthed all creatures.

"The mother listened to their complaints but denied their request," Thaddeus explained. "Most of the wolves accepted the mother's wisdom, but one group did not. Instead they attacked a tribe of humans, slaying them, and burrowing into their skin to try to steal their essence, something they'd learned from watching man steal animal essences."

"You're talking about skinwalkers?" Doc asked.

"Yes. Man cannot bear to see anything they don't have control over. So they discovered different ways to harness animals just like they found ways to harness water."

"I hate skinwalkers," Doc muttered.

"You only say that because Andrew hated them," Thaddeus chided.

"He said that Pecos said, and this makes sense, that there isn't much reason to wander around disguised as an animal unless you're up to no good."

"A valid point."

"The same could be said for shapeshifters except it would be impossible for them to function outside of the Hidden if they couldn't mimic humans," Doc mused.

"Anyway, as I was saying," Thaddeus broke in. "The wolves burrowed into the humans but nothing happened. The mother, however, saw their actions and laid a curse on them. They were fated to be neither man nor wolf, but to live in between both worlds, and neither world would ever accept them."

Doc considered this. "So that explains the wolves," he said thoughtfully, "but what about cyclopes and the Worms and the serpent people and—"

"Yes!" Thaddeus snapped. "I was getting there."

"I'll be quiet," Doc promised.

"Please do. As I was going to say, other creatures watched man as well and had the same thoughts. Some because they wanted power; some because they wanted the protection they thought being human would offer them. Little by little they studied humans and learned from them, they took on their mannerisms and adapted to be like them, but they were never able to leave their other part fully behind."

Thaddeus was silent for a moment, and Doc imagined him staring off into space with a thoughtful expression on his face.

"Of course there's another far more likely story," Thaddeus murmured.

"But you know I always bet on the long shot," Doc pointed out.

"Indeed you do, but that doesn't mean the long shot always wins," Thaddeus said severely. "In the other version of events, all the species were running around the earth minding their own business, but man kept getting stronger and more powerful, taking over more and more and more of the world, and by the time the other species realized there was a battle for supremacy going on, they had already lost the fight."

"Sounds about right," Doc grunted.

"In order not to be crushed underfoot, the other species turned to magic to protect them," Thaddeus said, ignoring Doc's statement. "Their witches or shamans, whatever they had, devised tokens of great power to shield them. Tokens that could turn them into humans, or more correctly, turn their forms into a human form."

"Tokens?" Doc asked, sitting forward. "Like an artifact?"

"Very similar, except these tokens were made from human bones and human skin and imbued with human essence and then bonded to each individual," Thaddeus answered, tone a tad more melodramatic than usual.

Doc let Thaddeus's words move through his mind, evaluating them and comparing them to what he had already observed. He knew for a fact that Dublin didn't have a token. He could change from wolf to human at will. However, the cyclops shifters had all muttered a strange word before they had shifted, which supported the second version of events.

"Why does everyone always think there can only be one truth?" Doc asked finally. "Why can't both stories be true?"

"You surprise me, John Holliday," Thaddeus murmured.

"I think if you're not careful you might turn into a philosopher yet."

Doc was dreaming. More or less. It was more of a memory, but as with all memory dreams, he knew it was both a memory and a dream.

He was inside that crazy door in Mexico. That door that didn't exist; the one that opened to a totally different world. A world that shouldn't be there.

But he was there in spite of that, playing five card stud, and for once he was losing. He was losing because he was playing against a tree spirit. A great, big, hulking tree spirit. Of course he only knew it was a tree spirit because he had asked and it had told him.

It or he, apparently, didn't look like a tree exactly. More of a mix between a tree and a man. He had green shimmery bark for skin and leaves for hair and acorns for eyes. Acorns. How could anyone see out of acorns? It didn't make sense, but see he did, because he was taking Doc for every dollar he had.

Only they weren't dollars. Jury had given them to Doc, and he had called them merlins and taliesins. The merlins were gold and had an impression of a wheel cut into four equal sections, each one representing a different element Jury had said. The silver taliesins had a similar symbol, but Jury had said it represented the layers of being, whatever the hell that meant.

Tree spirits, merlins, taliesins, elements. What was in that tequila? Could alcohol go bad?

Doc couldn't look away from the tree spirit's strangely branchlike hand as it swept the pile of winnings into a sack.

"Better luck next time, human," the spirit said, voice both verdant and rich.

Doc stumbled to his feet and walked through the strange streets in a daze until he reached the exit. He walked through the door, then turned around and stared at where it should have been. He could see nothing. Nothing at all. Just a solid wall.

He must be losing his mind. It was bound to happen eventually, wasn't it? Humans weren't meant to live forever, to stay young forever. Surely his mind would eventually break from all the memories and chaos.

He shook his head emphatically; that couldn't be it. He was only... Seventy-five or so. People lived to be seventy-five all the time. It had to be the tequila.

Even though he was asleep, Doc heard the door open in the physical realm, and he drifted out of his dream and listened carefully.

"I can't believe you went out without me," Jury complained as he dropped down onto the couch beside Doc.

Doc refused to let his lips grin. "You didn't want to come," he said sleepily.

"You didn't ask me to come!"

"You left. With rather harsh words if I recall."

"Please, you drink so much whiskey I'm surprised you can remember your mother's name."

"Alice."

"I didn't say you didn't remember it; I just said I was surprised you remember it," Jury countered.

"Remember when I lost all your money to that tree spirit?" Doc asked.

"That was a good time," Jury murmured happily. "Remember when you tried to get drunk afterwards?"

"I wish you'd let that go," Doc sighed.

"I can't. It was hilarious," Jury laughed. "To this day, I've never seen anyone consume that much tequila, and I don't think anyone else had either. I won a thousand dollars by betting you'd never pass out. First bet I ever won," he added proudly.

"And last," Doc snorted.

"So what's your plan?"

"I don't have one. Your dog is making it too difficult to think logically."

"My dog?"

"Yes. Your dog. The one YOU made from magic."

"Yeah." Jury took the whiskey bottle from Doc's hand and swallowed the last sip. "So remember when I told you that I didn't want to get married because you'd sleep with my wife, my kids would think you were cooler than me, and my dog would follow you home?"

"No," Doc lied.

"Sure you do. I must be a soothsayer because you slept with my wife and my dog is your dog."

"I did not sleep with your wife," Doc said irritably.

"You may as well have."

"You never had a chance with Babs," Doc replied. "She is way out of your league."

"Give me ten minutes alone with her," Jury argued. "Anyway, Boudica's yours. She likes you. She's mad at you, not me. Happy birthday."

This was not acceptable. One, it was not his birthday. At least he didn't think it was; he truly had no idea what month it was, let alone what day. Two, he did not want a dog. Dogs died. He studied Boudica's shimmering back. Or did they?

"Do witch hounds die?" he asked casually.

"She's made of magic so who knows," Jury replied.

"Hum," Doc said, standing and walking over to her. "I'm

sorry I left you alone for so long," he said, scratching gently behind her ears. "I didn't mean to. And I'm sorry I hurt your feelings earlier. I... I didn't know."

Boudica opened her big blue eyes and studied him. She tilted her head sideways.

"Honest," Doc said.

She shrugged.

"So we're good?"

She shrugged again, and Doc grinned.

"I can't tell you how irritated I am that you're apologizing to a dog," Jury ground out. "Sincerely at that."

"Get over it," Doc ordered. "Now let's make a plan."

"Not without food."

"I still don't see why we can't just break into Mitcham's house," Jury complained an hour later.

"I refuse to explain it to you again," Doc ground out.

"I'll do it," Thaddeus offered. "Doc theorizes that Mitcham is using every cryptid and magic at his disposal to both protect himself and build a network of spies."

"I still say if he was doing that, people would have caught on by now," Jury argued.

"It's like a car factory," Doc put in. "One person is cutting the spark plug wires into sections, another is putting those little cap things on them, yet another is attaching them to the plugs, and yet another is connecting them to the distributor. So not any of them see the whole picture from start to finish."

"I suppose that makes sense," Jury allowed. "But I still think your plan is stupid."

"I'm all ears," Doc stated.

"We could... No, we already went through that. What if... No, no. I suppose... On the other hand..."

"You're stalling," Thaddeus said.

"I'm not!" Jury snapped.

"Just do it already."

"I don't want to. If he doesn't ever have to apologize, I never have to say it."

"I don't care whether you say it or not," Doc said, "as long as we're in agreement."

"Alright then," Jury said.

"You should really be the bigger man," Thaddeus chastised.

"Shut up, Thaddeus!" Jury growled. "Who invited you anyway?"

"That wasn't very nice," Doc said, struggling not to grin.

"Fine! You're right!" Jury exclaimed. "Is that what you want to hear? You're right; you're always right. Goddamn it, I hate you!"

"I think that earned me some brandy," Thaddeus said, voice faintly amused.

"It certainly did," Doc laughed, pouring a bottle of brandy into Thaddeus's pot.

"Thank you," Thaddeus said dreamily.

"My pleasure."

"Can we just go already?" Jury demanded.

"Let me change," Doc said. He stood, then froze when he heard a suspicious click. "Give me your phone," he demanded.

"No," Jury laughed. "Besides, I already texted it to Aine."

"Why would you do that?"

"You slept with my wife."

"For the last time, Babs is not your wife!"

Jury's phone beeped; he glanced at it and burst out laughing. "Look, she sent a bunch of those laughing yellow faces."

"They're called emoticons," Doc said scathingly.

"You're both wrong," Thaddeus murmured. "They're emojis."

Doc and Jury both glared at Thaddeus's pot.

"What does he know?" Doc said.

"He's just a goddamn plant," Jury added.

Doc peered at Mitcham's closed front door and questioned his reasoning. If he calculated out all the odds, there was less than a ten percent chance his plan would actually work. But he couldn't calculate luck, which was one of his finest assets.

"This is truly one of your more ridiculous plans," Jury said even as he lifted his hand to knock.

"That's how you know it's me," Doc replied, "and not some villain glamoured to look like me."

"I suppose that's somewhat reassuring," Jury grunted.

Mitcham's Zeniu butler opened the door. His face didn't register any surprise to see them, and Doc bet himself the man had already known they were coming.

"Sir John, Sir Thomas," he said tonelessly, "this way if you will."

They followed him down the long hallway, nodded at the Takaheni guarding Mitcham's office door, and entered Mitcham's office.

Doc suppressed his normal confidence and tried to channel the anxiety of a person who has been on the run for eight months. He didn't speak, but waited just inside the door for Mitcham to greet them, mentally rolling his eyes when Mitcham made them wait two full minutes.

"Ah, Mr. Holliday, Mr. Jury. How very nice to see you. Take a seat."

"Thank you, Tetrarch Mitcham," Doc said as subserviently as possible. "It's kind of you to see us."

Mitcham waved his hand dismissively. "We have unsettled business; it's the least I could do."

Doc sat stiffly and said, "We were wrong before. We should have heard you out. It's obvious to us now that if you need something done, we shouldn't have questioned you. We just hope it's not too late."

"Gentlemen," Mitcham said with a pleased smile. "It's never too late. I'm so pleased you've come around. I was afraid after that unfortunate incident in the poor quarter's marketplace that I would have to put out an order to have you killed." He shrugged and added, "I'm relieved to see that's not the case. I absolutely hate to see talent go to waste."

Doc ducked his head and said with absolute sincerity, "You have no idea how happy I am to hear that."

Mitcham unlocked and opened one of his desk drawers and pulled out a folder. "The information on Bosch's family is in here," he said. "As well as an item belonging to his wife."

Doc focused on the folder, just barely keeping his eyes from narrowing. Mitcham had said it was urgent the last time they'd met, and that had been eight months ago. It was strange he hadn't already handled it.

"I want you to find and eliminate them as soon as possible," Mitcham added as Doc took the folder from his hand.

"Find them?" Doc asked.

"Yes."

"These are norms, correct?" Doc inquired.

"Yes, but Bosch learned quite a lot in his time at the Bureau, and he apparently put it to good use," Mitcham said, tone irritated.

"I see," Doc said. "So how am I supposed to find them?"

"That's really your problem, isn't it?" Mitcham said coldly.

Doc swallowed his annoyance and asked the more important question. "Will we be able to move about the Hidden unhindered?"

"You mean are you still wanted men?"

"Yes." There was a reason he hated dealing with politicians. They could never just answer direct questions, and no matter what, they were always angling for a way to utterly screw you.

"I'm willing to lift the bounty," Mitcham said thoughtfully.

Doc cast a sideways glance at Jury. Jury shrugged. So much for Jury doing the talking.

"What do I need to do?" Doc asked.

"I believe a show of good faith is required," Mitcham said. "Just so I'm certain where you stand."

"A show of good faith," Doc repeated. "Such as?"

"I've had a bit of trouble with a certain merchant, and it's become clear to me that his family does not have the Hidden's best interest in mind."

Doc waited, trying to read Mitcham's face without much success.

"Remove the LaRoche family," Mitcham ordered, "and I will lift the bounty and inform the Magistratus and the Hidden at large that you are no longer wanted men."

5

Doc kept his face carefully blank. "The LaRoche family?" he asked, as if he'd never heard the name before in his life.

"Yes," Mitcham said. "They operate out of the same section of the lower Hidden where you slew Thypon. I want you to eliminate the entire family; Sydney, Alma, Julian, and their norm pet, Lydia." Mitcham's tone twisted when he said norm, but Doc pretended not to notice.

"Alright," Doc said.

"You have until midnight," Mitcham added.

Doc nodded. There was no sense arguing or asking for more time. Mitcham had already made up his mind. If Doc didn't do this, Mitcham would put out a kill order on him. And if Doc didn't do the next thing, Mitcham would put out a kill order. It would never end.

"Bring me their ears," Mitcham said. "So I know you've done the task."

"Yes, sir," Doc said, working to keep the anger from his tone. "Thank you for giving us another chance."

"Don't fail me again," Mitcham commanded.

Doc bobbed his head, tapped Jury on the shoulder, and they both backed out of the room. They didn't speak until they were outside of the Hidden and standing on the sidewalk next to Doc's car.

"You sweep it?" Doc mouthed.

"What am I, new?" Jury mouthed back irritably.

"And?"

"Nothing."

"Did you look for plastic?"

"How do you expect me to do that?"

"I just assumed you could look for anything that was dead," Doc mouthed slowly.

"That's stupid," Jury replied silently.

"Is it?"

"Yes, but I'll try it, just so I can say you're wrong." Jury walked around the car several times before grunting and mouthing, "Waste of time. There's plastic all over the damn car."

"But does it belong there?"

"Goddamn it, Doc!"

"Just try," Doc urged.

"Fine." Jury faced the car and closed his eyes.

A group of pedestrians walked by, giving Doc and Jury a wide berth and watching them circumspectly. Doc grinned at them, and they hurried past.

After a long moment, Jury finally mouthed, "Check just inside the driver-side door panel."

Doc opened the door, cringing as he pried open the door panel, and snatched the little plastic disc hidden inside. "That wasn't so hard, was it?" he mouthed as he stood.

"It actually was," Jury mouthed angrily. "I've never tried to sort through plastic before. It's... exhausting!"

"But you did it."

Jury rolled his eyes. "Now what?"

"I say we discuss exactly how we're going to kill the LaRoches," Doc said out loud with a wink.

"Why can't we just get their address, show up, slice and dice, and be done with it?" Jury suggested as he climbed into the car.

"I feel like we should make an example, don't you?" Doc said. "Send a message to the lower echelons that Mitcham isn't to be messed with."

"You mean 'cause he'll ruin their lives?" Jury muttered.

"Exactly!" Doc exclaimed. "The sooner everyone falls in line, the easier it will be on everyone else."

He stopped at a red light and glanced over at Jury and mouthed, "Mitcham should like that, don't you think?"

"Try not to lay it on too heavy," Jury mouthed back.

"Did you release the fairy wasps?" Doc asked silently.

"Obviously. Wasn't that the whole point?" Jury mouthed, rolling his eyes as he did.

"Yeah, but I know how you get distracted."

"Like you?" Jury grumbled. "The light's green."

Doc laughed, and they drove the rest of the way in silence.

After Doc had parked the car, he texted Jervis and asked him to come to the parking garage.

"That car has a bug on the seat," Doc told Jervis when he arrived. "Leave it there so I can drive it back to Mitcham's later, but see if our guys can copy the tech or trace it or whatever it is they do."

"Certainly, sir."

"Also, how certain are you that the hotel is secure?"

"One hundred percent certain," Jervis said flatly.

"Could they have left bugs during their search?"

"Found them and destroyed them, sir."

"What about magic?"

"Impossible."

Doc frowned. He was obviously missing something. "Why's that?"

"Mr. Jury, would you be so kind as to listen in on the kitchen?" Jervis asked.

"That's not really my thing," Jury protested.

"I was under the impression you excelled at it," Jervis prodded.

"Fine," Jury huffed. He focused for a moment, then frowned. "I can't. Why can't I? The hotel is full of air; you can't just stop me."

"Can't I?" Jervis asked with an almost imperceptible grin.

"How did you do it?" Jury demanded.

"House secret," Jervis said. "But there you have it, sir. Completely secure."

"Exemplary work as always, Jervis. Give yourself a raise."

"If you insist."

"I do. Is Emily waiting for us?"

"As you requested, sir."

"Double your raise," Doc drawled as he headed for the elevator. "And come by when you're done with the car."

"Yes, sir."

"I still don't get it," Jury grumbled as they rode the elevator to Doc's suite.

"Get what?"

"How come I can't listen in?"

"You mean eavesdrop?"

"You know what the hell I mean!" Jury snapped.

"I don't know," Doc said. "It was news to me."

"Don't you think your hotel security is just a little over-the-top? I mean, Dulcis is more secure than the most hated man in the Hidden," Jury said thoughtfully.

"Well," Doc replied, "Jervis is extremely particular."

"Jervis is a sneaky devil," Jury muttered.

"You certainly wouldn't want to cross him," Doc stated.

Jury was silent, but Doc had a good idea what he was thinking. Jervis had always been a mystery to Jury, and he was a mystery Jury had no chance of solving.

Doc had been fairly surprised when Jervis had allowed Jury into the sub-subbasement. And he'd frankly been rather relieved that Jury hadn't poked around or even paid much attention to the decor. There were some things Jury was just better off not knowing.

Doc pushed open the door to his suite and walked along the spacious hallway to Bree's old room. He greeted Emily with a grin and asked, "Did our little gambit pay off?"

She nodded, eyes strangely unfocused. "I'm watching now."

"Excellent," Doc said.

She ignored him and wrote something down on the pad in front of her. "I do wish you had released a more manageable number though," she muttered when she was done writing. "A hundred was a little overkill."

"I wanted you to have access to the entire house," Doc said.

"And then some," Emily ground out.

"Let me know if you need anything," Doc whispered, backing slowly from the room.

She nodded vaguely, and Doc and Jury closed the door softly behind them.

"I don't think she's having much fun," Jury stated.

"Those damn bugs are so tiny," Doc replied. "I wanted to

make sure they didn't all get stepped on or vacuumed up. You think she's really inside all one hundred of them?"

"Couldn't say," Jury said. "I've never really understood what Myhanava can do."

"You and me both. I need a drink," Doc said, wandering into the kitchen.

"God forbid you go more than two hours without a sip," Jury snorted.

"If you recall, I went nearly thirty hours when I came to save you."

"That's a normal day for most people."

"And there you have it," Doc chuckled. "I hate to say this," Doc added as he sat down, "but Ahanu actually did us a favor." He shuddered. "I hope those words never come out of my mouth again."

"How so?" Jury asked.

"Mitcham thinks we've been in hiding for eight months, so he believes we're broken and willing to do heinous deeds in order to restore our former status."

"Idiot," Jury snorted.

"Having a file on someone is not the same as knowing them," Doc chuckled. "But if we'd only been gone two days, we would've never been able to pull off the whole 'we're so sorry, please forgive us' routine."

"So you want to send Ahanu a thank you note?"

"Hell no! I would never admit it to his face!" Doc exclaimed. "And if he brings it up, we'll just stare at him in confusion as if we have no idea what he's talking about."

"I really think he brings out your worst," Jury laughed.

"That's impossible," Doc drawled. "I don't have a worst." They looked at each other and burst out laughing.

Just then someone knocked on the door, and Doc knew it

was Jervis. He could always tell Jervis's knock; it was sharp and to the point. Exactly like Jervis.

"Come in!" Doc called out, still chuckling. Doc waited until Jervis was seated before asking, "What's keeping Mitcham from doing to us what we're doing to him?"

"Oversight," Jervis said.

"Explain."

"Dulcis employs over thirty Myhanava just like Emily."

Jervis didn't continue so Doc raised an eyebrow and said, "Do go on."

"What few insects or animals do make it past the wards inside Dulcis are immediately occupied by one of the Myhanava on duty," Jervis explained.

Jervis stopped again. Doc sighed and said, "I'm a little rusty on my Myhanava lore. Does that mean no one else can occupy it?"

"Precisely."

"I see. And Mitcham didn't think to do this?"

"Apparently not, sir."

"He probably thinks no one is stupid enough to try," Jury put in.

"He obviously doesn't know us," Doc said dryly.

"Obviously," Jury laughed.

Doc shuffled his cards and dealt out three cards face down, followed by three cards face up. Jury sighed, but checked his. Meanwhile, Jervis passed around the button bowl Doc kept in the middle of the table, and they each took a handful of buttons.

Doc tossed two buttons into the middle of the table. Jury and Jervis did as well, and Doc dealt out three more cards. Jury's eyebrow twitched, and Doc smiled inwardly. Jury obviously didn't like his cards. Doc tossed more buttons onto the pile.

"So you know that thing we had going in the seventies?" Doc asked Jervis.

"Yes," Jervis said evenly, matching Doc's bet.

"We still doing that?"

"Yes."

"So we still have the extraction team?"

"Yes."

"What the hell are you guys talking about?" Jury demanded.

"Dulcis business," Doc said dismissively. "Nothing overly important." He dealt another round of cards, and Jury sighed. "How have you not learned to control your tells by now?" Doc demanded. "We've been doing this for a hundred years."

"It's just frustrating," Jury said. "I mean, there're fifty-two cards! There's really no chance of getting anything worthwhile."

Doc shook his head. He already had a pair, but luck was on his side.

"I need to kill the LaRoches," Doc said casually as he threw in more buttons.

"Easy enough," Jervis replied.

"I also need to deliver their ears to Mitcham by midnight tonight."

"That can be arranged."

"I pay enough attention to know that not just any ears will do, so are you going to make fun of me if I ask how?" Doc inquired.

"Not to your face, sir."

"That's why I keep you on."

Jervis raised his bet, Doc met it, Jury folded, and Doc dealt the last cards.

"We acquire the appropriate number of ears, and then Mr. Jury enchants them," Jervis said as he threw in another button.

"Enchants?" Doc asked.

"It's not that simple," Jury interjected. "First, I need to have the LaRoches with me. Second, I have to do it in such a way it's not visible to another witch."

"But you can do it?" Doc questioned.

"Well, yes. I mean, I never have, but I'm pretty sure I can."

"It's rather fortunate really," Jervis said. "Not just any witch could."

"Didn't you know?" Doc asked, tone perfectly serious. "Jury is probably the single most powerful witch in North America."

"Well, I am," Jury grumbled. "And I don't know why you keep saying it like it's a bad thing. Did you enjoy your grunge phase? Because I know Aine and I did."

"I did, actually," Doc stated firmly. "It was like walking around with built-in air conditioning."

Doc revealed his cards and won the hand.

"It's always a pleasure playing against you, sir," Jervis said as he scooped the buttons back into the bowl.

"No need to lie, Jervis," Jury said. "He'd be lost without you."

"Hardly," Jervis replied. "Wait thirty minutes before going to the LaRoches, sir, and I'll have the extraction team ready for you. Mr. Jury, one of my men will escort you to the safe house. Are there any supplies that you need?"

"To turn eight fake LaRoche ears into eight real LaRoche ears?" Jury grumbled. "Yeah. I'm gonna need a shitload of sandwiches."

"Will that be all?"

"Hell no!" Jury snapped. "I'll write you a list," he added.

It didn't particularly surprise Doc to find that the LaRoches lived above the charm shop. It did surprise him how excited Selina, previously known as Lydia, was to see him when he arrived at the door.

She was the only one though. Mrs. LaRoche cast a very worried glance at Sydney, but he just shook his head. And in spite of his attempt to look nonchalant, even Julian looked concerned. Doc managed to pass Sydney a note before Selina tugged on his arm and started asking him questions.

"Where have you been?" Selina demanded. "Did Pops tell you how much you owe me? I haven't cussed in months. Ma doesn't allow it. Why are you here? Is Boudica with you?"

"Enough," Doc said. "One question at a time. I'll start with why I'm here." He met Sydney's eyes, hoping he'd had enough time to read the entire note, held his finger to his lips, winked, and said, "I'm afraid I'm here to kill you."

Selina's eyes went wide. "What?!" she exclaimed. "How can you even say that? That's not funny, you know. Not with everything that's going on!"

"And I'm going to start with your norm brat," Doc drawled. "I'm sorry," he mouthed and gestured to Julian. Julian seemed uncertain, and he watched Doc carefully.

"Norm brat!" Selina shrieked. Doc made a cut off motion and Julian clamped his hand over her mouth.

Mrs. LaRoche gasped, and Doc said, "That's what happens to norms in the Hidden."

"Why're you doing this?" Sydney demanded, tone tired and lacking his usual gruffness.

"Mitcham wants you gone."

"But why?"

"He didn't tell me; I didn't ask," Doc said. "But I'll make it quick."

Behind Doc, the door opened silently, and Doc's extraction team, all shadow phantoms, drifted into the room. Mrs. LaRoche whimpered, and Sydney gazed at them in awe. Doc could tell Sydney had a question he wanted to ask, but fortunately, he stopped himself from saying anything.

Doc gestured for Mrs. LaRoche to scream, and she did, very convincingly, in fact. At Doc's signal, Sydney clasped his hand over his wife's mouth, cutting off the scream in such a way that anyone listening might assume Mrs. LaRoche had just met her end.

"I'll kill you," Julian snarled.

"I doubt it," Doc replied. He began to move his feet across the floor as if he was fighting someone, mouthed "sorry", and struck Julian in the face. As Julian stumbled backwards, Doc knocked over a lamp and threw a vase onto the floor. And then he gestured for everyone to be silent.

He drew out his knife, made an apologetic gesture, and motioned for them to hold out their arms. Sydney immediately offered Doc his arm, and Doc made a narrow cut down the back of it, then flicked the blood onto the floor with his knife. Doc then handed Sydney a container of yarrow and motioned for him to put it on the cut.

When he turned to Mrs. LaRoche, she was trembling, but she bravely held out her arm, and Doc made his cut. Julian went next. Selina's eyes were stormy with anger, but she held out her arm defiantly. Tears rose in her eyes when Doc cut her, and he whispered, "I'm so sorry."

At this point the shadow phantoms moved silently forward, each of them depositing a dead body onto the floor.

It was a rather eerie sight; the four bodies, ears missing, lying in front of their live counterparts; and at the sight of them, Mrs. LaRoche began to cry.

Doc silenced her with a finger on his lips and pointed at the phantoms, then back at the LaRoches. Sydney nodded, although he was pale. The phantoms glided towards the family, and Julian squeezed Selina's hand, trying to calm her as one of the phantoms engulfed her.

Shadow phantoms were, without doubt, the best way to smuggle anything. They possessed the uncanny ability to envelop people, chairs, animals, rocks, whatever they felt like at the time, and move it with them. Furthermore, they were difficult to see under the best circumstances, but in the dark of night, even if you knew they were there, it was impossible to make out their form. Their crowning glory, however, was that they could drift through any type of wall or physical object, even if they were carrying something entirely solid. It was another one of those things Doc didn't really understand, but as long as it worked, he didn't need to know how it worked.

Without a sound the phantoms spirited the family away, and then Doc was alone with four dead bodies. He tried to make as little noise as possible as he stabbed each body in a vital place and arranged them just so. When he was done, he set the room on fire.

A careful investigation would probably reveal his deception, but he was betting Mitcham would only check the ears, not the bodies. But in either case, Jervis had supplied Doc with an accelerant that was helping the fire consume the LaRoches' home at a terrifying rate. With any luck, there wouldn't be much of the bodies left to examine.

6

"Here," Jury grunted, tossing a handful of human ears onto Doc's coffee table. "That was goddamn disgusting, and I don't ever want to do it again. And for the record, I do not enjoy traveling by phantom. It should be illegal."

"It is illegal," Doc drawled. "Couldn't you have put them in a bag or something?"

"I had to touch them so you have to touch them," Jury said, flopping down beside Doc and taking the whiskey bottle from his hand.

"I suppose that's fair." Doc glanced at the clock; it was already eleven seventeen. "Cutting it a bit close," he said.

"You try infusing ears with human essence and magic in such a way that no one knows you did it," Jury snapped.

"You have me there. Shall we?"

"Only if we go through the kitchen. You have nothing to eat in here," Jury complained.

"I'll meet you out front," Doc said.

It was precisely eleven fifty-six when Doc knocked on Mitcham's front door. The butler opened it and gestured for them to proceed to Mitcham's office.

"I was beginning to wonder if you were going to make it," Mitcham said severely when Doc and Jury stepped inside.

That was a lie. It was a lie because he had a bug in Doc's car, and he had heard them coming. Or someone had heard them coming. He had also "heard" Doc kill the LaRoches. So he'd known they were coming. He just didn't want them to know he knew.

"I apologize," Doc said humbly, placing the small box containing the ears onto Mitcham's desk.

"Sit," Mitcham ordered. He dumped out the ears and studied them for a moment, then he pressed a button on his desk phone and said, "Luke, bring in the expert. Did they give you much trouble?" Mitcham asked while they waited.

"No," Doc replied.

"I thought perhaps you chose to defy me and set their house on fire to cover your tracks," Mitcham said thoughtfully.

Doc pretended to look shocked. "Of course not," he insisted. "I set their house on fire to send a message."

"Convenient though, since there wasn't much left of the bodies," Mitcham countered.

"But I brought you their ears," Doc said, forcing his voice to sound confused. "I didn't think you needed the bodies."

"We shall see."

The office door opened, and a very wizened old man with a shock of white hair and dark wrinkled skin was led in by Luke, the butler. The old man wasn't blind; he was eyeless. He was eyeless because his eyes had been gouged out.

"Yes, my lord?" the old man said in a thickly accented voice as soon as he was near Mitcham.

"Examine these ears and tell me who they belong to," Mitcham ordered.

"Yes, my lord."

The old man shuffled closer and reached out to feel Mitcham's desk. Mitcham didn't help him in any way whatsoever; just watched with an air of impatience.

After a few seconds of fumbling, the man found the ears and scooped them up. A strange greenish-brown light enveloped his hand, ears and all; and he began to murmur soft words that were foreign to Doc.

The ears floated just above the old witch's hand and slowly circled through his thumb and finger one by one before splitting into pairs and circling once more. After a moment he said, "There are four people here. Three related; one not."

"Yes," Mitcham said. "But who are they?"

"I'm sorry, my lord; I'm getting there. Please be patient with me."

The largest pair of ears settled in the man's palm and vibrated there. "These ears," he said slowly, "belong to..."

Doc felt Jury tense, and he nudged him with his foot. "Relax!" Doc ordered with his eyes.

Jury breathed out slowly and forced his shoulders to relax.

"A man named Sydney LaRoche," the old man finally said.

Mitcham leaned forward in his chair and said, "Indeed?"

"Yes, my lord."

"And the others?"

The ears rotated again, and the old man said, "Alma LaRoche" and then "Julian LaRoche." He appeared to struggle with the final pair, but he finally said, "Lydia Smith. Also Selina LaRoche. Also Betsy Waters."

Doc cringed inwardly when the third name was uttered, but Mitcham seemed satisfied. "Excellent," he said. "Go now."

"Yes, my lord."

"You did not disappoint me," Mitcham said to Doc. "I will lift the bounty and repeal the arrest warrants."

"Thank you, sir," Doc said.

"I want Bosch's family," Mitcham said firmly. "And I want them soon. You have four days."

Doc argued because it wouldn't have been the least bit convincing if he hadn't. "But what if they aren't even in the States?"

"That's really your problem," Mitcham said. "If I were you I'd get right to work."

Doc and Jury didn't speak until they were back inside the sanctuary of Doc's suite.

"Who the hell was the witch?" Doc asked as he collapsed onto his couch.

"The oldest living witch," Jury uttered, face a mixture of confusion and awe.

"The oldest?"

"So they say. Rumor has it he's been alive since the dawn of time."

"Surely you don't speak of Thulan?" Thaddeus asked sleepily.

"Yes," Jury said.

"I was under the impression he had finally died."

"Not exactly," Jury said. "He disappeared, and everyone assumed he had died."

"And when did he disappear?" Doc asked, even though he was fairly certain he already knew the answer.

"It was about forty, forty-one years ago," Jury replied. His expression turned thoughtful, and he added, "Probably five years or so into Mitcham's first term."

"So if he's the oldest witch, wouldn't that make him one of the most powerful?" Doc asked.

"Technically, yes," Jury said, "but you have to understand, not all witches are the same. For instance, we Jurys are of warrior descent."

Doc snorted.

"Well, we are!" Jury snapped. "Whether or not my family actually remembers that is a different story. But there is peasant stock, merchant stock, healer stock. You understand?"

"That sounds like some elitist Jury tripe," Doc replied.

"I'm trying to make a point," Jury ground out. "Not everyone can bend the air currents to make a crushing wall. Some witches use the elements for other purposes. Thulan was never a warrior or a violent man. He was a... a thinker, a philosopher, even a philanthropist."

"Have you met him?" Thaddeus asked, voice full of envy.

"I have," Jury replied.

"When?" Doc inquired.

"When I was a boy and then again about sixty years ago."

"His eyes?" Doc asked.

"That's new," Jury confirmed. He shook his head and said, "I have a feeling Mitcham did that just to keep him under control."

"But he's a witch," Doc said. "Why can't he just... I don't know exactly, just witch his way out?"

"I don't know how to explain it," Jury said. "His area of specialty is unraveling knots and mysteries. He was known for identifying bones or unrecognizable bodies so the remains could be returned to their families."

Jury gestured expressively with his hands and said, "I wouldn't even know where to start with something like that. If I've met someone and noted their energy signature, I could easily identify their body, but someone I've never met? That's... That's insane. Somehow... He'd have to somehow... Well, he'd have to somehow know everyone who was alive or who had ever been alive," Jury said, voice full of awe.

"And that's not even all!" Jury exclaimed. "I heard that he could tell you every single person who possessed an item for more than a day. Someone tested him with a merlin once, and he wrote down three thousand names!"

"That is very specific," Doc muttered. "And also completely impossible to verify."

"You saw what he did with the ears," Jury pointed out. "You can't possibly say he can't do it."

"True," Doc allowed. "And naturally Mitcham would see him and want to control him, just like he does everything else."

"Quite," Thaddeus agreed. "Mitcham really is humanity at its worst."

"I don't think that's quite right," Jury said.

"But he is," Thaddeus argued.

"But he's not human," Jury countered.

"It doesn't matter," Doc cut in. "I understand exactly what you mean, old boy."

"Thank you," Thaddeus grumbled. "I'm glad someone does."

"Moving on," Doc said firmly, "do either of you have any idea how to kill a Zeniu?"

"No," both Jury and Thaddeus said.

"Alright," Doc said. "It's the ultimate challenge. In just four days, we have to figure out how to kill a Zeniu, build a case against Mitcham, and then kill him. Should be easy enough."

"Are you sure you're clear on the definition of easy?" Jury asked.

"Absolutely. It's when a task is really difficult and seemingly impossible, but we somehow get it done anyway."

"Sounds about right," Jury laughed. He yawned and added, "I'm going to bed; you can let me know what you figure out in the morning."

"Seriously? I thought you wanted to do more of the planning? Get more of the credit?" Doc pointed out.

"Turns out I like it better when you do the planning," Jury shrugged. "Finesse is all well and good, but it just... Well, it lacks your... panache." Jury grinned widely and scuttled out the door before Doc could respond.

"Lazy," Thaddeus muttered. "His father would be ashamed if he knew."

"Jury's not lazy," Doc retorted.

"Leaving in the middle of a brainstorm to sleep," Thaddeus intoned. "Lazy."

"Some of us use energy and actually need rest," Doc snorted. "We don't just sit around all day."

"As if I choose to sit around," Thaddeus complained. "What I wouldn't give to spend a day running around making messes like you do!"

"Making messes?" Doc laughed. "I didn't get turned into a plant for making messes!"

"I'm different now," Thaddeus snapped.

"Are you?"

"I refuse to be reprimanded by a reprobate."

"Walk away then," Doc drawled.

Thaddeus snarled, and for a moment neither of them said a word.

"You have probably changed," Doc finally said. "Right?"

Thaddeus grunted.

"Knowing what it feels like, I doubt you'd cage a cryptid anymore," Doc offered.

"I hope that's truly the case," Thaddeus said softly. "I really do."

"Me too," Doc said.

He pulled out his cards and began to shuffle. It seemed as if he was always shuffling cards, but it helped him think. Usually. He was impatient to get to it, but he didn't know where he was going or what he was doing.

First things first, he needed to kill Mitcham. He'd never killed a Zeniu, but how hard could it be? He'd killed lots of cryptids and creatures over the years. If one thing didn't kill them, you just kept trying things until you found the one that did.

Suddenly he could hear Andrew's voice, clear as day, speaking, and he closed his eyes, letting the memory take him, because he was afraid if he didn't, he'd accidentally turn and see that Andrew wasn't really there.

"It didn't stick the first time," Andrew said.

"That makes no sense," Doc argued. "You either killed her or you didn't."

"We did," Andrew insisted. "Or rather Pecos did. I just held her in place so she couldn't zap away. She died; I felt her die."

Doc waited for Andrew to go on.

"But she didn't. She slept it off. Or fed it off. I don't know." Andrew shrugged.

If only Andrew had known. If only he had known that it was Doc who had woken the Black Shaman. Maybe. Doc frowned. He hadn't exactly done it yet. There was a chance...

He shook his head irritably. First things first, he needed to kill Mitcham. Maybe if he slept on it, a more inspired idea would come to him.

Doc slept, drifting through dreams of lovely women before landing in a nearly forgotten memory. The air was just as sultry as he remembered, and he could still smell the warm fragrance of the dogwood trees, even though it was night.

He was young, and he could feel the inadequacy of his adolescent body and the rush of overpowering emotions that threatened to drag him under.

Even though he hadn't revisited it in years, he knew this moment. Francisco had just told him to come down, but he didn't want to. He wanted to stay up in this tree where things seemed far away and weren't quite solid or real.

So instead young John ignored Francisco's request and asked, "Do you believe in heaven?" His tone was desperate, and he knew it, but he couldn't seem to change it.

"Sure," Francisco said. "Now, come on down. Mother's worried, and besides, it's nearly midnight."

"I like it here," John lied. His legs were numb, and his fingers were raw from clutching the bark.

"That was a pretty good lie," Francisco said. "Next time try to keep your tone more even."

"Like you did when you said you believed in heaven?" John muttered.

Francisco sighed and started climbing up the tree; he sat on the limb beside John and gazed silently at the stars. "The thing is, pup," he finally said, "to believe in heaven, you have to also believe in hell."

"And you don't?" John asked, struggling not to yawn.

Francisco shrugged, not a motion he generally made. "There are a lot of evil people in the world," he said, "and surely some of them deserve to be tortured for a while. But for all eternity? Forever and ever?"

A bat flew overhead, and they were both quiet for a moment. When Francisco spoke again, his voice carried a trace of accent and sadness. "My great-grandmother believed that every person's spirit was just part of the Great Spirit, just little bits and pieces plucked from the vastness and dropped into waiting wombs. And she said that when we die we return to the Great Spirit, and the Spirit changes just a little."

John tried to visualize such a cycle and found it oddly soothing. "Like rain," he whispered.

"Exactly like that," Francisco replied.

A sudden shriek tore Doc from his dream, and he sprang up in bed, listening intently and sighing with exasperation when he heard Jules Baker say "sorry, Thaddeus" in a hushed tone. "I didn't mean to frighten you," she added. "I didn't realize you were asleep."

"One of the many perks of being a plant," Thaddeus complained.

"Is Doc up?" Johnny asked excitedly.

"I'm sure he is now," Thaddeus replied. "But you had better wait for him to come out. I'm afraid he doesn't hold with the puritan tradition of wearing clothing to bed."

Doc chuckled softly when he heard Frankie stutter, "Perhaps we'd better just go."

"But I wanna see Doc," Addison whimpered.

"Give me a minute!" Doc called out. He really didn't have time for the Baker children, but they wouldn't understand that. And furthermore, there was a slight chance Jules might know some obscure tidbit about Zenius that could be helpful. Since it wasn't yet six o'clock though, he was going to make them wait.

"How did the Baker children gain access to my suite?" Doc texted Jervis as he padded towards the shower.

"I gave them the code seven months ago so they could visit Thaddeus whenever they wanted," Jervis replied.

"Change the code."

"If you don't want them walking in on you, tell them so."

"Kiss your raise for the day goodbye."

Jervis responded with a yellow kissy face.

Doc raised an eyebrow and texted back, "Keep that up, and I'll think you have a sense of humor."

"Hardly," Jervis replied.

"Have Pierre send up breakfast, and make sure Emily gets what she likes."

"Her shift ends in an hour," Jervis responded. "At which point Randell will take over for her."

"I don't like Randell," Doc stated.

"You've never met Randell. Emily is not like you, sir. She can't stay awake for the next four days. She needs rest."

"We'll see," Doc replied.

He took a leisurely shower, allowing the hot water to soak fully into his bones, and by the time he was finished and dressed, he felt he could handle the Baker children with the patience they so required.

When he opened his bedroom door he heard Jules talking excitedly. "So the way the story goes," she said, "is that Holderman Luxury Suites, the name of Dulcis before it was Dulcis, was set to be demolished. I think the year was 1915 or something like that."

1914, Doc corrected silently.

"Anyway, the day before they started tearing it down, this flush business man walks in and buys the entire block. The sheets go up, the construction crews come in, and two years later, Holderman Luxury Suites reopens, only now it's Logan Luxury Suites."

Jules leaned forward and continued breathlessly. "It was so popular it was booked solid for the first five years."

"Only the first three," Doc drawled.

The children jumped, and Jules's face turned pale. Doc chuckled and said, "It looks as if breakfast has arrived. While we eat, why don't you tell me how you find these 'stories', Jules? But before we get to all that, how are you all?"

"Where've you been?" Addison demanded, giving Doc a tight hug. "You missed my birthday party."

"Sorry, love. Did I at least send you a present?"

"A big stuffed unicorn!"

"I have excellent taste," Doc said cheerfully. "Have you kept up with your lessons, Johnny?"

"Yes, sir."

"Good. I'll have to come see you in action. And you, Frankie, have you learned to control out-of-control witches yet?"

She blushed, and Boudica, whose head had been on Frankie's lap, turned to glare at him.

"I'm sure you'll get there," Doc laughed.

He gestured for them to head to the dining room, picked up Thaddeus, and followed them. "So Jules," he said, pouring himself half a cup of coffee and topping it off with whiskey. "How do you find your information?"

Jules glanced at Johnny. He shrugged and stuffed a piece of bacon into his mouth. Jules met Doc's eyes nervously and said, "I'm sorry; I shouldn't have been talking about you."

"I don't care about that," Doc grinned. "I'm just curious who your source is."

"Oh!" Jules's face brightened. "I don't have a source. It's

easy, really. I just searched the newspaper archives for Dulcis Requiem, and read through the articles until I found the old name, Logan Luxury Suites, then I followed that name back until I found Holderman Luxury Suites. It was purchased by a man named James Logan, and that's obviously you because the hotel is now owned by James Logan the third."

"A scholar after my own heart," Thaddeus sighed.

"And what did you find out about James Logan?" Doc asked.

"He's quite reclusive," Jules said. "He owns a handful of properties all over the States, but there're no photographs of him, just a description in one of the earlier articles, as well as, a description of his German manager."

Doc raised an eyebrow. "And what did it say about the German manager?"

"Nothing much," Jules said. "Just mentioned that he was apparently capable of producing modern miracles. I was wondering though—" Jules began, but Doc cut her off.

"Do you spend all your free time reading?" he asked.

"Yes. Well, no. I also practice magic. I mean I have to find an area I'm skilled in or I'll end up working a norm job," she explained with some amount of horror.

"I see. Can you use magic to research? Combine your two skills?"

"No," Jules replied automatically, then her brow furrowed. "Well... I mean... I don't think so."

"Maybe you should try. In the meantime, I'd like to hire you."

"Hire me? For what?"

"I need to kill a Zeniu."

Jules stared at him in confusion, then the blood slowly and completely drained from her face. "No," she breathed.

"Yes."

"No."

"Afraid so."

"You can't," she whispered, eyes humongous.

"Can't what?" Johnny asked.

"I'm going to kill Mitcham," Doc said easily.

"No!" Johnny gasped. "You can't!"

"Technically, as long as I can figure out how," Doc responded. "I really can."

Their signature purple bubble popped up around their heads, and the twins began to talk frantically. Doc didn't bother reading their lips because he had a pretty good idea of what they were saying.

"What's the big deal?" Frankie asked. "Don't you kill people all the time?"

"Mitcham is the head of the Hidden," Thaddeus explained. "If Doc kills him, but especially if he kills him without a compelling reason, he'll be hunted down and... destroyed."

"Oh," Frankie said. After a minute she added, "Then don't."

"I'm afraid I've come too far for that," Doc said. "He wants to control me, and I can't allow that. It's either him or me; I prefer him."

"Oh."

The purple bubble disappeared, and Jules said, "This is insane."

"Think of it as a calculated risk," Doc countered.

"But I don't know anything about Zenius!" she exclaimed.

"Learn," Doc suggested. "Quietly, of course. Apparently Mitcham has eyes and ears literally everywhere. And quickly; I need to know within two days."

"Two days!" Jules gasped. "I can't do that!"

"As a friend of mine once said, never plan to lose," Doc suggested.

Jervis knocked on the front door; and Doc stood and said, "Excuse me for a moment."

"This is Randell," Jervis said after Doc had opened the door. Doc studied the tall, broad man with suspicion. Randell stood perfectly still and smiled widely.

"Fine," Doc sighed.

"I won't let you down, sir," Randell said sincerely.

"It's not me you should worry about," Doc snorted.

Randell glanced sideways at Jervis and said, "Quite right, sir."

Jervis gave Doc a perfectly blank look, turned on his heel, and left.

"This way," Doc said, leading Randell towards Bree's room.

Emily was pale, with dark rings around her eyes, and she looked exceedingly relieved to see Randell. Doc felt a brief surge of irritation that her shift had been so long in the first place.

"I'm ready when you are," Randell said. She nodded and held out her hand. Randell took it, and they both closed their eyes, then Randell said, "Got them."

"Thank you," Emily breathed, sagging against the desk.

"Are you alright?" Doc asked in concern.

"Nothing a good nap and a steak won't cure," she replied. She picked up her notes and said, "You want me just to give you the highlights or do you want to read through it all?"

"Both," Doc said, gesturing for her to follow him to the sitting room. "Sit," he ordered. "Do you want my breakfast? I haven't eaten any of it yet."

"That's not really professional," she hedged.

"I won't tell Jervis if you won't."

She laughed and said, "Alright, I'll take it."

"Give me a second," he said. He walked into the dining room, interrupting Thaddeus's lecture about the heroic qualities of the first tetrarch.

"Stay in here," Doc ordered as he grabbed his plate. "I'll be back in a bit."

He handed the plate and a fork to Emily, sat across from her, and said, "Highlights?"

"To begin with, he feels absolutely secure in his home," Emily said.

Doc had noticed before that Emily was very careful not to say Mitcham's name, which annoyed him. He still didn't understand what Mitcham had done to inspire such terror, and so far no one seemed inclined to tell him.

She quickly ate half the omelet, then said, "After you left, he called in someone named Alex, and they talked about you for a while. I wrote it all down. He was really pleased you showed up groveling, and he said it was not a moment too soon."

Doc prickled slightly at the word "groveling" but reminded himself that's exactly how he wanted Mitcham to perceive him.

"A lot of what they said didn't make sense to me," Emily said, "but it sounds as if Bosch stole something that's integral to his grand plan."

Interesting. "Did he say what?" Doc asked.

"No," she replied. "But on the bright side, several of the fairy wasps infiltrated other areas of the house. A few rode out with that old man who read the ears. They keep him in a cell below the house." Her eyes grew troubled, and she said, "There are quite a few cells, but I can't see much. It's too dark down there."

"Who's guarding them?" Doc asked, just to make sure he could still trust Simon and his men.

"No one."

"No one?"

"The door to the basement is hidden behind a panel in the butler's pantry," she explained. "And no one goes down there but Luke, the butler."

Very interesting.

"His wife mostly stays on the second floor. I didn't see them interact with each other at all. And if he has children, they aren't in the house."

"How many servants?" Doc asked.

"Just Luke," she said. "There are two Takaheni guards at all times, but sometimes he sends them outside to do a perimeter check."

"So they don't see something they shouldn't," Doc murmured. "He doesn't trust them." That explained why they hadn't been there when he'd delivered the ears.

"Can you tell who's listening in on everyone?" Doc asked.

"No. I'm sorry."

"Don't be. You've done an excellent job, Emily. Tell Jervis to give you a raise."

"He said you'd say that, and he told me to tell you that I'm paid a fair wage so to stop interfering."

"Really?" Doc chuckled.

"That's what he said."

"Well then, how about a bottle of whiskey?"

Her eyebrow arched, and she grinned mischievously. "That's really more of a gift," she said. "I don't see how he can object to that."

Doc winked at her and went to get a fresh bottle.

After Emily had left, Doc rejoined the children at the

table. Now they were talking about the number of witches the tetrarch employed.

"Mitcham approached the council just last week about lifting the limit on witch households," Jules said confidentially.

"That's madness," Thaddeus snorted. "With your long lifespans and control of the elements you'd soon be in a position of strength that no other cryptids or humans could match."

"That's exactly what the council said!" Jules exclaimed.

"I've never paid much attention to how the Hidden government is set up," Doc drawled. "But I find it a little surprising that an eleven-year-old witch would be privy to council meetings."

Jules blushed.

"Let me guess," Doc said. "Another aunt?"

"No!" Jules retorted. "He's actually my cousin," she admitted softly. "Once removed."

"Ah. And he's on the council?"

"Of course not!" Jules laughed. "He's just a secretary."

"Does the council usually go along with Mitcham's plans?"

"It's mixed," Jules said. "Although they do often support his plans even if they don't agree with them. When he first took over, some of the council members who opposed him disappeared, but they were always replaced with staunch..." she paused and searched for the correct word.

"Unsupporters?" Doc supplied.

"That's not a word," she complained.

"But it's the right idea, isn't it?"

"I suppose. Anyway, even though they've blocked more than a few of his projects, none of the council members have gone missing in the last fifteen years."

"It must really irritate Mitcham that they stand in his way," Doc mused.

"He manages to find ways around them," Johnny said. "For instance, they didn't support his supplying of more cryptids to the norm government than the original contract requires, but he got around that by getting the cryptids to 'volunteer'."

"Clever," Doc said.

"And they always vote down his tax laws," Jules said. "So he just changes the wording and calls it a government remuneration for Hidden updates. He doesn't have to run remunerations past the council, you see."

"I'm beginning to think he's quite diabolical," Doc muttered. "In general, how long do Zenius live?"

"No one knows," Johnny said. "They've never been studied like so many of the other cryptids, and they are very closed mouthed about their species."

"Except for the six in power and their lackeys," Jules put in, "they all live in special communities built just for Zenius."

"Six?" Doc sighed.

"Yes," Jules said, her voice taking on her schoolmarm tone. "After Mitcham was elected as tetrarch of the United States Hidden, Zenius were also elected in Mexico, Brazil, France, Canada, Russia, and Spain."

"Tell me more bad news," Doc said irritably.

Johnny and Jules exchanged a glance, and then the purple bubble enveloped them once more. This time Doc watched their lips.

"Should we tell him?" Johnny asked.

"He should probably know," Jules said.

"I don't think he'll like it."

"No, but it's better than him finding out later."

"Are you sure?"

"Pretty sure?" Jules said, face not the least bit sure.

"You do it."

"You're older."

"But you're smarter," Johnny countered.

"You're only saying that because you want me to do it."

"So?"

"Fine."

The bubble dissipated, and they both studied the table in front of them.

"Just tell me already," Doc said.

Jules cleared her throat. "Well, the thing is, Mitcham's created a Hidden United Nations of sorts."

"Yes?" Doc said.

"And besides the six Hiddens run by Zenius, Mitcham has... um... convinced most of the other Hiddens to join."

"You mean coerced," Doc said flatly.

"I mean, who knows?" Jules said with a shrug. "I wasn't even born yet."

"Go on," Doc sighed.

"Well, they're having a summit here in Denver, and a bunch of the leaders will be there."

"Let me guess," Doc drawled. "This summit is happening sometime soon?"

Jules licked her lips nervously, played with her fork, and looked around the room a time or two before whispering, "In six days."

7

It took Doc another hour to send the Baker children on their way. He had them take Boudica as well so she wouldn't be lonely, but mostly so she couldn't keep looking at him with her sad eyes.

But even though it was quiet once they were gone and he could drink straight from his whiskey bottle again, he still couldn't think of exactly where to start.

"It's too big," he muttered, resting his head against the back of his couch.

He could almost hear Andrew chastising him. He'd say something along the lines of, "It sounds like you're planning to lose, Doc."

He wasn't though. He had every intention of winning; he just didn't know how yet.

"I know you never truly appreciate my advice," Thaddeus offered somewhat gloomily. "But perhaps you should pick the smallest task and start there."

"That's a great idea, but what's the smallest task?"

"I've never been one to interfere or tell you what to do," Thaddeus began.

"Since when?" Doc snorted.

"I've been an exemplary plant," Thaddeus snapped.

"Would you like me to get out the dictionary?" Doc laughed. "I'm pretty sure chastising the one who waters you is not exemplary."

"I never chastise Rosa."

"Point taken," Doc chuckled. "What were you going to say?"

"No, no, I wouldn't want to interfere."

"Please do. I'm not exactly getting anywhere on my own, and the clock is ticking down rather quickly."

"I was just going to say that, as you say, this is a rather large problem. Much larger than you're used to dealing with. You're about to take on not just the government of one Hidden but of almost all the Hiddens. It's a fool's errand. Or perhaps more aptly, a forlorn hope."

"You're making it look so much better," Doc drawled.

"Hush," Thaddeus commanded. "What I'm trying to say is this one might actually get you killed."

"I know," Doc sighed. "It's a little depressing. I don't think I'm ready yet."

"I'm not sure you will ever be ready. You live with a zeal few people can comprehend. However, you did make a promise to someone, and you may want to consider keeping it before you leap into the jaws of death."

"I still owe a few favors," Doc argued, "but I haven't made any promises... Oh. Right. Thank you. I was procrastinating because I forgot it's been eight months for everyone else."

"Anyway," Thaddeus said, voice infused with dreadful

fake cheerfulness, "complete a few small tasks, and you'll be much invigorated."

Doc couldn't say why it was so hard for him to knock on Bree's door. He'd known when he had taken her as his own that he would outlive her; he'd accepted it, and he'd thought he'd made peace with it but apparently not.

The pain was so much deeper, the fear more stark. It didn't matter how often he told himself he was being a fool, that he still had decades of good years with her, his heart ached every time he saw her. He couldn't bear the thought of her death, and so he avoided her, much like he'd avoided Francisco. It was time, however, to stop protecting himself and start protecting her.

He knocked, making sure it was loud enough for her to actually hear, and waited patiently for her to open the door.

"Doc!" she exclaimed in surprise when she saw him.

"See, I told you I would come by," he proclaimed cheerfully. She knew him better than anyone, but it was always easier to lie to someone when you were telling them what they wanted to hear.

"Come in!" she said happily. "Where have you been?"

"Do you remember the story I told you about the Grey Shaman?"

"Yes. He was quite mischievous, if I recall."

"He finally called in his favor."

"Oh dear," she said, green eyes wide with curiosity. "You'd better sit down and tell me all about it."

So he sat and told her about Ahanu's request, carefully leaving out any mentions of Mitcham.

"Are you going to do it?" she asked.

"I'm not sure I have a choice," he said with a shrug. "Not

if that's the way things need to happen." He frowned, then forced a grin. "That's a rather depressing story though, so let me tell you about Jury's fiancée."

"Jury has a fiancée?" she exclaimed.

"Well, he did."

She listened aptly, laughing uproariously at his description of the Jury family's defeat.

"It was quite fortuitous for Jury that the Baudelaires died just before the wedding," she commented knowingly.

"Wasn't it, though?" Doc said. "Marie would have made him absolutely miserable."

He told her all about the Bakers, and she nearly spit out her whiskey when he described the incident at Jury's apartment with long-legged Amy.

"They just put a bubble on her head?" she giggled.

"Until she passed out from lack of air," he said.

"And how old are they?"

"Eleven; unless they turned twelve and didn't tell me."

"Aren't you glad you're not the one raising them?" she laughed.

"Yes, although Jervis did give them the code to my suite."

"He didn't!" she gasped. "How could he?"

"I think he's recently developed a strange sense of humor."

"I don't believe it," she laughed, topping off his whiskey cup.

When he'd run out of things to say, she took over, telling him some of the highlights of the last six years.

"I went to Ireland," she said. "And visited every single castle."

"I'm surprised you're home then," Doc said dryly.

"It did take me a while," Bree laughed. "And when I got back I joined a fencing club."

He raised an eyebrow.

"It's fun," she said defensively.

"Not if you have to pretend to lose."

"I don't pretend to lose," she countered. He gave her a look, and she shrugged and added, "At least not very often."

"If you say so," he shrugged.

"I still work at the Banshee," she said at one point. "But Aine does a wonderful job, and she doesn't really need me anymore."

Doc watched her carefully. It seemed that all mortals eventually reached this point. The point when they no longer saw the point.

"I'm thinking about moving," she said softly. "Opening up a Banshee somewhere else."

"Where would you go?" Doc asked, heart clenching.

"I really liked Ireland," she said. "It... It felt like home."

"Ireland's nice," Doc said carefully. "The women there are fiery. And they can hold their whiskey."

She laughed. "So if I go, you'll come visit me?"

"Absolutely," he promised. Assuming I'm still alive, he added silently. "I always wanted to rent one of those picturesque cottages by the sea."

"No, you haven't," she giggled.

"Really," he insisted. "It's the best way to attract selkies."

"You're incorrigible," she laughed.

"I'm adorable," he countered.

He studied her naturally pale skin and remembered all the nights he'd stayed awake with her, comforting her while she fought the urge to shriek. Living in a city had been difficult for her because so many people and animals were always dying. It had taken Bree years, along with the help of several special stones, to be able to block out all the pain and fear she'd constantly felt.

He'd sometimes envied her because she had a unique view of life. Banshees saw things as they were dying, passing over, returning to the spirit or the mother or going wherever they went. They saw the moment before though, not the moment after, and when he remembered that, he remembered the way her family had died and grieved for her. How he wished he could somehow take the pain away.

But perhaps... He suddenly wondered if she'd ever felt a Zeniu die.

He picked up a notepad from her table and wrote, "I have to ask you a question."

She nodded and said, "Let me get some more whiskey," but she didn't leave the room.

He winked and wrote, "Do you know how to kill a Zeniu?"

He watched her eyes read his question. Over and over. Then she frowned at him.

"I have to do it," Doc wrote.

She raised one eyebrow.

"Trust me," he added.

She rolled her eyes and took the paper pad from him. "No, I don't," she wrote. "But I know someone who might."

"Who?" Doc mouthed.

"You said you'd visit me in Ireland," she wrote.

He snatched back the paper and wrote, "And I will. I have no intention of losing."

"You never do!" she wrote angrily.

"And I never have, have I?" Doc wrote back.

"As if you'd tell me!" she mouthed.

"Here's your whiskey," she said out loud. "Jervis accidently mentioned someone named Sami the other day. He seemed... flustered is the only word I can think of," she chuckled. "Have you met her?"

"I can't believe I forgot to tell you about her," Doc said, then he launched into a long description of Sami, watching as Bree wrote several paragraphs. It was definitely more than a name, which was interesting.

Bree laughed in all the right places, often making noises or comments. When she was done writing, she handed him a slip of paper, and he ended his story by saying that Jury was going to keep Sami on as his building manager.

"Thank you for coming by," she said sincerely. "I've missed you. Five years was too long."

"I know," he said. "I'm... I'm sorry."

She smiled brilliantly and said, "You never have to apologize to me; you know that."

"And you never have to tell me I'm right," Doc said.

"You're not right," she said with a dismissive shrug.

"I was right about you."

"Alright, sometimes you're not not right," she giggled.

"I'll take it," Doc said warmly.

She laughed, gave him a quick hug, and shoved him out the door. "Next time you come, bring Boudica," she ordered as she closed the door in his face. "And the Bakers!" she yelled through the door.

"You're not ready for the Bakers," he muttered softly as he walked slowly to his car. He climbed inside, rolled down his window, and began to read her curvy squiggles.

"After Billy died, I dated a man named Ian Comyn."

Doc had not known that. He obviously needed to pay closer attention; he didn't like the idea of her dating just anyone.

"And before you say it, I'm a grown woman. You don't get to interview my love interests anymore."

She knew him so well.

"Furthermore," she added, "you raised me to be strong, to be independent, to be fierce. And you know that I carry six knives on my person at all times. So just quit your worrying."

She had him there.

"I met Ian at the Banshee. He's quite a good gambler. But you'll be interested to know that he's a Zeniu although he lives on his own as a human. I believe he has some sort of glamour amulet. I don't know for sure, but since I can see through glamours, I was able to see him as he is."

He found it a little aggravating that he'd found out banshees could see through glamours from Aine, and he wondered what else Bree had kept from him. He sighed. He supposed she was entitled to a few secrets; he certainly had plenty.

"He owns a vintage record shop downtown," she wrote. "Tell him I sent you."

She'd included the address and a few other points, but then she stopped writing about Ian. There was a large space and then a single sentence. "I love you, Dad. Always."

Doc reread those last words, then carefully folded the sheet of paper and placed it inside his pocket next to his pack of playing cards.

Ian's record shop was located snugly between a brewery and an art gallery, and it had a large flashy sign announcing its name, "Vinyl Island".

Doc pushed open the door and was greeted by the clatter of a triangle and a barking dog. He gave the dog a very stern look, and it dropped its head, tucked its tail, and retreated to the back of the shop.

"I wonder why that doesn't work on Boudica," he mused as he walked up the center aisle.

The space inside the store did not match the storefront; it was easily triple in size, but Doc would hazard a guess no one had ever bothered to notice. Or if they did, they just passed it off as their mind playing tricks.

"Can I help you?" asked a skinny young woman with thick dreadlocks and a wide smile.

"Certainly," Doc said easily. "I'm looking for the owner, Ian Comyn."

"Ian just stepped out," she said with a shrug. "He could be back anytime. You can hang if you want. There's a record player over there," she added, gesturing towards the corner.

Doc glanced around the store. He liked music; but he couldn't see himself sitting in the corner with a pair of headphones jamming out to... He wasn't even sure what he'd be jamming out to.

"Mental note to self," he muttered as he walked down another aisle. "Start listening to music." He picked up a case and turned it upside down trying to figure out the transcendental imagery. "Or not," he chuckled, replacing the case.

"How about I leave him a note?" Doc asked.

"Whatever you want, dude," she replied, tossing him a notepad and a pen. "Pretty sure it's a free country."

Only if a politician didn't want something from you, but there was no point trying to explain that to her.

Doc wrote a to-the-point note, folded it around one of his cards, and handed it to her. "If you'd make sure he gets this right away," Doc divulged, "I would really appreciate it. It has to do with my daughter and is rather important."

"I'll make sure he gets it," she promised.

"Thank you very much."

She nodded distractedly, and Doc laughed softly as he headed for the door.

Just as he stepped outside his phone beeped, and Doc pulled up the text. "I'm calling in my favor, Bennie."

Of course he was. It's not like Doc had anything else going on right now.

"I just changed my phone," Doc texted back. "How do you always have my number?"

"I have my ways."

"Well?" Doc asked.

"I want you to kill a frat house."

"Is that all?" Doc texted back. "The actual house or the people in the house?"

"Don't be an ass. You know what I mean," Bennie replied, which surprised Doc because Bennie usually had more of a sense of humor.

"Can I know why I'm killing them?"

"Trying to flake on me?"

"You know me better than that; I just like to know why. Sometimes I make it quick. Sometimes I take my time. You know how it is."

"They hurt one of my daughter's friends."

"Hurt?"

"Goddamn, Doc! Do I need to spell it out? They raped her! She's in the hospital right now!"

"Give me the address," Doc replied.

It was true he had other things to do, but he was never too busy to kill a rapist.

Doc flipped a u-turn, which was no easy task on a busy Denver street, and headed towards the fraternity house. As he drove he worked out his plan. The best plans were made on the fly; Andrew had always said so.

Doc grinned, remembering this time they'd freed a bunch of orphan boys from a mining tycoon.

"So what's our plan?" Doc had asked Andrew as they crept through the snow towards a locked shack.

"I don't have one yet," Andrew whispered back. "It usually comes to me when I need it."

"You mean at the very last minute?"

"Pretty much."

"Is that why Doyle likes to hang back in the trees?"

"Nah. That's just 'cause he's grumpy, and the whistle his sniper rifle makes cheers him up," Andrew replied with a short laugh.

Doc doubted that. Doyle stayed in the trees so he could bail Andrew out of trouble if he needed it. Not that he would need it. Andrew didn't really need a plan or backup or help; he was a one-man army.

The memory shifted, and Doc was sitting in Andrew's ranch house, feet up on the hearth.

Andrew was sitting to the right of Doc, sipping at his coffee, a happy expression on his face. Andrew's wife, Jane, was in the other room with their son Bill, and their conspiratorial laughter was drifting down the hallway.

On the other side of Andrew, Doyle was carving something. Probably another cow. That man had very little imagination. Would it kill him to carve something he hadn't seen? Like an African lion or something?

"I still don't understand why you hold back," Doc said as he absently shuffled a deck of cards. "You could single-handedly defeat the entire United States army if you wanted to."

"I think that's laying it on a bit thick," Andrew said with a deep laugh.

"I don't know about that," Doc argued. "You killed twenty men in less than a minute, and I didn't even see you do it. I blinked, and they were dead."

"That's not true," Andrew pointed out. "I only killed fifteen of them."

"Still. I don't get it. How come you sometimes kill fifteen men like it's nothing and other times you just walk away?"

"The way I figure it," Andrew replied, "I wasn't always here, so everything I do changes something. What if I kill a whole bunch of bad guys, and the Black Shaman wakes up early? Or what if I accidently kill my grandpa? I mean, honestly, if I thought about it too much, I'd probably tie myself to my bed and never leave."

Doc tried to see the logic in that, but he wasn't sure he could. Ahanu could say time was like an ocean all he wanted; it still looked like a river to Doc.

"Anyway, I thought of a joke the other day," Andrew said.

Doyle groaned. "Boy, I have heard every single one of your jokes a thousand times. They don't get no funnier."

"Maybe not for you," Andrew laughed, "but Doc's never heard this one."

"I'm pretty sure he's glad 'bout that," Doyle growled.

"He loves my jokes," Andrew argued. "It's the only reason he sticks around. So anyway, this three-legged dog walks into a bar, he walks up to the man at the counter, and he says—"

"Says?" Doyle interrupted. "It's a dog, right?"

"It's a joke, Doyle," Andrew sighed. "In jokes, dogs can talk. In fact, I once met a real dog that could talk." He winked at Doc and shook his head. "I didn't really," he whispered. "A coyote though. Now shut up, Doyle. You nearly ruined the punch line."

Doyle snorted, but Andrew ignored him and went on, "So the dog, he was three-legged, you remember, walks up to the man at the counter and says, 'Hey, you the man who shot my paw!'" Andrew grinned widely. "Get it? Paw? Pa? It's like his dad, but it's his paw!"

Doc fought to hold back a chuckle because he didn't want Andrew to think he actually thought the joke was funny. It wasn't. But watching Andrew laugh until tears rolled down his cheeks was hilarious, and Doc finally gave in.

"Don't encourage 'im," Doyle grunted. "Next thing you know he'll be tellin' it to you over and over and over."

"I'd never do that," Andrew laughed. "Hey, Jane, come here!"

"I've heard it!" Jane yelled back. "Wasn't funny then; isn't funny now."

"Oh come on, Janey."

"You better hope you didn't just 'Janey' me!" she snapped from the doorway.

"I didn't," Andrew said, trying to make his face serious. "I swear."

"He definitely said 'Jane'," Doc put in with a grin.

"They're lyin' to you," Doyle stated.

"Why would you do that?" Andrew demanded. "I thought we were friends?"

"We were friends, but then you went and told that damn joke. Again."

The memory and laughter faded as Doc parked his car outside the address Bennie had texted him. He studied the house for a second, not really seeing it, but instead remembering them. They'd been his second family. And what a strange family it had been; composed of so many wanderers, lost souls, and strays, just like him.

He liked to believe they were all still together. Laughing and arguing. He couldn't stand the idea that they weren't, that they were all separate, tossed to the winds and scattered. In his mind they were all nestled safely against the mother's bosom, just waiting. Waiting for the rest of them to come.

8

Doc strode up the sidewalk towards the fraternity house and knocked firmly on the front door. After a long wait, a young man with messy hair and red-rimmed eyes answered.

"Whadda you want?" he mumbled.

"Name's Mackey," Doc said with an excited pitch. "Tom Mackey. Member of the ol' frat here. Three generations now. I'm in town for a day or two, and I want to throw a party for all you good ol' boys. There'll be women, booze, and all kinds of stuff that's good for your health." Doc gave an exaggerated wink and said, "You follow my drift?"

The young man did because he was smiling the half-smile of someone imagining a night of decadence.

"What's your name, son?" Doc asked.

"Ralph," he murmured.

"Fine name, Ralph, fine name. Now, listen up. I want you to bring all your frat brothers tonight, but frat brothers only. This is your day in the sun. Or night in the booze if you will," Doc said with a self-indulgent chuckle.

"Here's the location," Doc said, handing Ralph a card with

the address of one of his safe houses written on it. "Frat brothers only. You understand?"

Ralph nodded.

"At the end of the night I'm going to donate a hundred thousand dollars to your house," Doc said in an undertone.

Ralph's eyes went wide.

"Just think what you and your brothers could do with a hundred thousand dollars," Doc said. "But I'm not gonna give you anything if you don't all show up. Have to give honor to the old guard, if you understand me."

Ralph didn't, so Doc pointed towards his own chest with both thumbs. "This guy, right here. I'm the old guard."

"Oh," Ralph said finally. "I get it."

He didn't, but he'd show up, and that was all Doc cared about.

"I'll see you tonight, Ralph. Ten o'clock sharp. It'll be the best party of your life," Doc added with a grin.

Doc gave him a friendly pat on the arm, then ambled back down the sidewalk. He paused just outside his car, looked over his shoulder, and winked. He wanted Ralph to really see his fully customized Zenvo TSR-S. He wanted him to understand how much it had cost. Ralph saw it, and Doc could tell he understood the unspoken message.

Doc climbed inside, waved cheerfully out the window, and sped off down the street, chuckling softly. They'd be there. They'd be there with bells on.

"This day..." Doc trailed off. He'd been going to say it had been a complete waste of time, but it hadn't been. He'd thoroughly enjoyed his time with Bree; he hadn't realized just how much he'd missed her.

"Anyway," Doc amended. "I didn't figure out a damn

thing, and I have to pretend to throw a party for some frat boys tonight."

"What're you really doing?" Jervis asked, moving one of his pawns.

"Killing them. Bennie called in his favor."

"Not Bennie's usual style."

"They raped his daughter's friend."

"Did you verify?"

"Does it matter?" Doc shrugged. "He's calling in a favor."

Jervis raised a thin eyebrow. "That's not your usual style either."

"Ralph was a type," Doc insisted.

"You have a bit of a blind spot when it comes to rapists," Jervis said evenly. "If I wanted you to kill someone for me, I'd definitely tell you he was a rapist."

"What're you trying to say?" Doc demanded with a laugh.

"Would you like me to verify?" Jervis offered.

"If that will make you happy."

"It will."

"Go nuts then," Doc muttered as he moved his castle.

They played silently for a minute, then Doc said, "I have a problem."

"How to kill a Zeniu?"

"I mean besides that."

"How to prove Mitcham's evil?"

"Besides that," Doc growled. "Can I just tell you?"

"Please."

"I've been thinking about this a lot, I mean ever since Ahanu showed up and asked me to wake the Black Shaman, and there's something I just can't get past."

"And what's that?"

"It's like this, Andrew is from modern day. Right now he

could be sitting in his house several hours from here drinking coffee. Or maybe he's at the shooting range with his friend Vick. Or fighting the Death Bots." Doc paused to imagine that and almost smiled. "I don't know that Andrew though, the Andrew who's alive right now, the young Andrew. I met an older Andrew in 1888, after Ahanu had moved him permanently to the past."

"I'm well aware of how you and Andrew met," Jervis interrupted.

"Bear with me," Doc sighed. "I'm thinking out loud here."

"Carry on then."

"Before I met Andrew, Ahanu moved him back and forth between modern day and the 1800s, but Andrew said he hadn't always existed in the past. And since he didn't always exist in the past, his existence in the past changed time, so he was always really careful what he did. Well, not always, but you get my point."

"I'm not sure I do," Jervis replied.

"I'm not sure I do either," Doc said, rubbing his forehead. Just thinking about the messy web of reality was making his head ache. "What I'm saying is that the Andrew I knew believed it was possible to completely alter reality by say killing his grandfather or something like that. Some people might theorize that there is only one version of reality and since there is only one version, Andrew was always part of the past, and that's why the present is the way it is, therefore it wasn't possible for him to kill his grandfather."

"Time travel is not my area," Jervis broke in, "perhaps you had better spell it out a bit more."

"It's no one's area," Doc grumbled. "That's why this is such a mess. What I'm trying to get to is that Andrew disproved the theory that there is only one reality. He proved, without a doubt, that he had created a different timeline and that his existence in the past had changed the present."

"How so?" Jervis inquired.

"One of the times Ahanu sent him back," Doc explained, "Andrew actually set out to change time. He'd read about a village nearby that had been massacred, and he suggested they save it, and so they did. When he returned to the present, now or somewhere in here, he checked the history, and the massacre never happened. So you see, there is a timeline he wasn't in where the massacre happened, and a timeline he was in where it didn't."

"Why is that a problem?" Jervis asked when Doc didn't continue.

Doc glared at the chessboard. "My problem is that in one version of reality I never met Andrew because he wasn't there to meet. That's like saying I never met you," Doc added with a shudder. "Can you imagine?"

"I'd rather not," Jervis said flatly.

"Right?" Doc exclaimed. "But back to the point, how can I be what wakes the Black Shaman? I didn't even know Andrew when he defeated her even though it's in the future, my actual future." Doc tried to wrap his mind around that, but couldn't. "That statement doesn't even make sense to me," he sighed, "but I know what I'm trying to say."

Jervis took Doc's queen, which irritated Doc because he hadn't seen it coming, which meant he wasn't really paying attention.

They played for another silent moment, then Jervis said, "Checkmate."

"Indeed," Doc said sullenly. He had no problem losing; he just didn't appreciate that he was so distracted he'd let Jervis win.

"We'll have to play again when you're better focused," Jervis chastised.

"Sorry," Doc sighed.

"I can't say that I know anything about time travel or timelines or realities or anything like that," Jervis said slowly. "But I can say that regardless of whether or not you met Andrew in 1888, you always belonged to that time."

Doc leaned back and waited for Jervis to make sense.

"Andrew didn't change the course of your life," Jervis stated.

Doc opened his mouth to argue, but Jervis shook his head. "Just listen," Jervis said. "Señora Teodora saved your life, not Andrew."

"I don't suppose I can argue with that," Doc said.

"So in all versions of the timeline, you live until this day."

"Maybe," Doc allowed.

"At which point the Grey Shaman arrives and asks you to wake the Black Shaman," Jervis said. "Now if you had never met Andrew but had met the Grey Shaman, who also always existed or lived in all versions of the timeline, and you happened to owe the Grey Shaman a favor, you would have always been in this same position whether or not you knew Andrew. The only difference would be your feelings about it."

Doc tried to follow Jervis's logic. "So you're saying I've already woken her once before? Or a thousand times before?"

"Maybe," Jervis said with a shrug.

"I think we need a drink," Doc mumbled, pouring them both glasses of whiskey. He drank his entire glass before finally saying, "I suppose that makes about as much sense as anything. And you don't think I'll utterly mess up everything by getting involved?"

"I think Ahanu would have never asked you if that were indeed the case," Jervis replied.

"Good point." Doc drank another glass of whiskey, then said, "Do you think he just sits in his creepy out-of-time cabin and watches possibilities all day?"

"Couldn't say," Jervis said softly.

Doc could see being ready for death if that was his life. Just sitting there, watching time, hoping things all worked out in the end. If that were his life, he'd hop on the first death train out of there.

"Never mind all that," Doc said. "Tell me what you've been doing; eight months is a long time..."

"Not really," Jervis replied.

"I was just wondering if you, um... you know... played mancala with anyone while I was gone," Doc said with a wink.

"It would be quicker and more to the point just to ask if I've been seeing Sami," Jervis pointed out.

"Well, have you?"

"None of your business."

"I see," Doc grinned.

"You don't see anything. That's one of your biggest flaws."

"Maybe," Doc laughed.

"What are you doing down here in the basement, anyway?" Jervis demanded. "Don't you have things to do?"

"I do; I do. Speaking of which, since I'm throwing a party tonight at my place on Colfax, I'll need some beer and girls there..." Doc grinned widely. "Actually, I think I'll invite Ana and Ina. Yes, that should do nicely."

"You sure about this?"

"I'm always sure; that's why I do things."

"Questionable," Jervis said.

Doc laughed cheerfully and said, "I suppose I better hunt down Jury and make sure he's been staying out of trouble."

"I'm fairly certain he's not the one with the problem," Jervis muttered.

"Well?" Doc asked as he watched Jury devour his twentieth pancake.

"Well what?"

"You had your nap."

"And now I'm eating," Jury said around a mouthful of bacon. "After being in that creepy cabin and holding those glamours and enchanting all those ears, I'm beat. I need to keep my strength up," Jury pointed out. "And since I don't eat people's souls, this is how I do it."

"So you're going to be no help at all?"

"I could probably find Bosch's family," Jury offered.

"I don't see how that helps us," Doc ground out.

"Might help us know what Mitcham is planning. Whatever it is, it's obviously bad, so it might help us explain why you've killed him."

"Why I've killed him?" Doc asked.

"Obviously. We can't very well both kill him."

"Especially not if I kill you first," Doc drawled.

"Don't be like that. You know it's a good idea."

"I think you just don't want to leave your suite."

"That's not true at all," Jury said with an exaggerated air of hurt. "I have to go out and get supplies."

"Supplies?"

"You know, witch stuff. And I should probably stop by Millie's."

"Ah. Those kind of supplies."

"If you think about it," Jury said. "It's been over eight months, and it's not as if we can all go around sleeping with other people's wives."

Doc rolled his eyes and said, "Tell Millie hi for me."

"I don't think so. I'd prefer her to think of me."

"She doesn't even like me," Doc laughed.

"That's what they all say."

"That's hardly my fault," Doc complained as he stood. "Let me know when you find Bosch's family."

"Yep," Jury said, starting in on his omelet.

"It's no big deal," Doc muttered, opening the door and stalking into the hallway. "It's not like I'm trying to accomplish anything difficult here."

He meant to go up to his suite, but he ended up outside on the sidewalk instead. "Maybe I'm overcomplicating it," he muttered as he walked nowhere in particular. "Maybe what I should do is lure Mitcham into a cage and just leave him there. Then I don't have to prove anything to the council or anyone else."

He picked up a drifting piece of litter, tossed it into a nearby trashcan, and muttered, "But what about the other five Zeniu in power? And the Baudelaires?" He sighed. "I don't suppose I could I get away with saying 'not my problem'?"

He didn't bother answering himself. If he killed Mitcham and walked away, it was possible that the other Zenius might suddenly develop a sense of social consciousness; but more than likely, they would just follow in Mitcham's footsteps.

What really irritated Doc about Mitcham was that there wasn't any difference between him and the frat boys. Both of them were treading all over other people's no's, and Doc hated that. Absolutely hated it.

The Denver sidewalk blurred, replaced by a memory;

and in his mind, Doc was walking down another street in another time, a time when he was still mortal, still young, still expecting to make a difference in the world. He hadn't been Doc then, just John Holliday, dental surgeon in training.

He was heading wearily back to his lodgings after a long day of surgeries. Every now and then he wondered if the professors just used the students to do their work for them, but he'd never say that out loud.

He yawned as he turned a corner. If he was lucky, he'd be able to sleep three or four hours before he had to be back at the university.

A muffled whimper filtered through his tired mind, and he paused. He paused because it was the whimper of someone in pain. He was just a block from his bed now; he could just keep walking. But he couldn't, so he turned and started cautiously down the alley.

"Is someone there?" John called out.

Another whimper, and the short sounds of a scuffle, then silence. John kept walking, scanning the darkness for signs of life. A light suddenly flashed to life in one of the narrow windows up above him; and by its illumination, John could see the form of a man crouched on the ground.

"Are you hurt?" John asked.

"Go away," the man growled.

That's when John saw the legs beneath the man, struggling weakly.

"What're you doing?" John demanded.

"None of your goddamn business."

But it was too late now. The scalpel from his bag had already found its way into John's hand, and he rushed forward, lack of sleep making him wild and brave. He pulled the man backwards, stabbing his scalpel deep into the man's neck as he did.

The man howled in pain and slammed his elbow into John's face, knocking him to the ground. John scrambled to his feet and forced his tired legs into a wide stance as the man lumbered angrily towards him. John's hands were in place before he had thought to move them; and when the man dove towards him, fists flying, John ducked and came up with a solid strike to the man's jaw.

The man grunted and stumbled backwards, and John used the opportunity to leap forward and wrap his arm around the man's neck from behind.

"I'll kill you," the man snarled, ripping at John's arm. "I'll kill you, then I'll kill..."

His angry words trailed off, and he stumbled forward, dropping to his knees. John held the choke with one arm and pulled his boot knife with his other hand, stabbing it into the man's heart. A gasp slid past the man's lips, and his body fell forward, pulling John to the ground with it.

John rolled away from the dead man and crawled over to the woman. In the dim light from the upper window, he could see he was too late. Her pale face was a mask of fear, eyes stark, cheeks stained with tears.

John stared into her terrified eyes, asking himself questions he couldn't answer. What if he'd run instead of walked? What if he'd shouted? What if? What if? Could he have saved her? When he could stand the questions no longer, he gently slid her eyelids closed and tugged the hem of her dress down past her knees.

"I'm sorry," he whispered. "I'm terribly sorry."

Through his grief and anger, he still had the presence of mind to retrieve his scalpel and medical bag. He even remembered to roll the man over and remove his knife from the dead man's chest. Then he stumbled out of the alley towards home, stopping along the way to vomit in a flower bed. He'd never killed a man before, but what frightened him was not that he'd killed him, but that he wished he'd taken longer to do it.

Doc's mind returned to the present, and he focused on the actual sidewalk in front of him, slowing his gait slightly. His mind may have been in a different moment, but part of it had still realized he was being followed.

Doc stopped walking altogether, yawned, and turned around. The other pedestrians streamed past him. All except one man.

"Ian?" Doc asked cheerfully.

The man startled slightly. "How could you... I've never even..."

"It was just a guess," Doc said with a shrug.

"You're Doc Holliday."

"I believe I said as much in my note," Doc chuckled.

"And you came to see me because of Bree?" Ian demanded.

"Technically, I came to see you because Bree said you might have the information I need."

"Oh." For a second Ian looked disappointed, but he managed to lock it away fairly quickly and ask, "What information is that?"

"I'm planning to throw a party tonight, and I could use some guidance on the music selection," Doc said easily. "Would you be willing to come back to my place and help me pick some tracks?"

Ian's eyebrows shot up, and he studied Doc for a second before saying, "Alright?"

"Excellent. I look forward to hearing your suggestions," Doc said.

As they walked back to Dulcis, Doc asked inane questions like "What do you think of the weather this year?" and "Do you enjoy driving?"

Ian answered briskly and to the point. It was a very boring conversation, but hopefully anyone listening wouldn't know Doc well enough to realize he didn't believe in wasting time on small talk.

"That was exhausting," Doc sighed when they finally reached his suite. "I need whiskey. You?"

"Sure," Ian said, eyeing Doc strangely.

"I am actually throwing a party tonight," Doc laughed as he grabbed two bottles from the kitchen. "But I don't care about the music." He handed Ian a bottle and gestured for him to sit.

Ian looked between the bottle and Doc with an expression of complete bafflement.

"Sorry," Doc said. "Did you want a glass?"

"Um... I guess not," Ian replied.

"Sit," Doc ordered. "I apologize for that perfectly boring conversation. Apparently Mitcham has eyes and ears everywhere." Ian's face tightened, and Doc hastened to add, "Except in my hotel."

"Are you sure about that?" Ian asked softly.

"Quite."

"What exactly do you want?" Ian demanded.

"Tell me how to kill a Zeniu."

9

Ian stared at Doc, mouth slightly open like a fish, and Doc drank his whiskey, waiting patiently for Ian to recover his senses.

"Did you kill him?" Thaddeus suddenly asked.

"No," Doc chuckled. "He's just... Well, I think I shocked him a bit, is all."

Ian glanced around the room, eyes narrow with suspicion. "Who's there?" he demanded. "You said we were safe here!"

"We are," Doc said calmly. "Please meet my plant, Thaddeus."

"Your plant?" Ian muttered.

"Technically accurate, although I'm actually a man in plant form," Thaddeus corrected sulkily.

Ian still didn't seem to know where to look, so Doc gestured towards Thaddeus's yellow pot and said, "He's the plant, in that pot right there. Thaddeus, this is Ian. Bree dated him."

"Without your approval?" Thaddeus asked dubiously.

"Apparently she doesn't need my approval anymore."

"Hogwash," Thaddeus snorted. "A girl should never outgrow her father's approval."

"Privately, I agree," Doc said. "But please don't ever say that around Bree. I don't think I could bear to hear it."

"You're talking to a plant," Ian stated.

"And you're a Zeniu masquerading as a human; we all have our little eccentricities."

"Bree told you?" Ian muttered, tone injured.

"I'm sure she wouldn't have," Doc said consolingly. "It's just that I'm in the middle of something, and I really need to know how to kill a Zeniu. I've come up with a plan b, as it were, but I prefer plan a."

"Are you serious?" Ian exclaimed. "You actually think you can kill Mitcham?"

"Who said I wanted to kill Mitcham, and why not?"

Ian gave an exasperated snort, then said, "He's the only Zeniu around worth killing. Normally, I'd say go for it. Zenius aren't terribly difficult to kill actually, but in Mitcham's case... Well, plan b is probably the best you'll get."

"But Bosch said Zenius are hard to kill," Doc argued. "And I've asked around; nobody knows how to do it."

"It's not like we go around advertising," Ian snorted. "That would be pretty stupid, don't you think?"

Doc shrugged, feeling a little amused by the whole exchange.

"Talking to a plant," Ian muttered. "How's it talking? I mean, it doesn't have a mouth!"

People so rarely thought to ask that. "Your guess is just as good as mine," Doc drawled. "So why would it be hard to kill Mitcham?"

"Geez, man," Ian exclaimed. "We just met."

Doc grinned slightly. "Here's the thing, I've got about

three days, maybe, to figure out a loose plan here; and you just told me Zenius are fairly easy to kill, so you can either tell me what I need to know or I can experiment on the Zeniu I have until I figure it out."

Ian's blue eyes narrowed. "Did you just threaten to kill me?"

"No," Doc said easily. "I don't threaten; I was just clarifying your options."

"I've never met anyone as nice and accepting as Bree," Ian said.

"That's wonderful," Doc replied, "but I don't see how it relates."

"Are you sure you raised her?"

"Quite sure. I have the broken eardrums to prove it."

At that, Ian suddenly started to laugh.

"I think he's messing with you," Thaddeus grumbled.

"Perhaps," Doc agreed.

"You should see what happens if you poke a hole in his glamour."

"I'm shocked, Thaddy," Doc said, keeping one eye on Ian. "You're an intellectual man; not a man of violence."

"I don't like him," Thaddeus sniffed.

"Yes, but you liked Jefferson, so I'm not sure you're a good judge of character."

"He was one of the founding fathers," Thaddeus sputtered. "Without his efforts the Hidden would never have been formed!"

"Let's not get distracted," Doc said. "I have much more pressing matters to deal with." Ian hadn't quit laughing yet, so Doc took a minute to call Ana.

"Doc," she murmured when she answered. "I've missed you."

Doc grinned, letting his mind drift into Ana's lovely and talented arms.

"Doc?" she said.

"Sorry, I was... remembering." She chuckled sultrily, and he cleared his throat. "I'm afraid I called on business, love."

"I've never had a problem combining work and pleasure," she laughed.

"We'll see what we can do," Doc promised. "Are you and Ina free tonight? I have a frat house that needs... dealt with."

"The entire house?"

"I'm going to feel them out first, but probably."

"Sounds delightful," Ana purred.

"I'm rather looking forward to it. They're coming at ten, so nine-thirty?"

"We'll be there."

The way she said it sent a tingle of awareness over Doc's skin. "I'll text you the address," he said before disconnecting and studying Ian, who had finally stopped laughing and was now watching him.

"You really want to kill Mitcham?" Ian asked.

"Yes," Doc said, controlling his tone so his frustration didn't come through.

"Why?"

"He's a rapist."

"What?" Ian replied in a shocked tone.

"Of people," Doc clarified. "He forces them to do what he wants, takes away their no, subjects them to his will. It's not the same as physical rape," Doc went on, "but mentally it's comparable. When someone strips away your no and forces you to do something you don't want to do, it changes you, makes you less somehow. Shouldn't," Doc mused, "but it does. And so I'm going to kill him. And his lackeys. And when I'm done, the Hidden can run an election for a new tetrarch. One who actually cares about them."

"That's a noble sentiment," Ian said slowly. "It's just... Well, never mind. Like I said, it's not hard to kill a Zeniu, but it'll be almost impossible to kill Mitcham."

"Let's start with the easy part," Doc said.

Ian smiled vaguely. "Kinda figured you'd say that." He stood and removed a silver wrist cuff, and immediately his body shifted and his features faded, only to be replaced with the translucent blue color that was common for Zenius.

"We're corporeal," Ian said. "My head is just as hard as yours, my hand just as firm."

"But I can see through you," Doc argued.

"Can you?"

"Can't I?"

Ian laughed. "Not really. It seems like you can, but what you're really seeing is just my skin, better yet, my camouflage."

"You lost me."

"Traditionally, we live in or near water," Ian explained. "If I were to go skinny dipping in a lake right now, I would blend in fairly well and could probably convince you to come in for a dip."

"Maybe," Doc allowed. "If you had a sister."

Ian laughed and said, "But I'm super convincing."

"I hadn't noticed."

"Yeah," Ian sighed. "I think as a species, we've kinda lost our natural edge. But I'm still a hellavu salesman."

"Exciting," Doc drawled.

"We can't all live an adrenaline-charged life like you," Ian snorted.

"The world would certainly be a different place if it was filled with Doc Hollidays," Doc said.

"Perish the thought," Thaddeus moaned.

"Hush," Doc ordered.

"I still can't believe you have a talking plant," Ian said.

"Based on what you just said, you're essentially a talking puddle," Doc pointed out.

"Touché."

"So how do I kill you?"

"Just like that?" Ian asked. "You're not even gonna offer me money or, I dunno, dinner at least?"

Doc sighed and said, "No."

"Man, you're no easy customer," Ian muttered. "Just stab me in the heart."

"What?" Doc said. "That's too easy. Isn't it?"

"It's not easy actually because humans always think every species' heart should be in the same place as their own."

Doc chuckled softly and said, "Guilty as charged."

"Stab me here," Ian said, gesturing towards his chest, "and you'll just get some blue goo on your knife."

"Where's your heart then?" Doc demanded, getting a little tired of the merry-go-round.

"In my foot."

"What?" Doc exclaimed. "That doesn't make sense. What if you step on a nail?"

"It's encased in bone," Ian said with a shrug.

"But why your foot?"

"Who knows? Maybe our mother had a strange sense of humor. We are pretty... weird."

"Which foot?" Doc demanded.

"Both," Ian replied with a grin.

"Two hearts," Doc muttered thoughtfully.

"Absolutely fascinating," Thaddeus said. "I wish I could... No," he said firmly.

"No?" Doc inquired.

"It's nothing. For a moment there I... forgot myself."

"Hum," Doc said. In other words, for a moment Thaddeus had wanted to cut open a Zeniu so he could see those two hearts.

"So the hard part?" Doc asked Ian.

"You could stab Mitcham in the feet, but unfortunately, he's protected by so many charms and spells..." Ian shrugged helplessly.

"Can't I get him away from them?"

Ian shook his head. "Most of them are part of him or cast on him so they're quite permanent, and the ones that aren't... Well, they're still part of him."

"What does that mean?"

"Zenius can absorb pretty much anything and carry it around with them. Sort of like a shadow phantom, not that I've ever seen one, but I've heard the stories. Except we can't go through solid objects; 'cause we're corporeal. But I already covered that."

Doc wasn't sure that made sense to him. "Are you following this, Thaddy, old boy?"

"It's truly fascinating," Thaddeus said happily.

"Explain," Doc said, studying Ian's untouched whiskey bottle.

"A Zeniu's body is like a satchel. They can literally carry all their essentials with them, which is perfect for traveling through the water."

"Why can't I just cut open the satchel?" Doc demanded.

Thaddeus sighed. "Weren't you listening?" he chastised.

"Yes."

"Mitcham's protected by a multitude of charms and spells."

"You mean artifacts?" Doc asked.

"To use Mr. LaRoche's term, yes."

"So?"

"So, Mitcham would be rather shortsighted if one of the first spells he used didn't protect his skin, or his satchel, from being cut open," Thaddeus said pointedly.

"I see," Doc sighed. "Back to plan b."

"What is plan b?" Thaddeus asked.

"Lock him in a cage."

"That's actually... I think that could work," Thaddeus said in surprise.

"Thanks for your vote of confidence," Doc murmured. He brightened and said, "If I lock him in a cage, won't he eventually starve to death? Even Zenius have to eat, right?"

"Yes, we eat," Ian acknowledged with a barely perceptible cringe. "And probably not."

"Why not?" Doc demanded.

"There are spells that can... transfer the substance of one individual to another," Ian said darkly.

"Explain," Doc said. He understood perfectly what Ian was saying; he had a tattoo that did just that; he just didn't understand how it related to Mitcham.

"I have heard," Ian said, "that Mitcham... occasionally..."

"Out with it," Doc commanded.

"It's just..." Ian sighed. "I'm pretty sure Mitcham stopped eating a few decades ago."

"Because?"

"He consumes his meals quite differently now."

"Can you dance around the issue a little more?" Doc asked irritably.

"We eat people, okay?!" Ian snapped. "I mean, I don't, not anymore, but as a species, that's our food."

"Yes?" Doc prodded.

"Mitcham captures his prey, stamps them with a magic brand, and eats them via... osmosis?"

"God, that's incredible," Thaddeus breathed.

"Shut up, Thaddy," Doc snapped. "So, basically you're saying I can't kill Mitcham?"

"Basically," Ian agreed.

"Perfect," Doc muttered.

"Can I ask you a question?" Ian interrupted.

"Besides that one?"

"Yes."

"Well?"

Ian frowned at Doc, then said, "Bree never really talked about you, but...what are you?"

"Nobody," Doc said with a grin. "I'm nobody. Now a question for you. Why don't you live with the Zenius?"

Ian's blue face actually turned bluer, but then he slipped back on the wrist cuff, and his features shifted into a human once more.

"You still haven't bought me dinner," he said stiffly.

"Good enough," Doc replied. "Thank you for answering my questions; I appreciate it. I trust you can find your way down?"

"That's your way of saying you're done with me?" Ian asked, eyebrow raised.

"Pretty much."

"K." Ian stood and cast Doc a curious glance. "If you find that you need help with Mitcham, let me know."

"Are you a fighter?"

"No."

"Then why would I need your help?"

Ian gave a short laugh. "Touché, Mr. Holliday. Touché."

"It wasn't meant to be an insult," Doc said gently. "You have your music; I kill people."

Ian nodded and started to leave, but Doc stopped him. "Take the whiskey," Doc offered. "And if you like, I'll buy you dinner. The hotel has a French chef, you know."

"Just the whiskey," Ian replied.

As soon as the door had closed behind Ian, Thaddeus said, "He grew on me."

"I suppose," Doc said.

"It frustrates me though that people won't just tell you their entire life's story," Thaddeus sighed.

"Me too, old boy," Doc replied as he texted Jervis and asked him to keep an eye out on Ian to make sure he wasn't followed.

"Zenius are fascinating creatures," Thaddeus said thoughtfully.

"You mean people?" Doc corrected irritably.

"They're almost like a land version of the sirens," Thaddeus went on. "Instead of singing though, they use persuasiveness to trick people into going where they shouldn't."

"That doesn't make sense to me," Doc said. "If I'm passing by a bog, I'm not just going to walk into it because someone tells me the water's fine."

"Of course not," Thaddeus said. "But if you're walking along and it's quite foggy and you can't really see and a kind voice tells you to head a little more towards the left, you might."

"I suppose," Doc said. "I've never found Mitcham to be all that persuasive though. Every time he tells me to do something, I want to stab him in the eye."

"That's because you're you," Thaddeus said. "Your mind resists all forms of control. It's... What's that you say? Part of your charm?"

"Maybe," Doc laughed.

Doc glanced at the clock; it was still early afternoon. He could try to trap Mitcham now, but first he needed a cage. He sighed. Even if he managed to trap him, he still didn't have any proof that Mitcham was doing anything wrong. Which was ridiculous because everyone knew he was doing something wrong.

Perhaps it was time to go see Simon.

"I'm going out, old boy," Doc told Thaddeus. "Don't wait up for me."

"I never do, you hopeless wretch."

"Glad to hear you don't lose any sleep over me."

"You promised me you'd take me out," Thaddeus grumbled.

"I don't think... Oh. That I did," Doc said. "Now's probably not the best time."

"Of course not. Carry on then."

"Sorry, Thaddy. As soon as this is over."

"It's never over," Doc heard Thaddeus mumble just before the door closed between them.

Doc sighed heavily. It certainly felt that way lately. As if it was just one thing after another. He chuckled softly. Who was he kidding? It was always that way. He'd just forgotten. Spending five years locked in a room with an amorous vampire was bound to have some side effects.

"Worth every second," he sighed, remembering the feel of Ana's skin against his.

As Doc passed through the lobby, Jervis greeted him by saying "There was one pigeon on the roof, sir, but I took care of it. Mr. Comyn can rest easy tonight."

"Excellent work, Jervis. Give yourself a raise."

"No need, sir. I already had pigeon soup."

Doc swallowed a chuckle and walked out onto the busy sidewalk. The air was brisk, and there were skiffs of snow in the shadowy corners. He'd have to remember to wear his coat tonight. The cold and heat rarely troubled him, a side effect of his immortality no doubt; but he tried to keep up appearances.

He walked one block before leaning against a building and watching the traffic pass by.

After five minutes, Virgil Graves joined him. "So how long have you known?" Virgil asked.

"That you were following me? Since you started this morning." Doc paused, then added mischievously, "Alright, since you started last night."

"It's just a job," Virgil said. "Surely you can understand that."

"I do understand," Doc said. "If you quit following me, Mitcham'll break both your legs."

"Something like that," Virgil admitted.

"It's a good thing you and I are old friends then," Doc said cheerfully.

"Is it?" Virgil asked.

"Certainly," Doc said, suddenly ramming the back of his elbow into Virgil's forehead. Virgil's head tapped against the wall, and Doc caught him as he slumped forward. "If we weren't friends, I'd just kill you," Doc said as he wiggled Virgil onto his shoulder.

He walked back to Dulcis, smiling at passersby, greeting the ones who stared a little too long with "Poor man, can't hold his drink. Passed out at Mongo Bongos again." Then he'd chuckle when their heads dropped in embarrassment, like they were the ones who had passed out slipping dollars into some well-endowed woman's bra.

He pushed through the revolving door, being careful not to conk Virgil's head on the glass, and called over a Dulcis employee.

"Take this man to Jervis," Doc ordered. "And tell him that I don't want any more pigeons."

"Yes, sir, Mr. Holliday, sir," the man said, bobbing his head up and down.

"One sir is enough," Doc chuckled as he passed over Virgil.

"Very good, sir."

Now that he'd taken care of his pigeon problem, maybe he could actually get something done.

"Holliday," Simon said as he shook Doc's hand.

"I thought we agreed on Doc," Doc said.

"So we did. Sit. I'm surprised to see you," Simon said, pouring Doc a glass of whiskey. "After all, you've been on the run for eight months. You must have a mountain of work waiting for you."

"Quite. But you know how it is. Sometimes I need a good game to help me think."

"I'm happy to oblige," Simon said, handing him the pad of paper Doc had pointed to.

"Five card stud?" Doc asked.

"Let's change it up," Simon countered. "Seven card stud."

Simon shuffled the deck while Doc wrote a note. "If I kill Mitcham what sort of evidence do I need to present to the council so I don't have to kill the council as well?"

Doc took the cards from Simon and began to deal while Simon read the note.

Simon looked up from the notepad and raised an eyebrow. Doc shrugged.

"You have issues with authority," Simon said out loud.

"That's not in the least bit true," Doc argued. "I'm hunting down Bosch's family right now."

"That's what Mitcham wants from you?" Simon asked with a frown.

"I figured you already knew."

"I'm not privy to Mitcham's private dealings," Simon said. "Fold," he said, and then he began to write. When he was done, he took the cards from Doc and handed him the notepad.

"The council would be delighted if you killed Mitcham," Simon's neat handwriting said. "No evidence needed. However, I think you'll find yourself hard-pressed to kill him."

Doc had already forgotten about plan b. "Sorry," he wrote. "Instead of kill, I meant cage indefinitely."

Simon considered that, then wrote, "Killing would be better."

"I agree, but everyone keeps telling me that's not going to happen."

"If he just disappears, his second-in-command will take charge," Simon wrote.

"Just until an election can be arranged?"

"Yes, but he's well aware of Mitcham's tactics."

"You win," Doc said aloud.

Simon began to shuffle the cards again.

"I don't know why you're trying to make this difficult for me," Doc wrote irritably.

"Just trying to help you make legitimate business decisions," Simon replied.

"I don't even know why I like you."

"I ask myself that same question."

Doc grinned at Simon over the table and gestured for Simon to keep shuffling.

Doc reread through their conversation carefully. If the council didn't need proof that was at least one problem taken care of, but he still didn't know how to kill Mitcham. He could always start with plan b and move on to plan a. It was a little backwards, but it might work.

"What about the other Zenius?" Doc wrote. "Are they protected as well?"

"You mean the other tetrarchs?"

Doc nodded.

"Not that I know of," Simon wrote.

That was at least some good news. Maybe.

"My men have been charged with protecting the tetrarch, and they will do so," Simon wrote.

"I know," Doc replied. "I'll do my best not to harm them."

"I appreciate that. I cannot advise them of your actions."

"I understand."

Simon made a frustrated noise. "You win again," he said irritably.

"You have to play the people," Doc said.

"You don't have any tells," Simon grumbled.

"Sure I do," Doc laughed.

Simon began to shuffle again, and Doc tried to work out plan b. "Do you have Mitcham's calendar?" he wrote.

Simon nodded.

"Can I have a copy?"

Simon nodded again and handed Doc the cards. Doc finished off the shuffle and started dealing, keeping the cadence exactly timed for an actual game.

Meanwhile, Simon wrote out Mitcham's schedule.

"Thank you," Doc said when Simon was finished. "You've really helped me clear my mind."

"I'm sure we'll all rest easier when Bosch's family has been detained," Simon said.

"Definitely," Doc agreed, tucking the schedule into his pocket and shaking Simon's hand once more. "I'll see you around."

"Next time though, I'm winning," Simon declared.

"We'll see," Doc laughed.

10

"I swear Mitcham picked these venues on purpose," Doc muttered as he looked over Mitcham's schedule.

"What venues?" Jury asked distractedly.

"He's speaking at the witches' academy tomorrow, and then at the regular Hidden school the day after. He's also doing a speech to raise awareness about aging cryptids and the struggles they face. Other than that, he never leaves his house; and I'll look like a complete ass if I try to kidnap him at any of those."

"You already look like an ass," Jury mumbled.

"Goddamn it, Jury! You're not helping."

"I am," Jury said. "You just can't tell."

"How are you helping?" Doc demanded.

"I'm finding Bosch's family."

"I still don't see how that's helpful."

"Not my problem."

Doc sighed. It was possible that Lady Luck had finally abandoned him. Or at least taken a vacation. She'd probably taken one look at Ahanu and said, "Gotta go!" Doc didn't even blame her. What did luck matter when a time-traveling shaman was on the table?

"I've got three days to do this," Doc muttered. "Three days. I can do that. It's just one goddamn Zeniu. An invincible Zeniu who can't be killed or starved to death or anything."

"Would you be quiet?" Jury snarled.

Doc rolled his eyes. Jury was always testy when he was creating magic.

"I was going to invite you to my party," Doc said. "But now I'm not going to."

"I wouldn't go anyway. I know you. When you say party, you mean kill festival."

"That is not true," Doc insisted.

"Who's coming to your party?" Jury asked.

"Ana and Ina."

"And?"

"Some frat boys."

"Who's leaving the party?"

"Ana and Ina."

"Just as I thought."

"You didn't think anything," Doc argued.

"Go bother someone else," Jury ordered. "I'm trying to concentrate."

"Go bother someone else," Doc mocked as he left Jury's suite and walked down the hallway. "Like that's all I do all day, wander around bothering people."

He ran through his day in his head. "Alright, so maybe that is all I do. So what? People need me. Without me... Oh hell," he sighed. "I'm a goddamn pest."

"Hardly true, sir," Jervis said from behind him.

Doc controlled his startle and turned with a tight smile. "You know I hate that, Jervis."

"I do?" Jervis blinked slowly, his version of innocence. "I'm so sorry, sir."

"You know better than to lie to me," Doc said flatly.

"You're right."

"Stop it!" Doc snapped. "What do you want?"

"Just to tell you that Mr. Graves is awake and a little annoyed."

"He shouldn't have been following me," Doc grumbled. "You've not talked to him, have you?"

"Of course not. Winslow is handling him."

Doc stared at Jervis for a moment before asking, "Who's Winslow?"

"My right-hand man, sir."

"I wasn't aware you had a right-hand man."

"You don't know everything about me," Jervis said, one side of his lips slightly upraised.

"Obviously not," Doc replied, eyes narrow.

"Just like I don't know where you were from 1919 to 1922," Jervis pointed out.

Doc grinned. "Those were good years."

"I wouldn't know, sir."

"Have Winslow tell Virgil that I will release him in three days." Doc thought about that for a minute, then said, "Make it seven."

"Seven?" Jervis questioned.

"Mother always said there was no point in cleaning house if you didn't sweep under the furniture."

"I'm not sure I follow that."

"All you need to know is that Mother's house was always immaculate," Doc said with a wink.

"Very good, sir."

Doc opened the door to his suite and flopped down onto

his couch. Then he reviewed his mental list. He now knew how to kill a Zeniu. Unfortunately, that didn't help with Mitcham. Fortunately, he didn't need to bother finding evidence against Mitcham to present to the council. Unfortunately, that only worked if he killed Mitcham.

Doc shuffled the double deck of cards he kept on his sitting room table and wondered if Lady Luck would be coming back his way anytime soon. His longest run of bad luck had been in Russia in 1910. That had been one of the few times a woman had tricked him. She had been available, but she'd been playing quite a different game than him. She certainly hadn't been worth it, but it had been amusing watching Jervis decimate an entire Russian prison.

Doc laid out three rows of eight. Devil's grip was slightly more challenging than solitaire. If things were going his way, he'd win. If they weren't... Well, he still might win.

He began to move cards, thinking about Andrew as he did. For some ridiculous reason, Andrew didn't believe in luck.

"You can't tell me that my success at driving the cattle to market has anything to do with anything other than my men's skill at driving cattle to market," Andrew had argued once.

"Maybe not," Doc had conceded. "But the price you get once you're there might be influenced by luck."

"That's ridiculous!" Andrew snorted. "The price I get is determined by market value and the health of my animals."

"Just because you don't believe in something doesn't mean it doesn't exist," Doc pointed out. "Look at shamans. You think the majority of humanity believes in shamans? But that doesn't make them any less real."

Andrew had rolled his eyes and poured himself another cup of coffee. If only Doc had known about the Hidden when they'd had that argument, he might have won, but probably not. Andrew could be remarkably stubborn.

It wasn't that Doc actually thought luck was an entity wandering around touching people's shoulders. Or maybe she was. But regardless of whether luck was an entity or just a vagrant breeze, Doc had felt it with him his entire life. He'd felt its light touch when all hope seemed to be lost. He'd felt it shift the cards in his favor; he'd felt it move a knife a quarter inch to the left when it might have killed him otherwise; he'd felt it gust when Señora Teodora had strolled into his room.

No matter what Andrew said, luck was real. Maybe it never had helped Andrew; it's not as if he needed an edge. Maybe it only came to those who called it. Maybe it picked and chose who it served or didn't serve. All Doc knew was that he'd never really been without it, even when it seemed as if he was.

He topped off another stack of cards with a jack of clubs. He'd win the game; he could feel it. Maybe if Andrew had believed in luck, he and Pecos would have managed to kill the Black Shaman properly the first time around; and then Doc wouldn't have to figure out how to raise her from the mostly dead so Andrew could finish the job.

His hand froze as he tried to imagine the Black Shaman walking around free. What if he woke her at the wrong time and Andrew wasn't ready? Or what if he woke her and Andrew wasn't even here? Who would stop her then? Certainly not Doc. He wasn't that lucky.

"You can't imagine the power that oozes from her," Andrew had once said. "It's like drowning in a pool of evil. And people worship her, Doc. Worship her! Like she's a goddess." Andrew shook his head in disbelief. "Why? Why would they choose her? You'd be better off worshiping the sun; at least it's good."

"But the sun can't share its power, can it?" Doc had said softly.

Andrew snorted. "They're stupid if they think she'll share anything with them. She's greedy." Andrew tossed a stick into the fire and said, "I don't think she always was. Or maybe I'm wrong. Originally she said she wanted to remake the world without the white man, and there were times when I felt like I didn't even want to stop her."

The fire blazed suddenly, casting a strange shadow on Andrew's face. "But either she changed or she was always corrupt," he said softly. "Because she fed off the pain and fear of the city, and she loved it. She nearly won." He smiled crookedly at Doc and added, "But she didn't."

When Andrew had spoken those words, it had been years after he'd defeated the Black Shaman, but even then his posture had stiffened when he spoke of her, and Doc knew the Black Shaman still frightened him, at least a little.

He found it difficult to conceive of a creature or person Andrew Rufus was scared of. It didn't make sense to him because Andrew was a... a god. He'd become a god to defeat her, and Doc was certain there was no one, no one, who could challenge Andrew and win. But the Black Shaman had nearly won, and that made her very frightening indeed.

The memory of Andrew's voice faded, and Doc placed a queen on top of a nine and won the game. It had been a long time since he'd endured the bitter taste of true defeat. Like Andrew, he always assumed he'd win, and he almost always did. But life would be rather lacking in zest if it was always a sure thing. That's what made it so interesting; the knowledge that he could indeed lose.

"Speaking of losing," Doc muttered, "I think I'll grab Mitcham the day after tomorrow, just after he talks at the Hidden school. So I guess I need a cage. And a way to get the cage in and out of the Hidden."

He chuckled softly, then started to laugh.

By the time Doc left for his frat boy party, he was ready for something uncomplicated. Rapist equals bad. Bad equals dead. Easy. No hearts in feet, no artifacts or magic spells, just good old-fashioned killing.

Jervis had already confirmed and added to Bennie's version of events. Right now Abby Parrish was lying in a hospital bed in a deep coma. She'd not only been raped multiple times, she'd also been beaten so severely that several of her bones were broken. All Doc had to do was make sure all the frat boys were rapists, and then he and the girls could start killing.

Ana and Ina were waiting outside for him when he arrived at the house. "Thanks for coming," he told them as he unlocked the door.

"Thanks for inviting us," Ana purred. She ran her hand over his chest and kissed him lightly on the lips.

He pulled her inside the house, closed the door behind them, and kissed her thoroughly, pressing her gently against the wall. Her hands curled around his arms, and then her legs wrapped around his waist. He deepened the kiss, enjoying her feral energy.

"Ahem," Ina coughed from behind them.

Doc regretfully released Ana, lazily nipping her bottom lip as he did. "Later, love," he promised.

He turned to survey the room, raising his eyebrow as he did. "Looks a little trashy," he commented.

"It's perfect," Ana said. "Looks just like a frat party should."

"Really?"

"Absolutely," Ina said. "Jervis even set up a table for beer pong."

"That's good?" Doc asked.

"Yes," Ana laughed. "Are we killing everyone?"

"Probably, but let me feel them out first. Do you mind playing the damsels in distress for a moment?"

"I love that game," Ana purred.

"I know," Doc said with a grin. "Get ready to pretend to be tied to that radiator over there," he instructed.

"Yes, sir," Ana said, face a mask of innocence.

"And if you could at least try to look frightened," Doc advised.

Ana's and Ina's eyes both widened theatrically, and their bottom lips began to quiver. "Please don't hurt me," Ina whimpered.

"I'll do whatever you want," Ana added, a tear slipping down her cheek.

"Save it for the frat boys," Doc drawled.

They grinned at him, then went to stand by the radiator, stripping off their outer coats as they did, revealing two pairs of skimpy lacy underwear and lots of flawless skin.

He rolled his eyes. He'd be lucky if the frat boys heard a word he said.

The doorbell rang at exactly five minutes before ten. Doc flung open the door and grinned widely. "Brothers!" he exclaimed, quickly counting the heads. Forty-three; exactly the right number.

"Come in!" Doc ordered. "Come in! We're gonna have fun tonight!"

Once they were all inside, Doc closed and locked the door, then slid down a bar over the door frame. The boys didn't notice a thing; they were too busy staring at Ana and Ina.

"I just want to get some ground rules out of the way before we get started," Doc said loudly. "So listen up."

They managed to drag their eyes away and look at him.

Doc grinned. "Tonight's for you!" he exclaimed.

The boys cheered.

"We've got beer; we've got whiskey; we've even got some beautiful nose candy."

Another round of cheers.

"But most importantly," Doc went on, "we've got women!"

The boys hooted and hollered.

"Now my girls are a little shy," Doc said, "but we can loosen them up, can't we?"

Cheers all around.

Doc watched their faces as they cheered and high-fived each other, looking for anyone who didn't seem as enthusiastic as the others.

"I loved your work on the Parrish girl," Doc added.

Laughs and jeers all around. No one looked the least bit queasy at his reference to their latest victim. So be it.

"House leader goes first," Doc announced. "Pick a girl, pick a room."

A tall, athletic young man stepped forward. "Which one do you think'll put up more of a fight?" he asked.

The other boys gave each other fist bumps.

Doc grinned widely. "Definitely her," he said, pointing towards Ana. She was doing a fantastic job of looking scared, and when the leader went to collect her, she cried and struggled, forcing him to pull her down the hallway. She was so convincing Doc almost intervened.

"Music!" Doc exclaimed, hitting the remote control on the table. He flinched when the house was suddenly filled with the rough sounds of German rock. If he didn't know better, he'd say it was Jervis's idea of a joke. But, more importantly, it would do the job of covering up the sounds of the poor little frat boy's drawn-out death.

Doc tapped Ralph's shoulder, the boy he'd met just that morning, and pointed towards Ina. "You should take her."

"Me?" Ralph said in surprise. "I'm pretty new to the house."

"I don't think she'll fight much," Doc said, "but if you'd rather wait until some of the other boys have had a go..."

"No!" Ralph exclaimed. "I want her."

"Then go get her," Doc prodded.

Ralph and Ina disappeared down the hallway, and Doc started pouring drinks. He always preferred it when people put up a fight, but he knew how much Ana and Ina liked to play with their food.

A ping-pong ball bounced against Doc's head, and he smiled graciously and handed the offender another beer. Beneath the harsh thrum of the music, he could hear squeals of panic drifting down the hallway, but no one else seemed to notice.

Suddenly Ralph burst into the room, naked and covered in blood. "They're monsters!" he shrieked in terror.

"They're monsters!" everyone shouted.

"No! God, run!" Ralph sobbed. "They're fucking monsters!" He tried to force his way through the crowd, but it was too late. Ina was right behind him, long white fangs gleaming against her beautiful red lips.

Ralph began to wail and beg, and Ina watched him coldly. Doc knew what she was thinking. She was thinking of the women they had raped. The pleas and cries they must have heard. The tears they must have seen.

Ina reached down and lifted Ralph off the floor by his throat. She licked a trail of blood off his chest, then buried her fangs into his pelvic area. His scream of sheer horror filled the room, and the frat boys turned as one, eyes wide.

Ana was waiting for them. She grabbed the man closest to her and tore his neck open with ease. Blood spewed everywhere. Most of the frat boys watched in frozen horror, eyes hardly believing what they were seeing, but a few turned and bolted towards the door.

Doc was leaning against the door; and without even shifting his position, he stopped the fleeing boys dead in their tracks with several well-placed knife throws. As five bodies fell awkwardly to the floor, Doc's tattoo began to heat, and he sighed in satisfaction as the dead men's life force swept through his veins.

He breathed deeply, watching lazily as Ana and Ina worked their way through the shrieking frat boys. The sisters worked together, taking down their prey with a precision and viciousness that was rather beautiful to watch. Anytime one of the men tried to flee Doc killed them, but otherwise, he let the sisters have their fun.

A dismembered hand thunked against the wall near Doc's head, and he wiped a splatter of blood off his cheek. There was only one man still alive, and he took one look at the sisters and bolted towards Doc. Ana sped across the room, leaping over bodies, and grabbed the man from behind. She yanked his head back by his hair, and despite his screams of protest, buried her fangs deeply into his exposed neck.

After a second or two, the man's screams turned to whimpers and his eyes began to flutter. A moment later, he was dead.

"That was... delicious," Ana purred as she stood.

Behind her, Ina took one last drink from her final victim's chest, then dropped his body to the blood stained floor. "I haven't fed this well since..." She paused and grinned at Doc. "The last job you gave us."

"Are they all dead?" Doc asked.

"Yes," Ana replied, licking her fingertips.

"You're certain?"

"I can sense beating hearts," Ana said sleepily. "And there are only three hearts in this house."

"Actually," Ina said, "I think you might have some mice in the pantry."

"Fine," Ana laughed. "Three HUMAN hearts. People hearts. One human heart and two vampire hearts. Is that precise enough for you?"

"Better," Ina chuckled.

"Can you really tell the difference?" Doc asked. "Between my heart and yours?"

"No," Ana said as she licked the blood from her arm.

Doc glanced around the room. It looked... rather the worse for wear. "I suppose I'd better call the Worms."

"You promised me pleasure," Ana pouted, wrapping her arms around Doc's neck.

"Yes, but at the hotel," Doc said. "I'm not quite as enamored with blood as you."

"Too bad," Ana murmured. "If you were a vampire, you'd be perfect."

"I'm perfect for tonight," Doc assured her.

"Don't be long," she commanded.

The sisters collected their coats and left. Once they were gone, Doc circulated the room and stabbed everyone in the heart. Not that he didn't trust Ana and Ina, but they were a little blood drunk. Ana was right though; everyone was dead. Especially the house leader, the man who had gone off with Ana in the first place.

Once he was done, he called the Worms.

"Mortuary," someone answered.

"This is John Holliday," Doc said.

"Mr. Holliday!" the man on the other end exclaimed. "We were delighted to hear of your return to town."

"I'm sure you were," Doc said dryly. "I need a clean-up."

Doc gave him the details, and while he waited for them to arrive, he texted Bennie. "Done."

"Did they suffer?" Bennie replied.

Doc glanced around the blood splattered room. Having been on the opposite end of things, Ana and Ina hated rapists even more than he did; and they had not been kind, which is precisely why Doc had invited them to come. He snapped a picture of the room with his phone and sent it to Bennie.

"Thank you," Bennie texted back.

"Now that we're done with that, I'd like a cage, please," Doc texted.

"A cage?"

"I'm going on a catch-and-release hunting trip, and I need something large enough for a cougar."

"Really?"

"Maybe something with wheels?"

"And I suppose you want this by tomorrow?"

"That would perfect," Doc replied.

He could almost hear Bennie's huff of irritation when he texted back, "Fine."

"That's why you're the best," Doc said.

"Don't you forget that when you get my invoice," Bennie replied.

"I wouldn't dream of it."

11

Doc woke with a dismayed sigh and gently rolled Ana's naked body off his chest.

"It's early," she murmured. "Where are you going?"

"I have visitors."

She sniffed inquisitively. "Children?" she asked.

"Indeed."

"How did they get in?"

"Jervis gave them the code."

Ana's husky laugh filled the room, and Doc rolled his eyes. "Get dressed," he ordered. "I don't want you traumatizing Johnny."

"Oh, I don't think it would traumatize him," she purred.

"Don't be naughty," Doc laughed.

"I don't know any other way to be. I'll have to borrow some of your clothes," she added sleepily. "Mine didn't... survive."

"What's mine is yours," Doc said as he pulled on a pair of pants.

Ana kissed his cheek affectionately and strolled into his closet. He watched her backside sway until she disappeared.

"Doc?!" Jules called out.

"I'm coming," Doc replied.

"Wait for me," Ana said, exiting the closet wearing nothing more than one of his linen shirts and a tie cinched around her waist.

"Not what I had in mind, love," Doc chastised.

She winked at him.

Doc opened the bedroom door and walked out into the sitting room.

"I figured it out!" Jules said excitedly. She opened her mouth to keep going, but stopped, staring wide-eyed at Ana. "Who's she?" she demanded after a moment.

"Jules, this is Ana. Ana, this is Jules, Johnny, Addison, and Frankie."

"Lovely to meet you," Ana purred, Russian accent slightly thicker than usual.

Frankie glared at her, Jules dismissed her, Johnny gaped at her in delight, and Addison said, "Are you a unicorn?"

"No, sweetheart," Ana replied. "I'm a vampire." At that her fangs dropped down, somehow making her sultry expression even sexier.

Frankie gasped in horror, and Ana laughed lightly.

"Will you stay for breakfast?" Doc asked Ana.

"I'm still rather full," she said, red lips curving. "I'll see you around."

"Always."

She turned and picked up Thaddeus's pot. "I'm so sorry Doc refused to move you last night," she whispered. "There's always next time. I love your new pot by the way. Quite cheerful." Thaddeus sputtered some sort of ridiculous nonsense, and Ana laughed as she kissed one of his shiny leaves.

At the door, she ran her hand over Doc's chest and kissed him thoroughly, then she waved at the gaping children and closed the door behind her.

"She's probably not even Russian," Frankie grumbled.

"She really is," Doc countered. "She and her sister Ina kept my chandelier safe when I... brought it over from Russia." He glanced at the ceiling. Jervis had replaced the broken chandelier, and it was nice enough, but it just wasn't the same. He should have left Phillip Jury in his coffin a little longer.

"Ana and Ina?" Johnny asked, eyes wide with glee.

Doc winked at him.

"She's not really a vampire, is she?" Frankie demanded. "It's daytime!"

"So?"

"Vampires can't go out in the sunlight," Frankie scoffed. "Everyone knows that."

"They can't?" Doc replied innocently.

"No!" Frankie frowned and asked, "Can they?"

"Of course they can," Jules interjected. "That's just silly Hollywood stuff; I'll explain it to you later. And that's not why we came."

"You had a reason?" Doc asked.

"Yes! You asked me to figure out how to kill a Zeniu."

"And did you?"

"Yes! I mean, I think. It's not as if I can test it."

Doc gestured for her to go on.

"So it sounds as if most of their body is just kind of filled with goo. They have a sort of bone-like structure, but it's not the same as ours. More like cartilage."

"I hate to ask," Doc said, "but that's very specific. Where did you find this information?"

She bit her lip and wrinkled her nose. "It's not an avenue of research I usually take, but... well..."

"Yes?" Doc encouraged.

"There have always been those who... Well, I suppose they consider themselves scientists, but what they do is rather hideous."

Thaddeus made a strange choking noise, but Jules didn't seem to notice.

"Anyway, there was a Spanish man in the mid-1700s who made quite a sport of catching cryptids and dissecting them. On paper, he did it for the glory of Spain because he was under the impression that the only way Spain would ever be able to defend its people against the threat of non-humanity was if they were armed with as much knowledge about cryptids as possible. But he was not a good man," Jules stated firmly.

Thaddeus made that sound again, so Doc dumped some whiskey into his pot to shut him up. There was nothing to be benefitted by allowing Jules to find out about Thaddeus's past.

"Thank you," Thaddeus whispered.

"So he captured a Zeniu?" Doc asked, trying to move the conversation along.

"Yes. And he... Well, I suppose you know what he did. Anyway, as I said, filled with goo. They don't have the same organ system we have, but they do have a heart, two hearts, in fact."

"Go on," Doc said.

"But see, it's in their foot!" Jules exclaimed. "Or feet! Isn't that crazy?"

"Quite. How do they protect it?"

"It's surrounded by bone," Jules said. "I mean, each heart, in each foot, is encased in flexible bone. Traditionally, they lived in water," Jules added. "If you think about that, their feet would be at the far end of them when they were swimming towards their prey, so it actually makes a lot of sense."

"Fascinating," Doc drawled.

"I know!"

Jules was clearly very excited; the others didn't seem to share her interest, but Doc was actually quite impressed. In just one day, Jules had discovered something very few people knew.

"Where do you get your books?" Doc asked, thinking it was rather strange she'd even managed to uncover something so obscure.

"At the library," Jules said, eyes brightening.

"The library? And they just happened to have this man's journal?" Doc asked incredulously.

"Oh no," she laughed.

Johnny decided to jump in here. "Nearly all the Hiddens have some sort of library," he explained, "and they're all interconnected so that the knowledge of one becomes the knowledge of them all."

"I think this conversation requires whiskey," Doc muttered.

"But..." Jules started to say; she stopped herself, however, and just smiled at him.

"You're learning," Doc grinned. He grabbed a fresh bottle from the kitchen, sat beside Addison, and said, "Do continue."

"So there's an index," Jules said. "And it contains all the books from across all the Hiddens."

"Witches make all this possible," Johnny cut in. "In fact witches make the Hidden possible. Without witches there'd be no camouflage, no hidden spaces, no pockets of space where there shouldn't be space."

"What Johnny's trying to say is that witches built the libraries, and they're all connected," Jules interjected. "The librarian, obviously a witch, puts their hand into the request void, mutters the spell that includes the title or author of the book they want, and voila! Amazing, isn't it?"

Doc stared at them. "Really?" he finally said. "You're not just messing with me?"

"No," Jules said, clearly a little offended by the idea. "Why would we lie about that? I mean, how did you expect me to find out about Zenius? Did you just think I could go into some sort of trance and figure it out?"

"I don't know actually."

"So the library is like the internet?" Frankie suddenly asked.

"What?" Jules said, confusion wrinkling her brow.

"The request void is like the search bar?" Frankie inquired. "Right?"

That actually made sense to Doc, but the twins were struggling with the concept.

"No," Jules said. "It's not... I mean, the internet is not even there!"

"But it is," Frankie argued. "It's just invisible, like whatever links the libraries together."

"But that's magic!" Johnny insisted.

"As far as I'm concerned," Doc drawled, "so is the internet."

"The internet is technology," Jules argued.

"Same difference," Doc chuckled.

Jules and Johnny wanted to disagree with him; he could see it on their faces, but they didn't. Probably because they couldn't figure out an argument that would win.

"Anyway," Jules finally said. "That's how you kill a Zeniu."

"Good work," Doc said. "How much do I owe you?"

"What?"

"Owe you. For your work."

"But... No... I mean... No..." she stammered.

"Yes," Doc said.

"You pay for Johnny's lessons; I mean, we owe you."

"No. Johnny owes me a favor at an undetermined date. Will a thousand dollars cover it? Or would you prefer merlins?"

Jules's mouth dropped open in shock.

"I like merlins," Addison said. "They're pretty."

"They are," Doc agreed.

"Ana's pretty too, but I bet unicorns are prettier," Addison said.

"Every woman is special," Doc said. "There's really no comparison between them."

Frankie cleared her throat, and Doc looked at her. She shook her head, and he grinned.

"I'll have Jervis set up an account for you," Doc told Jules. "Since you live in the norm world, we'll do dollars, alright? But if you ever need merlins, just let me know."

"I don't... But..."

"I have some errands to run," Doc said, hoping to hurry them along.

"I need to get the kids off to school anyway," Frankie said awkwardly. "I'm sorry we keep barging in on you."

"You're always welcome," Doc said. "By the way, where's Boudica?"

Frankie's eyes darted to the side. "Um... She wasn't awake yet."

He was pretty sure Boudica didn't sleep, but he didn't contradict her. He'd never really warmed up to the concept of owning creatures, especially ones so clearly as sentient as Boudica. If she wanted to stay with Frankie, he'd not interfere.

"Did Ana bite you?" Addison asked curiously right before he closed the door on them.

"Not this time," Doc replied with a grin.

Frankie's cheeks flamed, Johnny's lips curved into a huge grin, and Jules rolled her eyes. "Come on, Addy," she said sternly. "Johnny and I will be late."

Doc winked and closed the door.

"She'll hate me," Thaddeus moaned.

"She won't," Doc sighed.

"You heard her. She said, 'He was not a good man'."

"And he wasn't," Doc said. "And neither were you, but we just covered this, and you said you'd changed."

"But what if I haven't?" Thaddeus exclaimed, voice thick with despair. "Because my first thought was how did he capture the Zeniu? Did he kill it first and then dissect it, or did he have to dissect it to kill it?"

"Seriously?" Doc demanded. "That was really your first thought?"

"Yes," Thaddeus whispered.

"It's a good thing you're still a plant then," Doc muttered. "I'm giving you more whiskey."

"I deserve it," Thaddeus groaned.

Doc poured in half the bottle, then drank the other half. Jules had confirmed what Ian had already told him, but that still didn't help him kill Mitcham. It also didn't help him figure out how to capture Mitcham.

His phone rang. It was Jervis. "Yes?" Doc said.

"Julia O'Connell is on the landline for you, sir."

"Thanks."

Doc picked up the handset and said, "Julia, darling, finally taking me up on my offer?"

"Absolutely," Julia said, voice just as chipper as he remembered it. "I'm leaving Dublin for you, but you have to raise the children as your own."

"We can't leave them behind? Dublin said they take after him, not you."

"That they do," she laughed.

"Eeeh," Doc said. "I've just realized I'm too old for you."

She laughed easily before chastising him. "Dublin said you might come by, but you never did."

"I was detained," Doc replied.

"That's what you always say," Julia snorted. "Anyway, the reason I called is that Theatrum Feriatum is opening a new play tomorrow night, and it would be wonderful if you would come."

"Hum," Doc said thoughtfully.

"I hate it when you say 'hum' like that," Julia sighed.

"You haven't heard me say that in years," Doc chuckled.

"Yes, but I remember the disastrous results."

"I'll tell Dublin you said that."

"I meant all the other stuff," she snapped.

"Hum."

"Stop that! What are you humming about anyway?"

"What's the play about?" he asked.

"We're actually doing the one we opened with. You know, the one you wrote, *The Corruption of Phineas Larimer*? It's our tenth anniversary."

"Has it been that long?" he mused.

"It's hard to keep track of time when you take vamp trank for five years," she said, amusement coloring her tone.

"Indeed," Doc laughed. "Send over four tickets, and set up a backstage meet and greet."

"Really?" she asked suspiciously. "What're you planning?"

"Nothing."

"I don't believe you."

"Believe me," he insisted. "It's better that way."

"I knew I shouldn't have called you."

"You love me," he laughed.

"I'm not sure I do today."

"See you tomorrow night, Julia darling."

Doc chuckled as he hung up the phone. For a moment he just stood there, thinking. Then he grinned. Lady Luck had never abandoned him because this might actually work.

He texted Jervis. "I need Mitcham's number."

While he was waiting for Jervis to respond, Doc wandered in to check on Randell. Only it wasn't Randell. It was Emily, and it was obviously near the end of her shift. Her eyes were tired, and she looked about ready to drop.

"Just ten more minutes," she said softly.

Doc nodded and left the room, feeling oddly self-conscious. He'd completely forgotten Emily was here, and there was no way she hadn't overheard Ana last night. Ana was a very vigorous lover.

His phone beeped. Jervis had sent him Mitcham's number.

"Give yourself a raise," Doc texted back.

"Done."

Doc went to his window and dialed the number.

"This is Mitcham," Mitcham said shortly.

"John Holliday, sir" Doc replied. "I'm sorry to bother you. I just wanted to give you an update."

"Yes?" Mitcham demanded.

"We're closing in, sir. I'm sorry for the delay; they've been rather difficult to find, but we're close."

"Good."

"Also, sir, I wanted to invite you to my theater tomorrow night. They're opening a new play for our tenth anniversary, and I thought you and your wife might enjoy it."

"Your theater?" Mitcham asked. "Are you referring to Theatrum Feriatum?"

"Indeed."

"I wasn't aware you owned any property," Mitcham said acidly.

"I apologize for the misunderstanding. I started the theater, but I no longer own it," Doc lied. "I still think of it as mine though."

"I see. My wife's been wanting to go; I just haven't had the time. Been up to my elbows in damage control."

"Shall we meet you outside the theater at 6:30?" Doc asked. "My box has the best view," he added, hoping to seal the deal.

"I suppose," Mitcham murmured.

"Looking forward to seeing you, sir." Doc said with a wide grin, then disconnected.

"I need to change my order," he texted Bennie.

"Of course you do," Bennie texted back. "It's not like I already have a cage sitting here waiting to be delivered."

"Charge me twice."

"I already was. What do you want?"

"I want a cage with a door front. It needs to look exactly like an interior doorway, only it's a shallow cage. Make sense?"

"You must be hunting a very clever cougar," Bennie replied.

"It's an experiment really," Doc wrote. "Trying to see if it's learned to open doors. You understand."

"I'll see what I can do."

Doc studied the city street below him. It was such a delicate balance that kept everything from descending into chaos. The norms lived in blissful ignorance, not even conceiving of the idea that there were cryptids walking among them. They had too many other things occupying their daily thoughts to notice anything odd like people suddenly disappearing from the sidewalks or the strange glimmer that sometimes occurred when the light hit one of the Hidden buildings.

Even he hadn't conceived of such a thing, and he had met shamans and Andrew and seen all manner of things already. He'd watched Andrew strip the cougar pelt from a dead skinwalker, revealing the human underneath. He'd wrestled summoned demons. He'd seen an ice giant first hand. And he'd still been surprised by the Hidden. Shocked actually.

If the norms ever found out... The thought was utterly horrifying. There would be a war, and in wars like that, there was never a winner.

He remembered Thypon's angry words about norms and wondered how many of the other cryptids shared his view. Doc had come to the conclusion that Mitcham was very anti-norm, and he had the feeling Mitcham was riling up the cryptids on purpose. Doc was fairly certain that the entire purpose of the Acolytes had been to anger the cryptids to the point that they would be willing to attack the norms. A tactical play Doc had neatly, and somewhat unintentionally, cut off at the knees.

He'd like to know what the overall atmosphere in the Hidden was right now. It had been eight months since he'd last spent time there. Perhaps he needed to go visiting. He'd have to be careful what he said though; he didn't want to accidently mark anyone for execution.

"Mr. Holliday?" Emily said from behind him.

Doc turned with a sheepish grin. "First, let me apologize for last night. I completely forgot you were here."

Her cheeks turned bright red. "I didn't... I mean... I wasn't..."

"It was completely my bad," Doc said. "I was a little caught up in the moment."

"It's... It's your house, sir." She cleared her throat and looked from side to side for a moment.

"Shall we just forget it happened?" Doc offered.

"That would be great! So about... um... the subject; Randell gave me his notes from yesterday, and I read them during the down times. I can't go outside with M... him, you know."

Doc nodded and gestured for her to sit.

"He's met several times with a man named Markus Johanns," she said.

"Who's he?"

"I've been hearing his name lately when I go visit my parents," she said. "He's some kind of movement leader."

"Let me guess," Doc drawled. "He's against the norms."

"I think so," she said. "He and Mitcham," she went on, flinching when she said Mitcham's name, "are working on some kind of campaign together, something they want to launch at the summit meeting that's coming up."

"Fantastic," Doc muttered. "Do you know what it is?"

"Not really," she said with frustration. "They're talking openly about it, but it doesn't make sense to me. It's all in the notes."

"Why is everyone so scared to talk about Mitcham?" Doc asked.

"Because he knows," Emily whispered.

"But how?"

"Who knows? He just does. I had an uncle who was avidly against Mitcham." She paused and swallowed awkwardly, then added softly, "He just disappeared one day."

"Do you think he's in one of the cages underneath?" Doc asked.

"I don't know," she said sadly. "The bug that went down there died. And yes, I was in it when it died," she added with a rueful laugh. "And here I am."

"Well, that answers one question," Doc replied with a grin.

"Sorry I don't have more to report," she said. "He's upset Virgil Graves hasn't checked in, but Virgil's daughter convinced him that the only reason he wouldn't check in is because he couldn't. He's hired another PI firm."

"I hate pigeons," Doc muttered.

"What?"

"Nothing. Anything else?"

"Not that struck me as important."

"Thank you, Emily. It won't be long now."

As soon as she was gone, Doc read over the notes. They didn't tell him much that he didn't already know. What he wanted to know was how Mitcham knew everything that was going on in the Hidden and what Mitcham's grand plan was. And he wanted to know why. Wasn't just controlling the Hidden enough? Why put everything at risk to obtain more?

12

Doc walked through the Hidden as nonchalantly as possible, observing people covertly as he went. He hadn't really paid that much attention the other day when he'd come to see Sydney, but looking around now, the underlying tensions were obvious.

It wasn't the same as the fear that had prevailed before he'd killed Bosch. Instead of fear, it was anger and hate. And it didn't seem to be directed at any one specific thing. It seemed to be directed everywhere and at everything.

Doc entered Kaasni's apartment building, jogged up the stairs, and knocked on Kaasni's door. She opened it without removing the chain lock and stared at him with her serpent eyes through the crack.

"Kaasni," he greeted, giving her a slight bow.

"Mr. Holliday," she said stiffly.

"May I come in?"

"I'm afraid not," she said.

That threw him. Kaasni had always been reserved but pleasant, but she was past reserved now; she was nearly rude.

"Have I offended you?" he asked carefully. "I had only thought to have our chess match."

"I don't play chess with norms," she said firmly, then shut the door in his face.

"Well, that was different," Doc muttered to the closed door. "There have clearly been some changes in the last eight months. I really wish someone would send me the memos."

Back out on the street, he continued to observe the residents. Nearly everyone here was a cryptid of some type, but they weren't behaving like a tribe of united cryptids. For instance, only Lutins were at the Lutin stand, even though Lutins were without doubt the best bakers around. There were a group of serpents huddled together by a fruit stand, and across from them were a group of humanoid cryptids. And they were all staring at each other suspiciously.

Doc studied them all with a frown because their behavior didn't make a lot of sense. If he were trying to start a war between the norms and the cryptids, he would definitely try to keep the cryptids focused externally, not internally. Instead of highlighting the differences between species, he would draw a line with cryptids on one side and norms on the other. If he wasn't mistaken, it had always been that way, so why shake up the balance?

If he wanted answers, he'd have to find someone to ask; but he didn't know anyone else in this area, so he headed for the exit, hoping Dublin could fill in some blanks.

The sign marking Dublin's gym was gone, but the code for the door was the same, so Doc entered, cautiously surveying the room as he went. The mats were still there, and overall, everything looked the same, but there was a general air of disuse.

"Dublin?" he called out.

The door in back opened. "Doc?"

"That's me."

"Come in," Dublin said.

"Are you closed?" Doc asked.

"More or less," Dublin said with a shrug.

"I just talked to Julia," Doc said. "She didn't say anything about the gym closing."

"I haven't told her," Dublin muttered.

"That's a terrible idea," Doc stated. "When she finds out..."

"I know, I know. But she's been working so hard on this tenth anniversary thing, and I didn't want to spoil it for her. Where have you been anyway?" Dublin asked. "Johnny Baker said you just disappeared one day."

"It's a long story," Doc sighed. "And it involves time travel..."

"Ugh," Dublin cringed. "Say no more."

"So why are you closed?" Doc demanded.

"To be honest... Oh hell," Dublin said. "I need whiskey for this conversation."

He opened a drawer in his desk and pulled out a bottle. "Here," he said, handing it to Doc. "You first."

Doc took a long swig, then gave it back to Dublin, and Dublin drained the bottle.

"About seven months ago, these anti-norm rallies started up," Dublin said. "People were speaking out against the inclusion of norms in the Hidden. You were even used as an example because at the time Mitcham was making you out to look like a psychopath."

Dublin looked longingly at the empty whiskey bottle, then went on. "Some of us, like me, are married to norms, and people were saying we shouldn't be allowed to be in the Hidden anymore. They argue that the more norms who know about us the more likely the Hidden is to be exposed, that sort of rot. We even had a riot," Dublin said wearily. "It's like the goddamn world has lost its mind."

"That's a strange tactic to take," Doc mused as Dublin checked the bottle for more liquid. "You, like most cryptids, don't even exist in the norm world. Pushing you out of the Hidden is more likely to expose cryptids than anything else."

"Already been argued," Dublin said.

"And?"

"Nobody seems to care. It's like they... They can't even think logically anymore."

"So what the hell happened?" Doc asked.

"One day Thypon and his crew came by," Dublin said. He paused and raised an eyebrow. "I believe you've met them."

Doc shrugged. "We didn't talk much."

Dublin laughed shortly, then said, "Anyway, I have a reputation as a fighter, and they wanted me to train them, but I refused. Why would I train someone who hates my wife just because she wasn't born a cryptid?"

"I see," Doc said.

"Thypon went on a campaign, telling everyone who would listen that I'm a norm-loving cryptid-hater. I mean, that doesn't even make sense!" Dublin exclaimed with irritation. "I'm a goddamn cryptid! My children are cryptids! And I hardly ever leave the Hidden."

"When people are riled up," Doc said softly, "things don't need to make sense."

"I know," Dublin sighed. "I have about ten clients still, but I managed to keep it from Julia. She operates in the upper echelon, and so far no one has said anything to her."

"So you've been blacklisted," Doc stated.

"Yep."

"And this is going on all over the Hidden?" Doc asked, remembering Sydney's closed shop in the middle of the day.

"Yep."

"Is there talk of war?" Doc asked.

"Not war exactly," Dublin said.

"Then what?" It was always something. You didn't rile people up just for fun; there was always an agenda.

Dublin glanced around the room suspiciously; and after a minute, he shook his head and just shrugged helplessly.

Doc studied him. Dublin was one of the fiercest people he'd ever met. Marrying Julia and having pups had certainly softened him, but Doc couldn't imagine him being afraid to speak. Something was really wrong.

"Have you met Markus Johanns?" Doc asked carefully.

Dublin's eyes narrowed. "He's the driving force behind the anti-norm movement."

"Why? To what end?"

"He insists that his main goal is simply to close the Hidden to future norms, like the strays you're always bringing in. You were mentioned specifically. Something about cryptid families raising norm children when cryptid families should be raising cryptid children."

Goddamn. He certainly hadn't done Sydney or Eloise any favors. At the time he hadn't realized all this was going on. He suddenly thought about Frankie bringing the Baker children down here all alone. So clearly a norm and so very vulnerable.

"Johnny said he's still coming by," Doc stated.

Dublin must have read his mind because he said, "No.

Ever since the Thypon incident, I've been going round to the Baker's house instead. I've never once seen their parents," he said as an aside. "Have you met them?"

"No. Frankie said she lives with them."

"Something strange is going on there," Dublin said. "But they haven't let me in on it yet, and I haven't pushed."

"Same here," Doc said. "Of course, I just lost eight months."

"You're immortal," Dublin laughed. "Eight months is nothing."

"Not to me," Doc sighed. "But it makes a remarkable difference to the mortals I know."

"Sorry," Dublin said sheepishly. "I wasn't thinking. Anyway, you should know that Thypon's crew is out for your blood. Mitcham announced you're under his protection though, so if they try something, it'll have to be sneaky."

"Sounds fun," Doc drawled.

"This isn't a game, Doc!"

"It's always a game," Doc replied.

"People are getting hurt!" Dublin exclaimed. "Just the other day, a merchant family was slaughtered in the lower three hundred. They had a norm girl living with them; that's why they were killed."

Doc couldn't afford to correct him. The LaRoches' lives depended on it.

"Just to summarize," Doc said thoughtfully. "I'm under the tetrarch's protection, but for all those in favor of the anti-norm movement, I'm persona non grata."

"Pretty much."

"I see. The hotel is always open to you and Julia if you need it," Doc said sincerely.

"It hasn't come to that yet," Dublin said. "I'm a little

concerned about the opening tomorrow night, but the show must go on," he added with a weak smile.

Doc could feel eyes following him as he left the Hidden, and he began to wish that Ahanu hadn't "helped" him in the first place. If Doc had just handled everything right away, maybe things wouldn't have gotten so volatile.

After talking to Dublin, he was a little concerned that killing Mitcham wouldn't actually solve anything; it might just make things worse. The straw that broke the camel's back. Furthermore, in spite of Simon's assurance, Doc didn't actually trust the council. They were politicians just like Mitcham, and they'd probably throw Doc under the train the first chance they got.

But there wasn't anything for it; he either killed Mitcham or learned to love the beach. He thought about all that gleaming sand and shrugged. He would miss Denver; it was home. Besides, he had a shaman to wake up and a war to start, and he couldn't possibly do that from a remote beach.

There was no point talking to anyone else from the Hidden because Dublin had told him everything he needed to know. And since there was no point talking to anyone else, Doc climbed into his car and drove back to the hotel.

As he crossed the hotel lobby, Doc stopped one of the uniformed clerks and said, "Send a tray of sandwiches up to Mr. Jury's room, please."

"Yes, Mr. Holliday, sir," the woman said briskly.

"And have Pierre whip up some kind of protein smoothie or malt or something like that."

"Yes, sir."

"And a couple steaks."

"Anything else?"

"That should do it," Doc said. "Thank you."

"My pleasure, sir."

A minute later, Doc was knocking softly on Jury's door. Jury didn't like to be interrupted when he was working, and that's why Doc was bribing him with food.

"What?!" Jury demanded, jerking open the door. The skin around his eyes was grey, and most of his hair was pulled back in a sloppy knot.

"I come in peace," Doc said. "I ordered some food sent up; it'll be here in a minute."

At the mention of food, Jury grinned. "I am hungry."

"Sandwiches," Doc said breezily. "Steaks, smoothies."

"I think I could eat a horse," Jury said, opening the door so Doc could come in.

"I hear it's tasty."

"I was kidding," Jury snorted.

"I don't see the difference between horses and cattle," Doc mused.

"For starters, one is a beautiful animal, the other's a cow."

"Technically only the females are called cows," Doc pointed out.

"You only know that because Andrew told you."

"That's true," Doc chuckled. "How's it going?"

"I found them," Jury declared.

"You did?"

"What? You didn't think I could?"

"I knew you could. I'm just surprised it was so easy."

"Who said it was easy?" Jury demanded. "I've been working my ass off."

"Apologies," Doc drawled. "I just figured Mitcham had been down every road."

Jury flopped onto the couch with a sigh. "You just don't get it."

"Get what?"

"Mitcham probably has been down every road," Jury snapped irritably. "But he hasn't been down every road with me."

"And that matters?"

"Goddamn it, Doc. I'm basically a freaking god, okay? I can do what it would take twenty or thirty linked witches to do. Do you know how many witches it takes to hide a building? A team of fifty. I can do a building on my own. It's not technically legal, but I can do it. Despite what you might think," Jury said sulkily, "I'm not a kitchen pantry witch."

"I never thought you were," Doc said sincerely. "So what you're saying is, on the power scale you're a fifty and everyone else is between one and ten."

"Pretty much."

"Fascinating," Doc said, sitting across from Jury. "Are there others like you?"

"Sure," Jury shrugged. "Just not in..." He glared at Doc for a moment, then said, "North America."

"I see. Why hasn't Mitcham ever tried to recruit you?"

"He did once, but I failed his test."

"You failed it?"

"Of course," Jury snorted. "I'm not stupid enough to actually advertise how powerful I am. I learned a long time ago from watching you that it's better to let people underestimate you. I can't tell you how many people think you're just an eccentric millionaire with three skills. Fucking, drinking, and winning."

"Billionaire," Doc corrected casually. "And those are fantastic skillsets."

Jury laughed and said, "Most people don't ever suspect that beneath your playboy facade lies a scheming, calculating genius."

"I was actually rather surprised that Mitcham did," Doc mused.

"Somebody must have told him."

"Maybe," Doc allowed. "I'm sorry I've never fully appreciated your skills as a witch. I don't really have anything to measure you against. You're the only witch I spend time with."

"What about the triplets?" Jury countered.

"We don't talk about magic," Doc replied with a smirk. "We're engaged in other pursuits."

"See? Fucking."

There was a knock on the door, and Jury yelled, "Come in!"

The same employee from the lobby opened the door and pushed in a cart loaded with food. Jury practically drooled.

"Thank you," Doc said, handing her a hundred dollar bill. Jury was halfway through a sandwich before the door closed behind her.

"So where are they?" Doc asked as he began to cut into his steak.

"They never left Denver," Jury replied around a mouthful. "Pretty clever really."

"But you found them."

"Yeah, but I would have found them anywhere. And it wasn't easy. It's like they're inside a plastic box."

"Maybe they are," Doc said.

"Gotta go out sometime though," Jury said, starting in on his own steak.

"Speaking of boxes," Doc said casually. "I need you to attend the theater with me tomorrow night."

"Why?" Jury demanded.

"Because I love the theater."

"And what's the real reason?"

"Mitcham and his wife will be accompanying us."

"And?"

"I just thought that perhaps we could take Mitcham backstage, he could walk into a door box, and then we could use my extraction team to move him to a different location where we could figure out how to kill him."

"Just that?" Jury grumbled.

"It's not much really," Doc said. "But if I don't succeed, you're going down with me whether you're there or not, so I thought you would want to be there to ensure my success as it were."

"Naturally," Jury said.

"Is your steak good?" Doc asked.

"You can't bribe me with food, you know."

"I can't?"

"No! But, yes, it's good."

Doc chuckled, and they ate in silence for a moment.

"What shall we do about Bosch's family?" Doc asked when he was finished eating.

"It might be good to know exactly what Mitcham wants," Jury said.

"Alright. We'll have to be careful though," Doc said. "I took care of Virgil, but Mitcham hired more people to follow us. His lack of trust is absolutely appalling."

Jury raised an eyebrow. "You're planning to kill him."

"Yes, but he doesn't know that, does he?"

"Shall we go now?" Jury asked.

"Not until you've showered," Doc said.

"It's only been a day," Jury said, sniffing his armpits.

"Two," Doc countered. "And maybe a nap? You look a tad... deranged."

"That hurts my feelings," Jury said. "If it weren't for you—"

"Yes, I know," Doc interrupted. "We wouldn't be in this mess."

"Well, we wouldn't," Jury complained.

"Maybe."

"Fine. I'll take a shower."

Doc cleared his throat.

"And a nap," Jury grumbled. "You're like a goddamn grandma," he muttered as he walked into his bedroom.

Doc stretched out on the couch, closed his eyes, and in seconds drifted off to sleep and into a dream.

His throne was occupied, and that annoyed him. It was his throne. And it was. He was the one sitting on it, just not him. And the woman with him... He would not have said he had a type, but even so, she was not it. She was... He didn't even know how to describe her. She was darkness, a shadow, a wisp of pure evil. And that's when he knew.

His heart slowed, and his lungs ceased to move. It couldn't be her. It just couldn't. He must have somehow conjured an image of her with his mind. She wasn't really there, in his head, handing that other him a chalice full of blood.

Her head swiveled, without really moving, and her fathomless black eyes pinned him in place. "Come here," she whispered.

Doc ran.

13

Doc woke with a gasp. For a moment he glanced wildly around the room, heart pounding like mad, but he was right where he had been. On Jury's couch, in Jury's suite. All was as it should be. Except...

Except the Black Shaman had been in his head.

"No," he muttered. "It's not possible."

He didn't even know what she looked like, and she was technically dead. Or at least mostly dead. He must have just imagined her because nothing else made sense.

He closed his eyes and forced himself to calm. "Everything's fine," he whispered, then allowed himself to drift off to sleep once more.

"There you are," she purred in his ear. She didn't purr the way Ana did, sultry and deep. No. Her purr was terrifying; it was a purr that said, "You're nothing but a worm, and I'm most likely going to eat you."

Doc turned slowly, trying to control his panic, trying to cover his fear. She was right behind him, and he stopped himself from stepping backwards. Her skin was pale, but the rest of her was black as night. Her hair, her eyes, her nails, the mist that seemed to clothe her. She was night. She was death.

"You smell afraid," she said, lips twisting into a smile. "Do you know who I am?"

"No," he lied.

"You are lying."

"I'm not. Who are you?"

"My name is Meli," she said, stepping closer and reaching out an ice-cold finger to touch his cheek. "I am lost. In the chaos. I cannot find my way out. But suddenly, I felt you. Or rather," she smiled grimly, "I smelled my brother on you."

"Your brother?" he asked calmly.

"About this tall," she said, indicating a spot just above her head. "Has a strange preference for grey. Rather meddlesome."

Doc couldn't help it. "You mean Ahanu?" he asked.

"Yes," she purred. "You do know him."

"I don't really. We met over a poker game; that's all."

"I see," she breathed. "Do you like him?"

"I'd like to kill him," Doc said emphatically.

"So would I," she grinned. "Unfortunately, I am rather dead. Will you help me?"

He'd rather die, and he almost said so, but then he remembered what he was supposed to be doing. "I'm not sure I can," he said truthfully.

"You will find a way, won't you?" she whispered, eyes beseeching and sad.

"I... I..."

"Wake up!" Jury snapped. "I'm ready."

Doc sat up, relieved to be free of her, relieved to feel the warmth of life again.

"You alright?" Jury asked. "You look... green."

He did feel a little ill. And he wanted a shower to wash away the taint of her touch.

"I'm fine," he said stiffly.

"You don't look fine."

"Are we doing this?"

"Don't tell me then," Jury grumbled. "It's not like I care."

"Let's just go," Doc said wearily.

"How do you plan to shake our tail?" Jury asked as they rode the elevator up to the parking garage.

"I thought you could glamour the car," Doc suggested.

"That's stupid," Jury snorted. "Nobody glamours..." He trailed off. "Actually..." he said thoughtfully. "And anyway, it'd be more of a camouflage."

Doc grinned inwardly. "But can you do it?"

"Can I do it? Please. I invented it."

"Pretty sure I invented it," Doc countered.

"No. You conceived of it," Jury said loftily. "I invented it, or at least I'm about to."

Regardless of who invented it, Jury did manage to perfect it rather quickly, because no one followed them when they exited the parking garage.

"It looks like I'm driving a Pinto," Doc complained as he caught a glimpse of the car's reflection in the windows along the street.

"Exactly. No one would ever suspect it," Jury said with a chuckle.

"I'd rather have a huge ass."

"You do," Jury laughed. "And anyway, it worked. We've circled the block six times. I'm pretty sure we're clear."

"That's because Pintos are stupid," Doc grumbled.

"We should have brought sandwiches," Jury said as Doc headed towards Littleton.

"Semper paratus," Doc said with a dejected shake of his head.

"It really is more of a glamour," Jury said, voice strained. "And it's bigger than a human, so between you and me and the car, it's like I'm doing six glamours all at once."

"Impressive," Doc said.

"It actually is!" Jury snapped.

"What makes you think I didn't mean it?" Doc laughed.

"Every time you say things like 'impressive' or 'interesting' or 'sorry', you just sound sarcastic," Jury complained.

"Interesting."

"Knock it off!"

They sat outside the Bosch's home for over an hour. No one came. No one went. But someone was clearly inside. The lights were on, and silhouettes occasionally moved past the windows.

"Shall I send in Winks?" Jury asked, licking a glob of icing from his fingers.

Doc considered strangling him. "You've had Winks this whole time, and you're just now asking if you should send him in?"

"Six glamours, Doc. I was exhausted. What's your excuse?"

"Just do it," Doc growled.

Jury rolled down his window and released Winks into the cold night air.

"He's inside," Jury said after a moment. "There're two women, three kids, a dog, and no obvious signs of magic."

Doc opened his door; he was sick of waiting. "I'm going; you coming?"

"Just 'cause there's no sign of magic," Jury said, hurrying after Doc, "doesn't mean there isn't any."

"So?"

"So?! Some of those spells can turn you inside out!"

"Not me," Doc said. "I have Amos the Betrayer's amulet."

"You have what?!" Jury exclaimed. "And you're just now telling me?!"

Doc knocked on the door without answering.

A haggard looking woman answered, eyes brightening when she saw them.

"Are you Mrs. Bosch?" Doc asked.

"Yes," she whispered. "Have you come to move us?"

"Move you?"

"Hiero said that if something happened to him, we had to stay here until someone came to move us." Her voice had a desperate edge, and her eyes were filled with tears. "Please tell me you've come to move us."

"I apologize for the confusion," Doc said smoothly. "We typically use the term extraction."

"Oh," she breathed, face nearly going slack with relief.

Jury elbowed Doc in the side, but Doc ignored him and said, "Before we work out all the details though, I need to speak with you about a few things."

"Of course," she said. "Please come in."

"Thank you, ma'am," Doc said. "By the way, my name is Tom Mackey, and this is my associate Thomas Birdwell." Jury made a choked noise, and Doc grinned inwardly.

"Nice to meet you," Mrs. Bosch said. "Please sit down."

"I don't want to upset you," Doc said carefully, "but I need to speak with you about your late husband."

Her pale face turned a brighter shade of white. "So he's... I wasn't..." The tears spilled over onto her colorless cheeks.

"I'm so sorry," Doc said. "I didn't know you didn't know."

"I assumed," she whispered. "But Hiero didn't trust anyone towards the end there. He was... He just..." Her eyes filled with tears again, and she said, "And then the night of the banquet, he never came home."

"Your husband tried to kill the tetrarch," Doc said softly, "and was killed instead."

"Oh," she whimpered.

"I'm sorry."

She wiped her eyes frantically and said, "No, I'm sorry. What was it you needed?"

"During his work at the Bureau, your husband stole something, and Tetrarch Mitcham is set on recovering it, no matter the cost."

Mrs. Bosch turned a sickly green color. "Did Mr. Mitcham send you?"

"No, ma'am. He hasn't been able to find you yet. We're here to move you, as your husband requested, but you won't be safe as long as you have what he took."

"I see," she said softly.

A pale boy peeked around the edge of the sofa, and Doc winked at him. Mrs. Bosch jumped, turned around frantically, and gasped, "Eddie! I told you to stay in your room!"

"But, Mom," Eddie whined, "I just wanted to see who it was."

"Go!" she ordered. "And take your brothers with you."

Three boys and a dog crawled out from behind the couch and, with sulky looks, wandered down the hallway.

"I'm so sorry about that," Mrs. Bosch mumbled. "They just... They haven't been outside in nearly a year now... It's been..."

"I'm sorry we didn't come sooner," Doc said sincerely.

"There's been a lot of unrest lately. But we can help you. My extraction team will move you."

"Hiero said if I left the house they would find me," she whispered in terror. "He said they could smell me."

"I have team for that," Doc said soothingly.

"You do?" Jury demanded.

"Of course I do. Otherwise, there would be no hiding people, would there?" Doc replied.

"But—"

"Hush," Doc commanded. "Mrs. Bosch, my men can be here within the hour, and you and your boys can have a new life."

"What about my sister?"

"She can go with you," Doc promised. "I just need for you to give me the item Bosch stole."

"He didn't steal it," she said softly.

"He didn't?"

"Not really. He worked with Edgar to create it, and, yes, they were building it for Mr. Mitcham, but that was before. It didn't ever belong to Mr. Mitcham."

"Before what?" Doc asked, curiosity spiking.

"Hiero was a scientist; he was in research and development," she said a little desperately. "He was trying to find a cell that when introduced to the human body could destroy cancer, but no one would fund him. When Mr. Mitcham asked Hiero to take over the BCA, he told him that he would be able to work with cryptids to try to find a cure."

"You mean experiment on," Doc said flatly.

"Hiero didn't know that at the time," she insisted. "And then he thought if he could just find the right thing, everyone could be stronger, better, more adaptable. Most cryptids don't contract the same diseases humans do," she said, voice pleading. "They have immunities, and Hiero... Hiero thought..."

She started crying again, and Doc nudged Jury.

"No," Jury mouthed. "You do it."

"Fine," Doc mouthed back.

He moved to sit beside Mrs. Bosch and patted her hand consolingly. "I'm sorry this is difficult for you."

"It's just that no one knows Hiero's side of things," she wailed. "Everyone probably thinks he was a monster, and he was just trying to help!"

"I'm certain he was," Doc said, tone comforting. "Can you tell me what happened?"

She blew her nose and said softly, "Hiero didn't tell me everything. All I know is that he developed a method of enhancing the cryptids' abilities, but at some point he realized that instead of just increasing the cryptids, maybe he could turn humans into cryptids. He thought it would change the world."

"Fascinating," Doc said.

"It was! He was so excited, but then he discovered something. Something horrible, and he was shaken, Mr. Mackey. Shaken to the core. He moved us here and told us that if anything happened to him, we couldn't leave the house. He told us we must never leave the house."

Her words were coming faster and faster, and Doc began to worry she would fall apart before she could give him whatever it was Mitcham wanted.

"Get Mrs. Bosch some water please, Birdwell," Doc said.

Jury gave him a furious look, but stood and left the room.

"I'm so sorry about your husband, Mrs. Bosch. I'm sure he had the best intentions. Can you tell me what turned him against Mitcham?"

"Don't you know?" she whispered.

"I really don't."

"Mr. Mitcham hates us," she said emphatically. "Humans, normal people. Despises us really. One night Hiero overheard him talking to one of his advisors, and Mr. Mitcham went into a rage about how when he was done humanity would once again occupy their proper place. As food for the greater species."

"Interesting," Doc said.

"He was just using Hiero," she whispered. "He didn't care for him at all. Once he had what he wanted, he was going to destroy the BCA and Hiero, so Hiero decided he had to find a way to stop him."

"Here's your water," Jury said grumpily.

"Thank you, Mr. Birdwell," she said, taking the glass with shaking hands.

"Straighten up," Doc mouthed at Jury.

"She's making him out to be a hero!" Jury mouthed back.

"So what? If it helps her sleep at night, it doesn't bother me," Doc said silently.

"Please go on," Doc encouraged, taking the empty glass from her hand and setting it on the coffee table.

"He thought he could turn himself into the ultimate cryptid, but it didn't work, I guess," she added weakly.

"I'm so sorry, Mrs. Bosch. What is it that Mitcham wants?"

"I'll get it for you," she said softly.

As soon as she was gone, Doc turned on Jury. "What is wrong with you?" he hissed.

"He was evil!" Jury shot back. "He hooked them up to that horrible machine and cut them into pieces!"

"Yes, but she didn't," Doc snapped.

"She thinks he was good!" Jury snapped back.

"It doesn't matter what she thinks," Doc said. "Besides, your family made the fetishes."

Jury blushed and grumbled something about being deceived.

"Here you are," Mrs. Bosch said, walking back into the room and handing Doc an octagonal metal box.

"What is it?" Doc asked, surprised at how heavy the box was.

"I don't know, and I don't know how to open it. Edgar and Hiero worked on it for hours and hours. They were so pleased when they were finally successful." She sighed and added, "But he wouldn't tell me what it was for."

"Thank you for all your help," Doc said. "Get yourselves ready; just one suitcase a piece. My men will be here soon." Doc took her hand and gazed into her eyes. "You will need to be brave, Mrs. Bosch. They are rather... alarming at first sight."

"Alarming?" she asked.

"Quite, but they will protect you. You must trust me."

"I do, Mr. Mackey."

"Excellent. One last question, Mitcham seems to have eyes and ears everywhere. Do you know how he manages it?"

She shook her head. "I'm sorry. All I know is that Hiero said this house was safe."

"Thank you, Mrs. Bosch. Remember, trust me."

Once they were back in the car, Doc called Jervis.

"Are you certain this line is secure?" Doc asked.

"Yes."

"In that case, I need the extraction team to conduct a removal and clean-up. Full scrub."

"Certainly, sir."

"I'll text you the address, and make it snappy."

"Snappy?"

"Quick, expedient, put a rush on it."

"It would have been quicker just to say so, sir"

"Excuse me for having a varied vocabulary," Doc snorted.

"You're excused."

"Hey!" Doc snapped. "That's my thing." But Jervis had already disconnected.

"Something's going on with him," Doc muttered.

"Jervis?" Jury asked.

"Yeah, but anyway, what do you think?"

"About?"

"Bosch?"

"I think he was a total asshole who joined up with another total asshole, and then he realized he was going to get screwed so he decided to be an even bigger asshole."

"Hum," Doc said. "Lot of assholes."

"You better believe it," Jury grunted.

"It sounds as if he and Edgar were working together pretty closely."

"Makes sense. They were both norms," Jury said.

"Do you think Cynric warded the house?"

"Possibly. If he did, he was careful not to leave a trace."

"I didn't know you could do that," Doc replied.

"Do what?"

"Not leave a trace."

"Sure, it's just really time consuming and takes a lot of effort. Usually there's no point." Jury grabbed the box of cupcakes from the floorboard and started eating the rest of them.

"You better not get any crumbs in here," Doc grumbled.

"You have people for that," Jury retorted.

"You still mad about that?"

"It only just happened, so yeah."

"Well?"

"Well, what?" Jury snapped.

"Are you going to ask or just be mad about it?" Doc inquired.

"I shouldn't have to ask," Jury grumbled.

"Please, I watched your video on mild compulsion the other day."

"It's not like I do it," Jury protested. "I was just explaining how it worked."

"I'm pretty sure I couldn't explain how to make love to a woman if I'd never done it," Doc countered.

"Fine, so maybe I've done it a few times. Emphasis on 'mild'," Jury tossed out.

"Have you done it to me?"

"No," Jury insisted.

"Really?"

"Really."

"I don't believe you," Doc drawled.

"Truthfully," Jury sighed. "I did try once or twice after we first met, but you're fundamentally opposed to compulsion. It just doesn't work on you."

"I reserve the right to punch you at a later date," Doc stated.

"Fine. Tell me about your 'team for that'."

"I sometimes... move people around."

"Like Ana and Ina?"

"Yeah, but I have gotten better at it," Doc said thoughtfully.

"How so?"

"Well, you met the extraction team."

"But you have... what, cleaners?"

"Something like that," Doc allowed. "You always said a witch could find you if they had your scent, so you can't just move people, you have to change their scent."

"Goddamn," Jury muttered. "You've been playing me this whole fucking time, haven't you?"

"What?"

"You act like you don't understand a goddamn thing I say, and here I am dumbing shit down for you so you can follow it because you're a fucking moron when it comes to magic; and meanwhile, you've been taking everything I say and figuring out how to use it against me."

"That is not true at all," Doc argued. "I figured out how to use it against others, not you."

"Sometimes I fucking hate you!" Jury snapped.

"But only sometimes," Doc prodded. "What about when I saved you from a loveless, abusive marriage?"

"I said thank you!"

"I'm just saying you didn't hate me then."

"No, but then you slept with my Mrs. Robinson, so I think we're square."

Doc burst out laughing. "Do you know how hard it was to kill Marie? I had an easier time with Elizabeth Haddock."

"Speaking of Elizabeth, where's Boudica?" Jury asked.

"I think she's left me."

"Seriously? For who?"

"Frankie."

"The norm babysitter?"

"Yep."

"That's embarrassing," Jury chuckled.

"It's not like I have time for a dog," Doc said carelessly.

"Hurts though, doesn't it?"

"We weren't close."

"You're lying," Jury snorted.

"I wouldn't lie to you," Doc lied.

"Ha! The way I figure, every other word out of your mouth is a lie."

"I'm glad you're here," Doc said with a grin.

"Fuck you too."

14

Doc and Jury parted ways in the parking garage. Jury headed down a level, and Doc didn't ask where he was going. One, he didn't particularly care what Jury was doing, and two, Jury still wasn't talking to him.

Doc went to his suite and sprawled on his couch, thinking over what Mrs. Bosch had said. She clearly wanted to believe that her husband was a good man, and Doc wasn't going to tell her differently. It wouldn't benefit her at all to know that Bosch had committed heinous acts and was planning to commit even more heinous acts. Furthermore, there was a part of her that already knew Bosch was evil; otherwise she wouldn't have tried so hard to convince them he wasn't.

Ultimately, no matter what she had said, Bosch had been a norm like his father, and he hadn't wanted to be a norm. He'd wanted to be special like his witch mother, and he'd figured out a way to get it.

Doc turned the octagonal box Mrs. Bosch had given him over in his hand. It was covered in strange carvings and markings, but there was no obvious way to open it. If all else failed he could get someone to laser it open, but since he didn't know what was inside, he'd save that for a last resort.

He ran his finger along a symbol. It looked like a rune, but that didn't particularly help him since he didn't know anything about runes. He wished he could take it to Sydney. If anyone could crack it, it would be him, but frankly, it didn't really matter what it was so long as Mitcham didn't have it.

Doc stood and took the box to his safe, placing it between Achaean's artifact that could raise the dead and Bosch's fetishes of cryptid power. He was getting quite a collection of artifacts that needed to be destroyed.

He stared at the fetishes for a moment, thinking about Bosch. There was a chance that, like Thaddeus, Bosch really had begun his work with good intentions, but Doc had a feeling he'd always had an agenda. Sofia's mother had hidden from him for a reason, but in spite of her efforts, Doc was fairly certain Bosch had killed her.

Doc closed the safe and considered his next move. There really wasn't anything he could do until tomorrow night. Which left him hours and hours to burn. There were probably a hundred things he should do, like check up on Ms. Goodhunt or touch base with Eloise, but he was trying to whittle down his problems, not add to them.

Perhaps he would stay in and read that Friedrich Nietzsche book he hadn't yet read. Or he could call the triplets. Or see if Jervis was free for a game. Of course the Banshee would be plenty busy right now.

After a brief argument with himself, Doc decided on the Banshee and spent several hours there dealing faro. By the time he returned home, the city was almost asleep. It wouldn't sleep long though; it never did.

He poured himself a glass of whiskey and drank it on his balcony overlooking the nearly empty street beneath him. He rarely had a truly quiet moment to himself, and he never knew what to do when he did. He wasn't like Andrew; he couldn't just gaze at the stars for hours.

On the surface, he and Andrew had been nothing alike. Andrew was a laid-back family man who only drank coffee and was terrible at poker. Doc enjoyed women, whiskey, and winning. But there had been a deep connection between them; they'd both looked death in the face more than once. Andrew literally, and Doc metaphorically.

More importantly, they both accepted the fact that the only way to deal with some people was to kill them. Perhaps there was such a thing as rehabilitation, but Doc wasn't willing to risk it. He refused to be the one to let a child beater walk free just to see if he'd been rehabilitated or not.

Andrew had understood that, but Andrew had never particularly enjoyed the kill; whereas, Doc enjoyed being the executioner.

It wasn't just about immortality. There was something very satisfying about killing people who deserved it. He sometimes felt that by granting him immortality with a required blood payment that Tozi had entrusted him with a sacred task. The task of protecting and defending those who couldn't protect themselves. He assumed he could kill anyone to fulfill the payment, that it didn't have to be someone evil; but Tozi had known him, and she had known he would seek out villains.

Doc turned from the window, removed his clothes, and placed them neatly over the back of his chair before sliding between his silk sheets. He should have taken that lovely blond up on her sultry invitation instead of returning home alone; he just hadn't been in the mood. Which was strange; he was always in the mood.

He closed his eyes and fell asleep wondering what was in Bosch's box.

"I knew you would come back to me," Meli whispered.

Doc swallowed the shudder that crawled his frame at her words and turned to face her. She'd changed her appearance. She was still pale with black hair, but the sharpness that had accentuated her features earlier was softened. She reached out a hand to touch his face, and he saw that even her fingernails were pink now, normal.

"What is your name?" she asked, cupping his cheek with her frigid palm.

"John," he replied, fighting the urge to push her away.

"John," she repeated. "A perfectly... mundane name."

"Yes," he agreed.

"But you are not a mundane man," she whispered. "I can feel your power, your strength. There is something... different about you."

He didn't bother to respond. He was too busy trying to conceal his revulsion of her. She didn't know him, but he knew her. She was evil. People were nothing to her but slaves. And a meal if she was feeling peckish. He wanted to tell her she wasn't going to win, that Andrew was going to destroy her; but he knew he couldn't, knew he couldn't say anything about Andrew, knew he needed to be very careful.

She studied him with curious eyes. "I feel... life in you. Life that is not your own."

"Where are you?" Doc asked, trying to distract her.

"I do not know. The in between space perhaps."

"In between what?"

"Life and death. Earth and spirit." She shrugged casually. "Dreams and awake."

That didn't help him at all.

"You glow," she said, eyes bright with interest. "Why?"

Doc forced himself to wake up.

He stared at the semi-darkness and consciously slowed his breathing. She couldn't hurt him. Probably. She wasn't likely to try in any case because she wanted his help. Maybe. He wiped the sweat from his forehead and desperately wished he could undo whatever he'd done to attract her notice.

His eyes narrowed as he wondered if Ahanu had somehow marked him. She'd said she could smell Ahanu on him. Had he done it on purpose? Knowing Ahanu, he probably had. Had Ahanu marked Andrew as well? Maybe Doc would go ahead and kill him. But he couldn't. Even if he could. Andrew still needed Ahanu.

It was one of those timeline things Doc hated. Ahanu and Meli had tortured Andrew for years, and Doc wished he could punish them for it. But even if he somehow could, he wouldn't because then the Andrew he knew would be gone. Maybe that was selfish, but Doc couldn't handle the idea that his Andrew would never exist. But beyond his own selfish reasons, he didn't think Andrew would thank him for it.

Which brought him back to this moment. He needed to fully wake the Black Shaman, but he needed to do it without losing his mind. The idea that she would be waiting for him every time he closed his eyes to sleep made him sick. It had been that way for Andrew, and some of the things she had done to Andrew in his dreams made dying look good.

"I don't dare sleep without my dreamcatcher," Andrew had once confessed. "I know she's not dead. She's out there somewhere, waiting; and I'm terrified that if I see her, I'll give something away, and everything will change. My god, Doc, can you imagine if I screwed it up now, after everything I've gone through to get here?"

They were silent for a moment, imagining it, then Andrew said, "I sometimes wonder if I could have changed things for the better. Saved her. Kept her from ever being. Even at the end there, I wanted to save her."

Angst crossed Andrew's face, and he made a frustrated sound. "Do you know how insane that sounds? She was... is... evil! She drank the blood of babies. She turned people into mindless slaves. She... She spreads death wherever she goes. Why do I still care?"

"I don't know," Doc replied honestly.

"She hated me. She was going to kill everyone I loved. She did..." Andrew paused, eyes distant, then said, "I should be glad she's dead. Or will be." He laughed. "Time travel is ridiculous. It makes no sense whatsoever. Do you think Ahanu's the only one?"

"The only one what?" Doc asked.

"The only one who can mess with time? I sure as hell hope so. I don't think the world could handle any more." Andrew paled slightly. "If there were more, they could screw up my timeline, and then I might never be born..."

"I don't think Ahanu would let that happen," Doc said with a chuckle.

"Probably not," Andrew agreed. "He is meddlesome. But the whole thing is impossible to wrap your mind around. It makes me sick sometimes, thinking about it."

That had been one of Andrew's darker moments. Most of the time you would have never guessed he'd faced the devil and lived to tell about it. Most of the time his eyes were twinkling with good cheer, happy just to be free and alive.

But Doc understood both sides of Andrew. He understood what it felt like to embrace life and at the same time wonder if just maybe you were supposed to be dead.

Doc stared at his ceiling, thinking of Andrew and the Black Shaman for a long while before he decided he may as well get up. It's not as if he'd get any actual rest if she was there, waiting for him, touching him with her freezing hands.

He glanced at the clock as he rolled out of bed. It wasn't yet six o'clock, but if he knew anything about the world, the Baker children would show up before too long. Which gave him just enough time to take a shower and order breakfast.

Just as he was finishing getting dressed, he heard his front door crack open. Right on time, he thought, wondering if this was the way things were going to be from now on.

"Morning, Thaddeus," Jules was whispering when Doc stepped into the sitting room. "We just wanted to say hi."

"Only to Thaddeus?" Doc drawled.

The children jumped and looked at him guiltily. "Frankie said you might not be awake yet," Johnny offered. "She said we probably shouldn't bother you... Just in case."

"Ana isn't here today," Doc chuckled.

"I like Ana," Addison said firmly.

"I like her too," Doc said. "I ordered breakfast, extra unicorn breath."

"Yum," Addison grinned.

As if he'd summoned it, someone knocked on the door.

"Come in," Doc called out.

"Your breakfast, sir," a Dulcis employee said, pushing in a large cart.

"Thank you, James," Doc replied.

James startled slightly. "You remember me, sir?"

"Certainly."

"But its been almost six years, sir."

"I don't forget a face," Doc said easily. "Or a name. Glad to see you're still here."

James beamed as he laid the covered trays on the table. "I'd never leave Dulcis, sir. Thank you, sir. Have a wonderful day, sir."

"You as well, James," Doc said cheerfully.

"Don't you ever get tired of being 'sirred'?" Jules asked testily.

"Not at all," Doc laughed. "In fact, I rather enjoy it. It's a nice change from 'reprobate' and 'pleasure seeker'. Isn't that right, Thaddy, old boy?"

"I prefer hedonist," Thaddeus said stiffly.

"That you do," Doc chuckled.

Jules's expression became thoughtful. "So how's it work?" she suddenly asked.

"How's what work?" Doc asked.

"The hotel, the staff," Jules said. "Do they all know you're immortal? Dulcis isn't in the Hidden, so I don't see how they could know, but it's kind of obvious so I'm not sure how you're hiding it."

"I'm not," Doc replied.

Jules glared at him. "I told you how to kill a Zeniu, the least you could do is explain it to me."

"I paid you," Doc said, grinning. It seemed that Jules, like Thaddeus, hated it when she didn't know the answer to something.

"Stop torturing her," Thaddeus grumbled. "It's not as if it's important."

"It could be extraordinarily important," Doc countered.

"Senselessly cruel," Thaddeus sighed.

Doc laughed. "I suppose it is. I have two types of employees," he said. "Norms who work with norm patrons and are turned over every ten years or so, and cryptids who can work here as long as they like."

"I see," Jules said thoughtfully. "So Jervis is a cryptid?"

"Naturally," Doc said.

"And all the employees who come up to your suite."

"For the most part."

"But Pierre?"

"Norm," Doc said sadly. "He has two years left on his contract."

"Too bad," Johnny said. "I like his chocolate pudding."

"I believe he prefers the term 'mousse'," Doc said.

"Yuck!" Addison exclaimed. "Why would you want chocolate moose?"

"It's French—" Thaddeus started to explain.

"Never mind," Doc said, cutting him off. "Let's eat." He sipped his whiskey and watched them eat for a moment before asking, "How come you didn't mention the unrest in the Hidden?"

"Why would we?" Johnny said, trying to eat his bacon and sausage at the same time. "It doesn't really affect you."

"You don't even live in the Hidden," Jules added. "Why would you care?"

Before Doc could respond, Thaddeus started laughing. All four children stared at Thaddeus, mouths open in shock.

"Is he... laughing?" Frankie whispered. "Is he alright?"

"Funniest thing I've heard in decades," Thaddeus giggled. "Actually that one thing with Abigail Jury was pretty funny, but this... this takes the cake. 'Why would you care?' Oh God, it's hysterical!" Thaddeus's laughter filled the room, and Doc fought to keep his face impassive.

Addison tugged on Doc's sleeve and said in a hushed tone, "Is Thaddeus sick?"

"Nah," Doc said. "He's just feeling amused at the moment."

"Why?"

"Why?!" Thaddeus cackled "Why?!"

"This could go on for a while," Doc said. "We may as well finish our breakfast."

Except for the sound of Thaddeus's chuckling, they ate in silence. Finally Thaddeus wound down. "Thank you, children," he said with a hiccup. "I needed that."

"I still don't understand what we said that was funny," Johnny muttered.

"I know," Thaddeus said. "That makes it even funnier. Granted, you haven't known Doc long, and you're not privy to everything that goes on, but Doc has never met a problem he didn't try to fix. He can't help himself. It's a compulsion, I think."

"You can't just fix warring factions in the Hidden," Jules said stiffly.

"Maybe you can't," Thaddeus corrected gently.

"That's ridiculous," Jules countered. "He's just one man. One literal man. He's not even a cryptid."

Doc poured more whiskey into his coffee cup and let them argue around him. He never bothered trying to explain himself; no one ever listened. But if Thaddeus wanted to waste his time trying to describe Doc's unfortunate addiction to meddling, he could have at it.

"I'm rather ashamed of you, Ms. Baker," Thaddeus chastised. "You should know by now that what you are has very little to do with who you are."

"Yes," she snapped, "but we're not just talking about

Tetrarch Mitcham here; we're talking about the Hidden at large. There have been riots and protests all over the nation. How's Doc going to fix that?"

"I don't know," Thaddeus admitted. "Shall we ask him?"

"Would you look at the time?" Doc cut in. "I've got a meeting with Jervis I need to attend, and I'm sure you have school to get off to." He stood and gestured towards the door. "Out with you."

When they were gone, he closed the door with a sigh. "That was rather naughty of you, old boy," he said.

"They're completely clueless!" Thaddeus exclaimed.

"I'm not sure if you've noticed this, but that's the way I prefer it," Doc pointed out.

"I apologize," Thaddeus muttered.

"It doesn't matter."

"How are you going to fix it?"

"Goddamn, Thaddy! How the hell should I know?"

"You don't have a plan?"

"I have a hopeful solution lined up for tonight. But only for Mitcham," Doc admitted. "I haven't gotten to the rest of it yet."

"You don't sound overly confident."

Doc sighed. "I just... I've felt just a tad luckless lately, and my plans usually require a certain amount of... well, luck to succeed."

Thaddeus made a noise, and Doc felt as if he was shaking his invisible head. "I've been watching you for a while now," Thaddeus said solemnly, "and of one thing I am certain."

"What's that?" Doc asked.

"You make your own luck."

Doc spent the rest of his day working out the details for his ridiculous plan. He examined the door cage Bennie had delivered, he met with his extraction team, he studied the blueprints for his theater, and he bribed Jury with more food.

Two hours before show time, Doc showered and strapped his knives into place, then he dressed meticulously in a crisp tuxedo.

"I need you," he texted Jervis as he studied his reflection.

A moment later Jervis was at his door. "After all these years," Jervis sighed, "you still can't tie your own tie."

"It's a failing," Doc chuckled.

"It gives me something to do," Jervis said, thin fingers deftly tying Doc's tie into place.

"If things don't go as planned tonight..." Doc began.

"They never do," Jervis said.

"I know, but if things go really sideways..." Doc paused. He couldn't let things go sideways. He just couldn't. There were too many lives at stake. Frankie and the Baker children. Dublin and his pack. The LaRoches. Brad and Tami. Not to mention all the cryptids who simply looked like norms, such as Emily and Randell. If the Hidden fell apart, too many people would suffer. Too many people would die. He couldn't fail. He simply couldn't.

"Never mind," he said. "If things go sideways I'll just figure out a way to get it back on track."

"Excellent plan, sir," Jervis said solemnly.

"One of my best."

"Are you seriously smoking?" Doc demanded as he and Jury entered the four hundred block of the Hidden.

"I'm antsy as hell," Jury snapped. "I need something to calm my nerves, and I didn't figure I could walk into the theater with a basket full of sandwiches. I mean, we're about to... Goddamn, Doc. We're about to break the fucking Hidden."

"No," Doc corrected. "We're fixing it. And stop stressing. Mitcham will be able to see right through you."

"You know I'm not good at this," Jury grumbled. "You should've left me at home."

"I need you," Doc said.

"You better hope this works," Jury said gloomily.

"How can it not?" Doc replied cheerfully.

"I thought of twenty-nine ways on the way over," Jury snarled.

"Only twenty-nine?"

"I got distracted by that lady wearing the short skirt."

"That was a very short skirt."

"She smiled at me," Jury said.

"Pretty sure she smiled at me," Doc stated. "After all, I was the one driving the supercar."

"She didn't care about supercars," Jury argued. "She wanted to touch my hair; you could see it in her eyes."

"Whatever makes you feel better."

"Oh shut up," Jury snapped, stubbing out his cigarette with the toe of his dress shoe. "Let's just do this."

Doc could understand why Jury was nervous. Jury couldn't bluff worth a damn, but Doc bluffed for a living, and even he felt on edge.

They greeted Tetrarch Mitcham and his wife, also a Zeniu, and entered the brightly lit theater, leaving Mitcham's stiff Takaheni guard just outside.

"Doc!" Julia cried out when she saw him. "I'm so glad you came." Her eyes widened when she recognized Mitcham, and she started stuttering. "Oh... Tetrarch Mitcham... I wasn't aware... I mean... I didn't know... I'm so glad you're here! Doc has the best box in the theater."

"Mrs. O'Connell," Mitcham said in that gracious tone he

had, the one that made you feel important if you didn't notice the flatness of his eyes. "Delighted to finally meet you; I've heard so much about you from my associates."

Julia blushed and said, "I sincerely hope it was good things."

"Only the best," Mitcham assured her.

Mrs. Mitcham had yet to say a word. She just held onto Mitcham's arm and looked from side to side occasionally, a set half-smile on her face.

"Do enjoy the show," Julia said enthusiastically. "Afterwards Doc can take you backstage; the cast would be absolutely thrilled to meet you."

"Sounds wonderful," Mitcham said.

Doc knew Mitcham was lying, but he couldn't say how he knew because Mitcham didn't have a single tell. Doc could just sense it.

As they sat in Doc's box waiting for the play to start, Mitcham said casually, "You and I are wolves, Mr. Holliday. We tolerate the sheep; but, ultimately, we are above them."

Doc wasn't sure how to respond to that, but fortunately, he didn't have to.

"Tell me about Bosch's family," Mitcham said. "Have you found them?"

"Yes," Doc said. "I didn't call because I knew I'd be seeing you tonight, and I didn't want to waste your time. They were in Littleton, and they've been eliminated."

"How so?"

"I killed them, sir," Doc said softly. "Just as you ordered."

"All of them?"

"Yes. All five."

"Five?"

"Yes," Doc said. "Two women, three children, and their dog."

"That would be six," Mitcham corrected.

"I wasn't sure you'd count the dog, sir," Doc said apologetically.

"Indeed." Mitcham practically vibrated with impatience. "The house?"

"I didn't burn it, if that's what you mean," Doc said, making his tone defensive. "I cleared out the bodies because they were in norm territory, but I left the house intact."

"Excellent work," Mitcham said. He handed Doc his theater program and said, "Write down the address."

Doc nodded and scribbled it down.

"I'm pleased you're so efficient, Mr. Holliday. And not a moment too soon. I look forward to working with you again," Mitcham said.

Just as Doc had suspected. Once a politician had his teeth in you, he was never done with you.

Mitcham was so obviously impatient during the play that Doc began to worry he wouldn't go backstage, but when the play was over, Mitcham said, "I believe we were promised a backstage pass."

"Yes, sir," Doc said, standing to open the door. "There's a VIP stairway right this way."

He led Mitcham and his wife down the hallway towards the fake doorway, controlling both his step and his breathing. If this didn't work, they were in for a hell of a fight. Doc glanced at Jury, then opened the door. On the other side, a set of stairs led down into the back of the theater.

"After you, sir," Doc said subserviently.

Mitcham and his wife stepped through the doorway onto

the illusion of the stair landing that Jury had created, and Doc quickly shut the door behind them, shoving the now visible bolt into place.

"Seal it!" he ordered.

"I know what I'm doing!" Jury snapped. After a moment he said, "It's done."

"Now!" Doc called out softly.

At his command, a shadow phantom drifted out of the wall and settled over the doorway. Then both the phantom and the doorway cage disappeared, leaving behind an empty hallway.

"I can't believe that worked," Doc whispered.

"It was quite a convincing glamour," Jury said.

"I thought it was a camouflage," Doc countered.

"Why get hung up on vocabulary?" Jury muttered. "It worked; that's all that matters."

"Put on the glamours, and let's go," Doc said.

"We went over the plan a hundred times," Jury ground out. "I know what I'm doing."

"Then get on with it," Doc ground out.

"Done."

Doc glanced down. He was still wearing his tuxedo, but his hands were wrinkled and old looking. "What's this?" he asked.

"I tried to guess at what you'd look like if you looked your age," Jury said with a smirk.

Doc shrugged. "I can work with it. You on the other hand... You're bald."

"I know," Jury said. "It's like the Pinto of hair styles. No one would ever think it was me."

Doc laughed as they hurried down the hallway towards the exit. It just so happened that Doc owned a safe house only a block from the theater, and that's exactly where the phantom had taken Mitcham.

Doc and Jury walked casually down the sidewalk, chatting about the play, and pretending they weren't in any hurry at all. When they reached the house, Doc said, "Come inside for a brandy, won't you?" He unlocked the door, and they both stepped inside.

The phantom was waiting, door cage beside him.

"Thanks, Enoshi," Doc said. "We couldn't have pulled it off without you."

"The pleasure is mine," Enoshi said, voice oddly hollow. "I will leave you to your business now." And he literally drifted into the wall and disappeared.

"Goddamn, they freak me out," Jury hissed.

"Imagine how they feel about us," Doc replied.

"What?"

"I mean, we have to use doorways," Doc said sarcastically. "How baroque."

"I refuse to get into this with you. What now?"

"We open the box and kill him," Doc said hopefully.

"Right."

Jury stepped up to the cage, put his hand on the side, and closed his eyes. After a moment, his eyes popped open and his face drained of color. "Holy fucking shit," he hissed.

"What?" Doc asked, dread filling him.

"He's not fucking in there."

15

"What?!" Doc demanded, certain he'd somehow misheard Jury.

"I said he's not FUCKING there!" Jury exclaimed.

"No," Doc said firmly. "That's not possible. You did all that magic to seal it and everything."

"I know," Jury said.

"And we... Fuck!" Doc exclaimed. "How the hell did he get out?"

"How should I fucking know?" Jury snapped. "All I know is that we are now royally, one hundred percent fucked."

Doc stared at the door cage in shock. It didn't make sense. There was simply no way Mitcham could have escaped. It was a metal box, lined with wards and more wards and then some more wards. The bolt was still in place. There were no holes. But he was gone.

"Are you sure?" Doc asked one more time.

"Yes! I'm fucking sure! Open it if you don't believe me."

"What about Mrs. Mitcham?"

"There's no one in the box," Jury ground out.

Doc studied the innocuous looking door with concern. There was a chance Jury just couldn't see Mitcham. Maybe what made Mitcham alive was different than what made other species alive, and Jury just couldn't sense it.

Doc pulled back the bolt with excruciating slowness. The bolt snapped free, and he took one step back, knife in hand, waiting. Nothing happened. After a long minute, he stepped forward, swung open the door, and looked inside.

"Goddamn," he said.

"What?"

"You're right; Mitcham's gone," Doc said flatly. "And I've no idea how to make luck out of this."

"What?"

"Just something Thaddeus said. See for yourself."

Jury pushed Doc aside and looked into the box. "Oh holy fucking shit. He killed her?"

"No, we killed her."

"What?"

"At least that's what Mitcham will say when he puts out the kill order on us," Doc said.

"Fuck, fuck, FUCK!! What was so wrong with just taking out human traffickers and crime bosses?" Jury demanded. "Those were good times. What fucking possessed you to get involved in politics? It was your number one fucking rule! Stay the fuck out of fucking politics!"

"You're going to give yourself an aneurysm if you keep it up," Doc said calmly.

"An aneurysm is the least of my fucking problems!" Jury yelled.

"It's not all bad," Doc said. "We tried something, and it didn't work. We can think of something else."

"Are you out of your goddamn mind?! There is nothing

else! I'm not even sure if dropping a bomb on Mitcham would kill him."

"In any case, we don't have a bomb," Doc pointed out.

"That's not the fucking point!" Jury snarled. "The point is, he's invincible."

"No," Doc said thoughtfully. "No one is invincible. Andrew taught me that. There's always a way."

He stared at Mrs. Mitcham's dead body crumpled on the cage floor and felt a surge of sorrow for her. She had trusted Mitcham, and he had sacrificed her to further his end game, discarded her like a worthless pawn.

"I'm sorry," Doc said softly. "I would have done it differently if I had known." He closed the cage door and said, "I'm going to see if the kitchen has any whiskey."

"That's all well and good for you," Jury muttered. "I need a goddamn sandwich."

"You should install one of those hole thingys into the kitchen at Dulcis," Doc suggested.

"I could just see Pierre's face if I did," Jury snorted.

Doc laughed and opened a random kitchen cabinet. Fortunately, Jervis was extraordinarily thorough, so there wasn't just one bottle of whiskey, but five. Doc popped the cork on one, sat on an end table, and stared morosely at the cage.

"I really thought Lady Luck had my back on this one," he said soberly.

"You think she's hot?" Jury asked, lighting a fresh cigarette.

Doc didn't bother telling him to put it out. They were dead men, drinking their final shot, smoking their final cigarette. It was over. He hadn't planned on losing, but he had. Mitcham wouldn't bother with warnings or threats; he'd send the entire Magistratus after them and that would be that.

"Beach?" Doc asked "Or mountains?"

"Mountains," Jury replied.

"I was afraid you'd say that. I think I have a cabin in Montana."

"A cabin or a mansion?" Jury snorted, blowing smoke out through his nostrils.

"I couldn't say," Doc shrugged. "On the other hand," he mused, "Mitcham will go after everyone we've ever known, so I suppose we'd better go down fighting."

"I like the idea of going out in a blaze of glory," Jury agreed. "I have a few tricks up my sleeve I've never had a chance to try. Kind of figured they would blow off the top my head so I was saving them; you know how it is."

"I really don't," Doc laughed.

His phone rang, and he glanced at the screen. It was Jervis. "Yes?" Doc said, answering it.

"Mitcham's called out a hit on the O'Connells," Jervis said quickly.

"What?!" Doc hissed, pure fury exploding in his mind.

"Emily just called me. She overhead him call in the order."

"Did you warn Dublin?" Doc demanded.

"I can't reach him."

"Goddamn!" Doc hissed, disconnecting. "Let's go," he said, discarding his jacket and vest on the floor.

"What's wrong?" Jury asked.

"Mitcham called out a hit on Dublin's family."

"We better hurry," Jury said.

"I know."

They were in the five hundred block section now; Dublin lived in the six hundred block section, but to get there they would have to cross this section, use the connecting door, then go all the way to the other side of the six hundred section. And if they weren't fast enough... It didn't bear thinking.

Doc threw open the door, and they started to run. The few people still out and about scrambled to get out of their way, although one man actually tried to stop them because Jury hadn't bothered with glamours.

"Stop!" he shouted as they dashed past him. "By order of Tetrarch Mitcham, I demand you stop!"

Doc didn't bother to respond, but when the man tried to apprehend them, a cobblestone jerked free from the ground and conked the man on the head.

"Nice aim," Doc said as they turned the corner.

"Thanks," Jury replied.

"It helps if you're not drunk," Doc drawled.

"You'd be able to run faster if you stopped talking," Jury snapped.

"I don't know that that's true."

"Shut up."

They rushed past a crowd of tree people arguing with a group of sprites. Someone yelled something, but Doc didn't understand what was said. Not that it mattered. Nothing was going to stop him from reaching Dublin. Not even the Magistratus team guarding the connecting door in front of them.

"Are we killing?" Jury asked, breath starting to sound labored.

"I'm afraid it's the fastest way," Doc said.

"I'll aim for the obvious cryptids," Jury suggested. "You take the humanoid ones."

"See?" Doc chuckled. "You do love me."

"Halt!" the Magistratus captain yelled. "You're under arrest for murder!"

Four knives had already left Doc's hand by the time the captain finished speaking, and from the corner of his eye, he saw the flash of Jury's gun. Seven members of the Magistratus had dropped before the captain yelled, "Fire!"

A bullet ripped through Doc's chest just as his tattoo began to burn, but he ignored the mild pain and hurled knife after knife. In under a minute, the entire Magistratus team was dead.

Doc paused in front of the door for a moment. "You alright?" he asked Jury.

"Just a few flesh wounds," Jury replied. "You?"

"Already healed," Doc stated.

"I hate you."

"I am extraordinarily lucky," Doc laughed as he pushed the number to designate which neighborhood he wanted and walked through the connecting door.

A strange feeling washed over him, prickling the edge of his senses and raising the hair on his arms. Doc knew this odd sensation was a result of the magic moving him to another location, not entirely unlike Ahanu's transportation, but knowing it didn't change the fact that he hated it. He had never been able to understand how magic could simply move a person from one spot to another, and anyone who said they did understand was lying.

The darkness cleared, and Doc stepped into the plaza on the other side of the magic doorway. He glanced around, relieved to see there were no Magistratus waiting for them, and as soon as Jury joined him, Doc took off running once more.

Doc heard the sounds of fighting when they were still a block away, and he pushed even more speed into his legs.

"Goddamn it, Doc," Jury wheezed. "I'm bleeding here."

"I'll sew you up later," Doc promised as he burst onto the street in front of Dublin's house.

Dublin was doing his best to guard the entrance to his home, but even in wolf form, five cyclopes, a pair of serpent men, and three tree men would ultimately be too much for him. He was already limping and bleeding from his muzzle, but he was still on his feet.

"Take the trees!" Doc ordered.

"What?!" Jury exclaimed. "They're fucking trees!"

"So burn them!" Doc snapped, running across the street and leaping onto the first cyclops' back. He used his knives as pegs to scramble up the giant, and when he reached the man's neck, Doc shoved a knife as deeply as he could into one side and ripped it across, severing the vertebrae. For good measure, Doc drew another knife, placed it at the base of the cyclops' head, and hammered it through his skull.

The giant began to wobble, and Doc leaped from his back, landing gently on the cobblestones. Doc judged the distance and angle, then rammed his shoulder into the back of the cyclops' knee. The cyclops swayed for a second, then dropped like a tree, knocking over one of the other cyclopes as he did.

Doc ran up the dead cyclops' arm and jumped onto the other's chest. The giant tried to knock Doc to the ground, but Doc ducked the sloppy blow and straddled the man's gigantic neck, wrapping his legs tightly around the sides.

The cyclops groaned and grabbed at Doc with his humongous hands, but Doc slashed viciously with his knives, shredding the cyclops' hands each time they came near to him, while applying as much pressure to the neck as he could with his thighs.

The giant began to buck frantically and tried to roll, but

the dead one was still on top of his legs, pinning him to the ground. He batted his bloody hands at Doc, trying to dislodge him, but Doc just took the hits, knowing it wouldn't be long.

The cyclops' movements grew slower and slower until he finally collapsed with a sigh. Doc didn't loosen his legs; instead he started counting, flinching as his nose popped back into place and healed. When he was certain the cyclops was out cold, he slashed open his jugular vein. Only then did he loosen his legs and drop to the ground, moving just in time to avoid a massive fist that slammed into the ground where he'd just been.

"You killed my brothers!" one of the remaining cyclopes howled angrily.

"You don't get the contradiction at all, do you?" Doc drawled. "You were intent on killing my people, what did you expect? A lovely little note asking you to stop?"

The cyclops blinked his one gigantic eye in confusion. "What?" he said.

"Exactly," Doc snapped, hurling a knife straight towards the man's eye.

The knife spun point first into the cyclops' eye, and the eye burst, spewing gelatinous goo into the air. The cyclops shrieked in pain and stumbled around wildly, knocking into several buildings. Doc dodged a falling brick and threw three more knives. Every single one of them disappeared inside the bloody mess that had just been an eye. Doc hurled one more knife, and as it tore the eye completely in half, the cyclops' scream died abruptly and he collapsed to the ground, landing with a crunch on his dead brothers.

"Three down," Doc muttered. "Two to go."

He glanced quickly around the street. Dublin was tearing out one of the serpent's throats, and Jury was in the middle of a firestorm, surrounded by tall burning forms. The remaining cyclopes, however, were trying to rip off the front of Dublin's house. Doc could hear the terrified screams of the children inside, and Julia was standing in one of the upper windows, hair loose around her head, cutlass in her hand, slashing away at one of the cyclops' hands.

Doc bolted towards the cyclops nearest Julia, growling with frustration when a huge hand grabbed him and slammed him to the ground. He swallowed a groan as several ribs cracked and focused on breaking free. He had seconds at best before the other hand came down on his head.

He tucked his feet in towards his back and bucked as hard as he could, dislodging the fingers just enough to roll to the side. As he leaped to his feet, he grabbed a knife and drove it through the gigantic palm, temporarily pinning the cyclops' hand to the stone road.

He ducked, gasping as his broken ribs rubbed against each other, and barely escaped a smack from the other huge hand. Then he bounded up the cyclops' pinned arm, launching himself from the bicep straight at the giant's neck. Doc speared the soft spot between the man's collarbones knife first, thrusting his whole body forward and driving the knife, his hand, and his entire arm through the cyclops' throat.

With a strange gurgle, the cyclops dropped, taking Doc to the ground with him. They crashed to the street, jarring Doc's slowly healing ribs. Doc yanked his bloody arm from the giant's throat and turned, looking for the final cyclops, heaving a sigh of relief when he saw that he was already dead, his corpse splayed across a nearby garden, a large wooden beam protruding from his eye.

Doc took quick stock. The serpents were a mass of bloody parts, the trees were piles of smoldering ash, and all the cyclopes were dead. Dublin was leaning heavily on Jury, but they were both alive. Doc glanced back at the house. Julia was still standing in the window, tears streaming down her cheeks.

Doc turned and surveyed the street. It was lined with houses, and the houses were lined with windows, which were lined with faces. He growled, suppressing his sudden urge to kill them all.

"What is wrong with you?!" he shouted instead. "You were just going to watch out your windows while a family of innocents were brutally slaughtered?! And what would you have told yourselves as you went to sleep tonight? 'They had it coming?' 'He should have never married a norm?'"

The spectators didn't move, just glared at him, guilt and cowardice filling their faces.

"You disgust me!" Doc yelled. "Your minds are so weak that anyone can come along and tell you lies, and you believe them. What wrong has Julia O'Connell committed? What crime has she perpetrated that is worthy of sentencing her entire family to death?

"If someone comes along and tells you to hate your neighbor, you should turn your hatred on them because you don't know them!" Doc shouted. "They don't care about you; they're only using you! Using you for their own ends!"

"What do you know?" someone shouted from the shadows. "You're a bloody norm!"

"Want to come down here and test that theory?" Doc snarled. "While you powerful cryptids cowered in your homes, I killed four cyclopes with my bare hands and a pair of knives. If you're an example of what a cryptid is, I want nothing to do with you."

Feet pounded, and a Magistratus team three times the size

of the team that had been guarding the door lined the street, completely surrounding Doc and Jury.

Doc began to laugh. "How fortunate. Now your self-appointed ones have arrived on the scene, and you can disappear behind your curtains and say comforting words to yourselves. 'The law will sort it out.' 'Justice will prevail.'"

The Magistratus officers closest to Doc pulled their guns and aimed.

Doc grinned widely and said, "I warn you, anyone who stands between me and the door, dies."

"Shoot him!" someone yelled.

"Yeah! He's a filthy murderer."

"He's a norm!" someone else accused. "A norm murdering cryptids in our own streets! It's just what we were warned about!"

Doc surveyed the faces plastered to their windows, meeting eye after eye. "You're not worth the trouble," he said sadly. "All this time I thought you were worth it, but you're not."

He shook his head with complete disgust and called out, "Julia, come down with the pups and get behind me." Then he faced the Magistratus once more. "I'll give you one more warning. Stand down or die. You might find Mitcham frightening, but I'm here right now, and I will kill you without mercy."

The ranks of officers wavered slightly.

"We are leaving," Doc said firmly. "Stand aside."

One of the officers raised his gun, moving his finger on the trigger, then the gun dropped from his dead hands, and he crumpled to the ground, one of Doc's knives buried to its handle in his skull.

"Anyone else want a go?" Doc offered.

Several guns moved, but Doc was faster and his knives flew straighter. Five more officers fell to the street, their guns clattering to the stones.

A hush filled the street, a quiet so intense that Doc could hear the remaining Magistratus officers' panicked breathing. The captain stared at Doc. Doc stared at the captain.

Without warning, a woman opened her door and stepped out onto the street, pushing boldly past the Magistratus. She walked across the open stones and, body trembling in fear, stood bravely beside Doc.

Doc grinned at her.

More doors opened, and more people joined them. Some looked like humans, some serpents. There were several Lutins, a wood sprite, a handful of Worms. Before long, Doc, Jury, and the O'Connells were completely surrounded.

"What will you do now?" Doc mocked the captain. "If you fire, the people will turn on you. Mitcham's army killing the people he's sworn to protect? Badly done."

"Weapons down," the captain ordered harshly.

The Magistratus lowered their weapons and moved to the side, and Doc began to lead the way towards the exit. While he walked, he texted Jervis. "I need a van and a car at the main six hundred entrance."

"Certainly, sir," Jervis texted back.

Inside Doc was seething. He knew he shouldn't make decisions when he was mad, but this wasn't just mad. This was fury; the type of fury that remade nations, that rebuilt cities, that pulled down tyrants.

It was the kind of fury that changed the world.

16

"Where are we going?" Jury demanded as Doc sped through a red light.

"Mitcham's."

"You sure about this?"

Doc didn't respond. He was through playing Mitcham's game. He was going to end this. Now.

"Can I ask how exactly you plan to kill him?" Jury asked carefully.

"It'll come to me."

"Alright. Well, I guess I have to die sometime," Jury shrugged. "A hundred and twenty-five years was a pretty good run."

"We're not dying today," Doc said firmly.

"Glad to hear it," Jury laughed.

Doc parked outside the upper block and stalked into the Hidden, palming two knives as he did. There were six measly Magistratus officers near the entrance, and they all pulled their guns as soon as they saw Doc. Their efforts were futile though; Doc was faster and more accurate, and they fell like little dominos as his knives pierced their hearts and throats.

"You didn't leave any for me," Jury grumbled.

"I'm kind of in a hurry," Doc replied, fury pulsing like a living thing inside him.

His tattoo was warm under his shirt, and part of his mind enjoyed the rush of power flowing through his veins. The rest of his mind focused on the task in front of him.

"You can have the butler," Doc offered, climbing the stairs and readying his hand to knock.

"Better than nothing," Jury sighed.

"Double tap to each foot," Doc instructed.

"The foot?" Jury replied.

"Apparently. I heard it from two reliable sources."

"If you say so."

Doc knocked, and the door creaked open, the butler's stern face appearing in the gap. Doc hit the door with his shoulder, pushing the butler backwards; and Jury's bullets made a muted noise as they tore through the butler's feet and into the floor. Doc caught the dead butler as he fell and eased him down gently.

"Lock it," he ordered Jury. "And put a spell on it. I'm going after Mitcham."

Doc strode down the hallway, startling the four Takaheni guarding Mitcham's study door.

"Stand down," Doc ordered as they drew their swords.

"We're charged with protecting the tetrarch," the leader said, moving his feet into a solid fighting stance.

"Mitcham is dead," Doc said. "And if you stand in my way, so are you."

"We cannot abandon our post," the leader said regretfully. "We are the honor guard."

"So be it," Doc said. "Just remember, when you fall down, don't get back up." Several knives sped down the hallway, glinting in the dull light and spearing each guard in the thigh.

The leader grunted in pain and surprise, but still managed to step towards Doc.

"Fall down," Doc ordered. "I won't ask again."

Doc watched the struggle cross the leader's face. He didn't want to protect Mitcham, but he had been ordered to. He wanted to fall down, but he could still fight.

"There is no honor in dying here, protecting him," Doc said softly. "Fall down."

The leader fell slowly backwards into the hallway and away from Mitcham's door, and after a brief hesitation, the other guards did likewise.

"Very good," Doc said, and he kicked in the door.

Mitcham looked up from his desk and observed Doc with a cold smile.

"I was afraid it would come to this," Mitcham said regretfully. "It's a shame really. You would be such a useful asset."

"You shouldn't have gone after them," Doc snarled.

"How else would I have drawn you out?" Mitcham inquired. "I did not want you to go into hiding for another year. That was very tiresome. And why do you care?" Mitcham asked curiously. "They're just cattle. All of them. We are the predators, you and I. They should live to serve us, not the other way around."

"You and I are nothing alike," Doc snarled.

"No, I see that. But we could be. Now tell me where it is."

"Where what is?" Doc asked blankly.

"The artifact Bosch stole from me."

"I don't know what you're talking about," Doc said with a slight grin.

"It's not in the house," Mitcham said, voice seething with anger. "And I know you took it."

"Can you describe it for me?" Doc asked. "That might help me recall it."

"I weary of your arrogance," Mitcham said. "After I kill you, I will tear down everything you don't own until I find it."

Doc chose not to roll his eyes and demanded, "Seems like a lot of work for a bauble. Why do you need it anyway? What's your plan? You already run the Hidden. What more could you want?"

"To restore the balance," Mitcham said simply.

"How?" Doc asked, curiosity stepping in front of his fury for a moment.

"Simple really." Mitcham stood and circled his desk until he was only a few feet from Doc. "I have cryptids in place within the government." He smirked and added, "All the governments, really; and at the summit, I will convince the holdouts of the necessity of change." His eyes glazed slightly, and he stared past Doc. "Can you see it?" he whispered. "I can. I can see it so clearly. The whole of humanity caged like the animals they are."

Mitcham focused on Doc again and said, "At my word, the Hiddens all over the world will revolt, removing the norm powers and replacing them with a much higher authority." He smiled grimly. "Me."

"Whole world takeover," Doc said skeptically. "You don't think you're biting off a bit much, do you?"

Mitcham glared at him. "Of course not," he snapped. "I've been planning this for years. Since the very beginning.

Everything is in place; everything is perfect; absolutely everything is accounted for."

Doc shrugged. "The thing is you can't account for wild cards."

Mitcham laughed harshly. "You still think you can defeat me, Mr. Holliday? Compared to me, you are nothing, less than nothing. You might defeat my butler and my guard, but you will never defeat me. I'm protected by so much magic it would take a veritable god to defeat me."

That's true, Doc thought, feeling his lips twitch in amusement. So wasn't it incredibly lucky that he just happened to be on speaking terms with several veritable gods?

"Take away your magic, though," Doc said casually, "and you're just a Zeniu with a heart in each foot."

"I'm going to enjoy killing you," Mitcham said, picking up his letter opener from his desk.

"I doubt that very much," Doc drawled. "You see, you're just a small fish. You think you're the biggest fish, but there are much, much bigger fish doing much bigger things, things you can't even conceive of. And these fish are watching, just to make certain these things happen as planned."

"You're a mad man," Mitcham sneered.

"We'll see."

Doc leapt forward, knocking the letter opener from Mitcham's grasp and pinning Mitcham's arms to his sides. He wrapped one arm tightly around Mitcham, holding him still, and with his other hand tossed a knife at Mitcham's foot. The knife rebounded, nicking Doc's cheek as it did.

"You can't hold me forever," Mitcham laughed.

"No. Just long enough," Doc said. "AHANU!" he shouted. "I need you! NOW!!"

For a long, breathless moment nothing happened. Then the air shimmered, and Ahanu stepped out of nothing into the room.

"You called?" Ahanu said, lips curved in amusement.

"I need a quiet moment at your cabin," Doc said.

"Are you taking your friend here?"

"Absolutely."

"Just clean up your mess," Ahanu said with a long sigh.

The air around Doc began to glow, like the light was shaking. Mitcham gasped and started to fight against Doc's hold, but forty-some years behind a desk had weakened him.

Mitcham's office faded into grey nothing, and when everything settled, they were standing in the center of Ahanu's out-of-time cabin.

Doc released Mitcham and faced him with a wide grin. "Take away your magic, and you're nothing," Doc said. "Take away my magic, and I'm still one hell of a good killer with a lucky edge."

Mitcham's eyes looked around the cabin desperately as he tried to figure out what had happened. He didn't understand. He couldn't understand, but he'd understand soon enough.

"I think I'll take my time," Doc drawled. "If only because you deserve it."

He stepped forward and shoved a knife into Mitcham's chest. Blue goo exploded out onto his hand, and Mitcham stared at the gaping hole in horror.

"It's not possible," he stuttered. "It's not. I'm invincible. You can't touch me."

"Just did," Doc said, stabbing into Mitcham's chest again.

"No!" Mitcham screamed, backing away. "No! This isn't how it's supposed to go! You can't do this to me. I've worked too hard, too long! I've thought of everything!"

"You shouldn't have thought of me at all," Doc snarled. "I am not a puppet. I do not have strings. You can't call me like a dog and send me out to fetch your paper."

Mitcham touched his chest wounds in fascinated disbelief. "I don't understand," he said dully.

"Understand this," Doc snarled. "You're about to die."

He thrust a knife through Mitcham's eye, feeling a grim satisfaction when Mitcham screamed in pain and terror.

"I'm going to leave your other eye intact," Doc drawled. "Just because I want you to see it coming."

Mitcham was stumbling around the room, wailing and screaming, and Doc stepped towards him, stabbing him repeatedly in the torso.

He wanted to drag it out, he wanted to cut Mitcham to pieces just to punish him for all the terrible things he'd done, but he didn't want to push his luck. At any moment Ahanu might pull them back or Mitcham might recover his wits and think of something clever.

So even though Mitcham hadn't suffered enough by any means, Doc pulled two knives, dropped to his knees, and slammed them through Mitcham's shiny-toed shoes.

Mitcham's remaining eye widened, and his mouth opened in shock. A horrifying scream emerged from somewhere deep inside him, then he stumbled backwards and fell across Ahanu's wooden table. He shuddered once, twice, then the air slid from his mouth in a sigh, and the life left his eye.

"It's out of time, see," Doc said softly. "There's nothing here. Time doesn't exist. Magic doesn't exist." He shrugged and said, "I wasn't actually sure it would work; I just took a gamble."

The air around Doc began to tighten, and light spun past his face like little shooting stars. Ahanu's sparse cabin faded into nothing, and after a breath, Doc was once again in Mitcham's office, the dead tetrarch on the floor at Doc's feet.

17

Doc studied Mitcham's body and embraced his rising feeling of victory. He'd done it. He'd killed Mitcham. Mitcham was dead.

"Did you clean up?" Ahanu asked, shattering Doc's moment.

"No," Doc replied.

"Typical. I believe you owe me another favor now."

"Not hardly," Doc snorted. "Eight months you moved us, without even a warning."

"Time's tricky like that," Ahanu said with a wink, and then he was gone.

"What the fuck?" Jury said from the doorway. "You killed him? How the hell did you kill him?"

"Sleight of hand," Doc replied.

"That's all you're going to say?" Jury snapped as he stalked forward and gazed at Mitcham's corpse.

"I just took a little trip to an out-of-time cabin. It was your idea, really."

"That's... brilliant," Jury mumbled.

"I'm glad you thought of it," Doc drawled.

Jury gave him a hard look and said, "What now?"

"Well," Doc said, "Order some sandwiches and take a really, really, really good look at Mitcham here."

"Because?" Jury asked, eyes narrowing suspiciously.

"The summit is in two days, and until then, I'm going to be Mitcham. Fortunately, I'm just about the right height."

"Please tell me you're kidding," Jury pleaded.

"Afraid not," Doc replied. "We need to infiltrate the summit so we can take out the trash, quite literally, and the easiest way to do that is by posing as Mitcham."

"This is a bad idea," Jury said, even though he was currently kneeling beside Mitcham and studying his face. "I've never glamoured someone to look like someone else before. Let alone a completely different species. And the voice?" Jury exclaimed, starting to sound a little panicked. "What if I sneeze and the nose moves or something?"

"You won't," Doc said. "Besides, you yourself said you're the most powerful witch around. I'm pretty sure you can do it."

Someone cleared their throat, and Doc turned. The Takaheni leader was standing in the doorway.

"Sir," he said awkwardly.

"What's your name?" Doc asked.

"Nick," he replied.

"Excellent, Nick. No one comes in or goes out of the house until I say so. I need you to securely alert Simon of Mitcham's death and tell him that I will be posing as Mitcham until the summit. When you're done with that, you and your men need to come in here so I can stitch up your wounds."

"Sir?"

"Can't have you running around bleeding, can I?" Doc said cheerfully. "It would stain the carpets."

Nick jerked his head slightly and left the office.

"Sorry to interrupt, Jury," Doc said, "but I need my kit."

"Get it your own damn self," Jury muttered.

"Can't; we're kind of doing a thing here."

"Where is it?" Jury grumbled.

"Kitchen. Bottom cabinet, left of the sink. Get me some whiskey while you're there."

"Get me some whiskey," Jury mocked softly.

A blue surge of magic burst from Jury's hand, and a strange, wobbly grey hole opened in front of him. He thrust his hand through it, and when he pulled it back out, he was holding Doc's medical bag.

"Don't forget the whiskey," Doc said.

"Don't forget the whiskey," Jury muttered irritably. But he put his hand back through the rift and pulled out three bottles of whiskey.

"I love you," Doc said happily.

"Don't even start," Jury snapped.

Doc chuckled softly as he popped the cork and took a swig. "That never gets old," he sighed.

"Shut up!" Jury demanded. "I'm trying to concentrate."

"Take a picture," Doc suggested. "It'll last longer."

"I said shut up," Jury ground out.

Doc shrugged and sat in Mitcham's chair, swallowing a laugh when he saw Jury pull out his phone and start snapping photographs of Mitcham's face.

"I'm so glad you could join us," Doc said softly, testing Mitcham's tone of vague condescension. "I would have so hated to have to kill you. After all, examples must be made." He adjusted his posture, throwing back his shoulders marginally and adopting Mitcham's overall stiffness.

"We're ready, sir," Nick said.

"Here," Doc said, standing, "have a chair and drop your pants."

Nick raised a furry eyebrow.

"I can stitch your pants to your leg if you like," Doc said casually. "I just thought you might prefer if I didn't."

Nick slowly lowered his pants and sat in Mitcham's desk chair; Doc inspected his fur-covered leg in dismay.

"This should be interesting," Doc muttered. "I've never... Well, anyway. Hold still."

He poured some of the whiskey over the wound, pushed Nick's fur carefully out of the way, and began to stitch. It didn't take long, and when Doc was finished, he softly rubbed some yarrow over the stitches.

"Done!" Doc announced. "Next!"

Doc quickly stitched the other guards' wounds, and then he turned to check on Jury. "Are you about done?" he demanded.

Jury glanced from Mitcham to Doc and back again, then Doc felt a whisper of magic, and he held up his hand. It was blue, and it shimmered strangely in the light.

"I don't like it," Doc said.

"It looks good," Nick said. "I can't tell the difference. I can smell the difference though."

"And if I look," Jury added, "I recognize your essence."

"I didn't think of that," Doc said softly. "I suppose we need a scrubber."

Someone was pounding at the door, and Doc figured it was the Magistratus.

"We'll have to deal with that later though," Doc said. "The Magistratus probably won't be looking that carefully. Jury, glamour Mitcham to look like me; glamour yourself to look like anyone but you. Nick, you and your men will carry

Mitcham out, announce that Doc Holliday has been killed, let everyone get a good look at him, and then... Oh hell, you don't have a car. What would you normally do with a dead body?"

"I'd call the Worms," Nick said.

"That won't work," Doc muttered. "Alright, I've got it. Let them come in, have a look around, see me, Doc, dead, then shoo them off, and say we're keeping the body for examination. If anyone asks questions, we'll say I'm curious to know how he, me, lived for so long. Knowing Mitcham, that's probably pretty believable."

"Sounds good, sir," Nick agreed.

"Let them in," Doc said. He sat behind the desk once more, breathed deeply, and tried to think like Mitcham. Superior. Judging. Annoyed.

Several Magistratus officers rushed in, and Doc raised an eyebrow. "Finally decided to join us?" he stated, trying to use just the right amount of acid and apathy.

"I'm so sorry, sir," the captain stuttered. "He killed the men I had stationed inside the entrance."

"Perhaps the Magistratus has outlived its usefulness," Doc intoned.

The captain paled. "No, sir, I mean, I'm sorry, sir. It'll never happen again, sir. Men, carry out this piece of scum!"

"No," Doc said firmly. "My men will take him."

"Sir?"

"Are you questioning me?" Doc asked, voice perfectly placid.

"No, sir!" the captain stuttered.

"I thought not. I want to examine him; discover his secret. Now go. Before I decide to demote you."

"Yes, sir. Sorry, sir, Right away, sir."

The captain and his men shuffled backwards out of the door, and Doc turned to Nick. "Escort them to the exit."

"Yes, sir."

"What now?" Jury asked once they were gone.

"Lock the doors again, take the bodies downstairs, and see who's locked up down there."

Nick had already returned, and he asked, "Downstairs?"

"Yes," Doc replied.

"There isn't a downstairs," Nick argued.

"There is."

"What's down there?"

"We're about to find out," Doc said easily.

"But first," Jury said, "I need you to change clothes."

"What?" Doc questioned.

"It will be easier to hold the glamour if you're wearing his clothes. Besides that, the clothes you have on are covered in blood and goo."

"I don't want to wear his clothes," Doc replied. "It's hard enough hearing his voice coming out of my mouth."

"I don't care what you want," Jury growled. "I'm working my ass off here, and that will make it easier. Go goddamn change!"

Doc glowered at Jury and started to say something about Jury's messed up clothes, but somehow Jury's clothes were perfectly clean. Just like always.

"How exactly do you manage to kill people without ruining your clothes?" Doc demanded.

"It's a gift," Jury said.

"But how?"

"You have luck; I have clean clothes."

"I'd rather have luck," Doc muttered. "Except in this one instance, when I'd much rather have clean clothes." He turned to Nick. "Can you show me Mitcham's room?" Nick nodded, and Doc followed him upstairs.

"Put on another man's clothes," Doc muttered as he looked through Mitcham's closet. "That's... It's a disgrace. These aren't even well made."

He picked a suit and cringed as he changed into it. It was slightly loose, and the pants were just a tad short, but he figured Jury could fix it.

"It's itchy," he complained.

"Sorry, sir."

"And feels cold, like Mitcham. What did he smell like, anyway?"

"Death," Nick said.

"Like a corpse?"

"A rotting corpse," Nick replied.

"Interesting. I hate that I always have to kill people before I can torture them for information. I'd like to know the entirety of his plan. I'd also like to know how he always knew what everyone was saying about him. And I'd like to know how he got out of the damn cage."

"Cage?"

"I caged him," Doc said sullenly. "But it didn't take."

"I'm afraid I can't answer any of your questions," Nick said.

"No worries," Doc said with a loose shrug, heading back downstairs. "I'm used to it."

Jury was waiting for them outside Mitcham's office.

"Where's the butler's pantry?" Doc asked.

"I'm not sure," Nick said. "We don't usually move about inside the house."

"It's probably outside the kitchen," Jury said.

"To the kitchen," Doc declared.

"Yes," Jury said, eyes lighting with hunger. "To the kitchen."

"I don't know," Doc shuddered. "Eating his food might be even worse than wearing his clothes. Why don't you just ask one of Nick's men to go get you some food?"

"I already did," Jury replied.

"And you can't wait?"

"Three full glamours, Doc!"

"Yeah, for three whole minutes," Doc drawled.

"So now you're an expert?"

"No," Doc laughed. "Eat his food if you want to."

"This is it," Jury said, pausing outside a locked room. He put his finger to the lock, closed his eyes, and after a few seconds, Doc heard the lock click.

"Can you see the entrance?" Doc asked "Or shall we have Nick hack up all the walls?"

"It's right there," Jury said, pointing at a section of the inner wall. "I can see the air moving into it."

Doc felt the panel, looking for some kind of latch, but after a minute he turned to Nick and said, "Would you mind making that into a doorway?"

Nick drew his sword, stepped forward, and carefully drove it through the paneling. He buried the sword to its hilt, pulled it back halfway, and began to cut upward.

"I can do it quicker," Jury said.

Nick nodded, withdrew his sword, and stepped back.

Jury's hands flared blue, and the entire section of paneling ripped from the wall, revealing a steep, narrow staircase that dropped down into the darkness.

"Evil secret dungeon, check," Doc murmured. "Can you give us some light, Jury?"

"Too hungry."

Doc rolled his eyes. "Give us some light, damn it! You can eat later."

"What if someone shows up, and I have to glamour you and me for like five hours?!"

"I can only hope you'll dive deep and find the strength to do so," Doc drawled. "Because otherwise, all our work thus far would be meaningless."

"Fine," Jury grumbled. "It's no easy task though, making light out of nothing."

"It's not nothing," Doc said patiently. "I watched your video on using air and dust to create a magical orb of light. And if I recall correctly, which I do, you said it was a simple children's trick."

"Goddamn it," Jury muttered. "I'm taking down those goddamn videos."

"You can't do that!" Doc gasped. "You have a hundred and two followers."

"You mock," Jury growled. "But it's more than your I Hate Doc Holliday club."

"I'm not sure that's an accurate comparison," Doc laughed.

"Are we going down?" Nick demanded, voice terse.

Doc and Jury both looked at him. Doc sighed.

"No one understands the process," Jury complained.

"I know. It's so frustrating," Doc replied.

A large orb of blue light suddenly appeared at the top of the stairs. Doc drew a knife and followed the glowing ball down into the dark. When he reached the bottom, he glanced around, trying to see where the echoes of light ended, but he couldn't.

"I have a bad feeling about this," he said softly.

"Yeah," Jury agreed.

They walked forward slowly, releasing the occupants of

the first ten cells, one of which held Thulan, the blind witch who had read the ears.

"We didn't know this was here," Nick repeated over and over, angst filling his voice.

"I know," Doc said as he helped an old woman and her three children out into the hallway.

"The tetrarch?" the old woman wheezed.

"Dead," Doc said simply.

"He cannot be dead," one of the shadowy figures whispered. "He cannot die."

"Turns out he can," Doc said cheerfully. "You just have to pick the right venue. Nick here will take you upstairs. I'm afraid you can't leave yet, but we'll get you home as soon as possible."

There was a torch attached to the wall, and Nick lit it and gestured for the freed prisoners to follow him.

"Well?" Doc said as soon as they were out of earshot.

Jury shook his head.

"Shall we check anyway?"

"Why not," Jury said.

They followed the orb down the hallway, unlocking cells as they went so the remains of the prisoners could be removed.

"How many cells do you think there are?" Jury whispered after a while.

"If I had to guess, forty-six years' worth," Doc said flatly, remembering what Ian had said about Mitcham eating through osmosis.

"I wish you had taken your time," Jury growled.

Doc didn't respond. A hundred years of torture wouldn't have evened the score. He heaved a sigh of relief when the light began to bounce off a wall ahead of them.

"Hold up," Jury said after he'd unlocked a cell and pulled open the solid door. "I... I think this one's alive."

"How could he be?" Doc asked.

"I don't know, but I sense... I sense life."

The orb drifted into the cell revealing a strangely-shaped shadowy form on the cell floor.

Doc's eyes narrowed as he studied it. "It's a tree spirit," he finally said, kneeling beside it. "Are you alive?" he asked gently.

"I do not know," a dry voice whispered.

"What do you need?" Doc asked.

"I do not know."

"Can you move?"

"It took many years for my roots to force their way through the leaden floor," the tree spirit rasped. "I have not seen the sun in... ages. I fear the stars are gone; the moon, gone; my people, gone."

"I'll carry you to the light," Doc promised.

"Doc!" Jury hissed. "You can't do that!"

"I can," Doc said. "There's a walled yard at the back of the house. No one will see us there. And it's not like anyone's stupid enough to spy on Mitcham anyway. What's your name?" he asked the tree spirit.

"Shwaelishminaree, but you may call me Min."

"Lovely name, Min. My name is Doc. Wrap your arms around my neck, and I'll carry you outside."

The floor began to creak ominously, and the portion under Doc's feet sunk as Min removed her roots from the ground beneath the floor. Once she was free, her rough arms twisted around Doc's neck, and Doc lifted her into his arms.

He'd never carried a tree spirit before, but given their large size, he would have guessed they were quite heavy. Min, however, was so slight, she weighed less than a human.

"Steady now," Doc murmured as he maneuvered her through the door. "Check the rest of the cages," he told Jury.

The blue orb split in two, and one floated back the way they had come. Doc followed it, silently wishing hell really existed and that he'd just sent Mitcham there.

Nick met him halfway, eyes stark with grief. He glanced at the form in Doc's arms and exclaimed, "A tree spirit? How?"

Doc didn't answer, just continued walking through the darkened prison, and when they reached the stairs, they carried her up together. In the light of the house, Doc could see that her bark was grey, her twigs brittle and dry, and her limbs twisted in, like a hand afflicted with arthritis.

Doc carried her past the other prisoners and out into the walled yard. As soon as he stepped outside, Min's face turned and lifted towards the sky.

"Sorry," Doc said. "I forgot it was night."

"Stars," she whispered. Then words poured from her mouth, words Doc didn't understand.

"Set me down," she commanded softly.

Doc carefully lowered her legs towards the ground and held her gently in place.

"Bring some water," he ordered Nick.

Nick nodded, and when he returned, he poured a pan of water around Min's feet. She sighed happily, and her arms extended to touch the wet ground. Her chest moved as she breathed deeply, and she began to straighten, branches stretching out and flexing. In the beam of light from the doorway, Doc watched as her grey skin slowly became a shimmering green.

"I never thought to live again," she said happily. "I just hadn't made up my mind to die yet. Thank you."

"How long have you been down there?" Doc asked.

"My roots tell me it was forty-three years."

Doc closed his eyes, regret coursing through him. He should have at least cut off all Mitcham's parts before he'd killed him. He should have pulled out his teeth, broken all his bones, crushed his skull.

He wished he had, but he hadn't, so he'd do the next best thing. He would destroy everything Mitcham had built. He would destroy Mitcham's name. He would destroy Mitcham's legacy. When Doc was done, Mitcham would just be a dead Zeniu discarded in his own damn dungeon.

18

Doc left Min in the yard. He would talk to her at some point and find out exactly why Mitcham had locked her away, but there was no need to interrupt her moment of happiness.

He walked through the house, stopping to survey the crowd of tattered people in the parlor. There were seventeen of them, and they all looked about ready to drop.

"Get them fed," he ordered Nick. "Bring in some fresh clothes, and they can get clean if they like. Whatever they want. They just can't leave the house. Also, let's keep them on the second floor. Mitcham is bound to have visitors at some point."

"Yes, sir," Nick said.

"After they've recovered a bit, have someone interview them. Find out why Mitcham locked them up, and ask them what they know about Mitcham."

Nick nodded.

Doc met Jury's eyes and gestured towards Mitcham's office.

"I need Emily's notes," Doc said once the door was closed behind them.

"Why're you telling me?" Jury asked.

"You know why."

"For someone who hates witches you sure use me a lot," Jury grumbled.

"I do not hate witches," Doc stated. "I just hate your family. Actually, I only hate some of your family. Have you talked to them since we got back?"

Jury shrugged.

"And?" Doc asked.

"Margaret said things are good. Father, Edward, William, Charles, and Edmund went to England. Mother is... She's mad, I guess, that they left."

"Livid, I should think," Doc said.

"Probably," Jury replied. "Anyway, Margaret and Caden are working on breaking the marriage contracts, and Gwenna is traveling. That's about it."

"To be perfectly clear, I hate hypnotists," Doc said. "That's not the same as hating witches."

"Pretty sure we'd moved past that," Jury pointed out. "Where're the notes?"

"In Bree's room."

The wobbly hole materialized, but before Jury could reach in, a hand pushed its way through, holding a pile of papers. "That's a little creepy," Jury said, cautiously taking the papers.

"I expect she heard us talking," Doc said. "Good work, Emily. I assume you're keeping Jervis apprised?"

Emily's muffled voice drifted through the hole. "Yes, sir."

"Thank you."

Doc took the notes and sat behind the desk, straightening his back the way Mitcham did.

"No one's here," Jury said, sitting across from Doc and propping up his feet on the desk.

"It's best if I stay in character," Doc replied absently.

"What're you looking for?"

"I want to know who Mitcham meets with, what they talk about, and how he interacts with them."

"Good thing you took all those acting classes, huh?"

"Uh-huh."

"I always thought you were taking them because you wanted to sleep with Hedy Lamarr."

"I was, and I did," Doc said. "Now, would you please shut up? I'm trying to read."

"I'm bored," Jury complained. "And frankly, this house gives me the creeps."

"Go eat a sandwich," Doc suggested.

"I already had a sandwich."

Doc sighed. "Then how about one of those smoothie things?"

"Not in the mood."

"Goddamn it, Jury!"

"No need to get pissy," Jury chuckled.

"Just go," Doc sighed.

Doc read and reread Emily's and Randell's reports. He practiced saying what Mitcham had said. He memorized the topics of discussion, and he committed the names to memory. Now he just needed to know who was who.

"Nick!" he called out.

Nick poked his head in the doorway and said, "Sir?"

"Sit down. It looks as if Mitcham meets consistently with five people, and I want you to describe them to me."

Nick nodded.

"Let's start with Markus Johanns," Doc said.

Nick's lip curled back slightly before he managed to smooth his features. "He's older," Nick said. "Maybe mid-sixties. White hair. Very affable face if you don't look too carefully."

"But he's obviously a cryptid?" Doc asked.

"He claims he is a Lougreselli," Nick said with a shrug.

Doc searched his memory, but came up blank. "A what?"

"A Lougreselli. They can turn into creatures of the night. Bats and owls mostly; although I have heard of one who could turn into a bobcat."

"Interesting," Doc said thoughtfully. "I've always found it strange that cryptids who can walk among the humans without suspicion chose to be part of the Hidden."

"Perhaps they don't always want to hide what they are," Nick suggested.

"Perhaps. Has anyone ever seen Markus turn?"

"Not that I know of."

"So he could easily be a norm?"

"I suppose," Nick allowed. "But I don't know why he would lie. He's vehemently against norms; and besides that, he doesn't quite smell like a norm."

Doc nodded thoughtfully and asked, "What about Attikus?"

"Attikus is Thypon's father, and also the leader of the North American cyclopes."

"I did gather that from Emily's reports," Doc said. "And I made sure to mark him down in the enemy column."

Nick nearly smiled.

"What does he look like in his human form?" Doc asked.

"Rather plain," Nick replied. "Flat brown hair, mid-height, mid-weight, plain brown clothes."

"Should be easy to spot," Doc mused. "And how about William? I don't know his last name."

"William Grakstone. He's the head of the Magistratus."

"Wonderful."

"Not just the Denver head," Nick went on. "The head of the United States Magistratus. He's a vampire. Originally from France, I believe."

"Naturally," Doc drawled. "His brother Harold Grakstone is probably the head of the French Magistratus. Never mind, I forgot it was a Baudelaire," Doc said with exasperation.

"What?"

"Nothing. What does he look like?"

"Thick, bulky man. Usually walks around with his fangs out."

"Classy."

"He's got black hair and a thin mustache," Nick added.

"What about Ella Glass?"

"Cruel-looking woman," Nick said without inflection. "She always wears a woman's business suit."

"What species?" Doc asked.

"Shapeshifter," Nick said. "Anaconda."

Doc stared at Nick for a moment before saying slowly, "Anaconda?"

Nick nodded.

"I did not know that was a thing," Doc said.

Nick shrugged.

"As in big enough to swallow people alive?" Doc asked.

Nick nodded.

"Yikes," Doc muttered. "And what about Alex? No last name."

"I don't know," Nick said. "I've never met an Alex. Of course people come and go, and I don't always know who they are."

"Do you know who handles Mitcham's surveillance?"

Nick shook his head.

"Alright, but do you know who doesn't handle Mitcham's surveillance?"

"What?"

"Do you know if Grakstone or the Magistratus does?"

"Oh," Nick said. "I don't think so, but I can't be sure."

Doc nodded, filing away everything Nick had said. "Anything else I should know?" he asked.

"Hard to say," Nick said with a shrug. "Do you really think this will work?"

"I wouldn't be doing it if I didn't," Doc grinned.

Nick raised an eyebrow. "So when you burst in here you had a plan?"

"Absolutely; win."

"And that works for you?" Nick asked.

"Almost always."

Nick made a strange noise, then said, "The shift changes in an hour."

"Simon has, of course, let the others know what's going on?" Doc asked.

"Yes."

"Excellent. I guess we're good then. Do you think the scent will be a problem? I can call in my scrubbers, but I rather think I like my scent, and perhaps neutral would be worse?"

"I doubt anyone will think to check," Nick said. "What are scrubbers?"

"My cleaning crew," Doc said vaguely. He'd long ago decided it was always best to tell people less than they wanted to know.

"I'd better look through Mitcham's planner," Doc said. "See what I'm getting into today."

Nick stood to go, but paused as he reached the door. "Mr. Holliday?"

"Yes?"

"Thank you for... wounding us, and also for..." He was silent for a moment, then he said swiftly, "I'm glad you killed Mitcham."

"Me too."

The day proved to be long and tiresome, reinforcing what Doc already knew. Politicians were insane, because who would willingly do this for a living?

There were six appointments on Mitcham's calendar, none of which required Doc to leave the house. He dealt with the first two while Jury sulked in the corner, glamoured to look as plain as possible. No one spared Jury a second glance, even though he did chew rather loudly.

William Grakstone forced his way in between appointments two and three.

"Tetrarch Mitcham," he growled. "There are rumors you killed Holliday."

Doc affected a truly bored look. "Are you just now hearing these rumors? Because if that is the case, I fear you are getting a bit slow on your feet."

Grakstone's face turned red. "No, I... There was a matter that required my attention, sir."

"I see. And have the O'Connells been dealt with?"

Grakstone cleared his throat. "The thing is, sir, of course, you're aware of this, I'm sure, Holliday interfered with the private team sent to kill them."

"What about the Magistratus teams that were sent in afterwards?"

Grakstone cleared his throat, and Doc could tell he was

regretting his decision to come. "See, sir, um... The thing is... The residents rallied around the O'Connells, and there wasn't much to be done."

"Could you not have made an example?" Doc asked, laying one hand on the desktop and slowly tapping his index finger, something he'd seen Mitcham do when he was irritated.

Grakstone's eyes darted to that finger, and he paled. "I wasn't aware we were at that stage, sir. I apologize. I should have known."

"That is true," Doc said evenly. "I have someone else in mind to take care of the O'Connells. Someone who won't fail. I want you to see to the security of the summit."

Mitcham and Grakstone had talked a lot about security at the summit over the last few days, so Doc figured this was a safe thing to say.

"Yes, sir."

"Go now. I have an appointment with someone who had the foresight to call ahead."

Grakstone's face pinched, and he rushed from the room.

Doc waited until he was sure Grakstone was gone before saying, "I don't think he's all that pleased to be Mitcham's watchdog."

"There are only so many places of power," Jury said philosophically. "Grakstone is practically number two, and unless he's prepared to overthrow Mitcham, he's stuck."

"True," Doc said. He took a long drink of whiskey, hid the bottle back in the drawer, and waited for his next appointment.

He dealt with the interim head of the Bureau and the merchant's council before it was time for the appointment he'd been waiting for.

Markus Johanns. Leader of the anti-norm movement.

From reading over Emily's notes, Doc knew that Mitcham's relationship with Markus was very different than his relationship with the other cryptids; he just wasn't sure why.

"Ambrose!" Markus said excitedly as he sat across from Doc. "I gather you killed the fly in your soup last night."

"That I did, Markus," Doc said with a slight chuckle.

"Put up much of a fight?"

"He certainly tried to."

"The real question is..." Markus leaned forward. "How did he taste?"

Doc had not expected that question, but he managed to keep his expression even. It took him just a second to formulate a response, but he finally said, "Like victory."

Markus laughed. "I love it! I've been going through the sections this morning, riling up the sheep. All they need now is a little push."

"Excellent," Doc said. "What do you suggest?"

Markus shrugged. "I say we stick with your original plan."

That did not clear it up at all, so Doc tried again. "No adjustments?"

"I don't see why. If it hadn't been for Holliday saving all those children Edgar kidnapped, the sheep would be knocking down the fences. It's taken a little extra effort, but we've still got them where we need them. One solid push, and they'll jump."

"Good," Doc said vaguely.

"I'd better go," Markus said as he stood. "I've got another rally to lead in the slums. I've convinced them that the reason they're so poor is because the norms are holding them down." He laughed sharply. "It's embarrassing really. They can't even see the illogicalness there. I mean, how could the norms possibly affect them? Sheep!"

"Hold on," Doc said as Markus stepped away from the desk. "Birdwell, stand up."

Jury didn't move, but Markus looked around the room in confusion. "Who's Birdwell?"

"My new secretary," Doc said irritably. "But I'm not sure he's going to work out. Birdwell!"

"Sorry!" Jury jumped to his feet. "What?"

"Watch your tone, Birdwell," Doc snarled. "Stand over by Markus here."

"What's going on, Ambrose?" Markus asked.

"Nothing. I just wanted to check something."

Jury was standing next to Markus now, and Doc visually measured them against each other. They were nearly the exact same height. "What are the chances?" Doc murmured.

"What?" Markus demanded. "You're not quite yourself today. Is something wrong?"

"Of course not," Doc drawled. "In fact, everything is perfect."

He stood and walked around the desk. Jury was glaring at him, eyebrows raised in question.

"You're the same height," Doc said slowly.

"So?" Markus demanded.

Jury shook his head and shrugged his shoulders.

"You are... the same... height," Doc said again, emphasis on "height".

"Ohhhh," Jury murmured. "I get it."

"Finally."

"Ambrose?" Markus demanded.

Doc smiled widely. "And since we're not on a time table, maybe we can get some answers from him."

"Ambrose?" Markus was starting to look worried.

"Let's drop the pretenses, shall we?" Doc said meaningfully to Jury.

Jury shrugged, and Markus gasped as the glamours faded. "Where's Ambrose?" he demanded.

Doc ignored him and told Jury to inform the guard to cancel his last appointment. "This particular meeting is going to run long," he added cheerfully.

"I don't understand," Markus said. "Where's Ambrose? What have you done?"

"I killed him," Doc drawled.

"You couldn't have. That's not possible!" A note of panic entered Markus's voice, and he looked frantically at the doorway.

"I did, and I'm going to kill you too, but first, I'd like some answers. Please sit."

Markus suddenly bolted for the door, but Doc grabbed the back of his jacket and yanked him to the floor. "I didn't get to take my time with Mitcham," Doc drawled. "A fact I dearly regret."

Doc dragged the struggling man back to the chair and shoved him into it. "You politician types never know how to fight," Doc said conversationally as he studied Markus. Markus sat there, not even trying to escape, just staring at Doc in shock.

"This is awkward," Doc muttered. "I don't have anything to tie you up with."

"You can't do this," Markus blubbered. "You can't... Did you really... Ambrose can't be dead."

"He is," Doc said. "Ah, I've got it."

He pulled a knife and held Markus's arm still while he thrust the knife through Markus's hand, pinning it to the chair. Markus screamed, and Doc stared at Markus's hand in confusion. Instead of red blood, blue goo was oozing around the knife blade.

"I did not see that coming," Doc mused. "You clever, clever bastards."

He pinned Markus's other hand, then used Markus's belt to strap his torso to the chair back.

"Let's have a little talk," Doc said. "First of all, I see you are a Zeniu."

Markus hurled a string of curses at Doc. Doc waited patiently, and when Markus was panting from his exertion, Doc asked, "I take it you and Mitcham were close? Brothers perhaps?"

Another string of curses.

Doc sighed. "Perhaps we should start over. I'm going to kill you... eventually. I have every intention of torturing you for hours to get what I want. In fact, I once tortured a man for, oh, some fifteen hours."

Markus's face turned pale.

"Long time," Doc mused. "He was just a mess of flesh and blood by the time I was done with him." Doc drew another knife and purposely ran the cold blade over Markus's hand. "I don't particularly enjoy torturing people," Doc continued. "Although it does serve its purpose. If you'll just tell me what I want to know, I will make it quick and fairly painless. I do want you to suffer at least a little bit, given what you've done."

"I haven't done anything!" Markus snarled. "We're making the world a better place! We're going to purify it, return it to balance. There are always fools who oppose change, even if it is for the better."

"Better for whom?" Doc demanded. "Certainly not for the

people Mitcham locked away to rot in his dungeon. Certainly not for the norms or people like the O'Connells or the LaRoches."

"Scum!" Markus spat. "Mixing cryptid blood with cattle! Bringing cattle into the Hidden, breeding with them, protecting them, telling them our secrets! Dublin O'Connell betrayed us first!"

Doc sighed. He hated it when people were religiously committed to their cause. It made it much more difficult to break them.

"It's obvious to me that Mitcham didn't share his invincibility with you," Doc said, hoping to frighten Markus. "Sad really. You could use it right now. I've never tortured a Zeniu, but I expect the mechanics are about the same. I'm going to start with your face and work my way down to your feet." Doc put a special emphasis on feet, and Markus began to sweat.

"What is your plan to push the cryptids into attacking the norms?" Doc questioned.

Markus snarled defiantly and didn't say a word.

"So be it," Doc said, slicing off the outer ring of Markus's ear.

Markus gasped in pain and struggled weakly against his bonds. "You won't get away with this," he hissed.

"I already have," Doc shrugged. "And, unfortunately for you, I can do this all night. First this ear, then the next, then a finger or two, three or four, then maybe I'll pull out the letter opener and poke some holes in you."

"Filthy norm abomination," Markus ground out. "When we're done, the Hidden will be purified of your taint."

"What are you not getting about this?" Doc sighed. "You're dead. There is no we."

The door opened, and Jury poked in his head. "I'm going to sit this one out," he said. "Torture always puts me off my appetite."

"Did you get a good look at him?" Doc asked.

"What's that blue shit?" Jury asked as he carefully examined Markus's face and clothes.

"He's a Zeniu," Doc replied.

"Oh. That actually explains a lot," Jury murmured.

"My thoughts exactly."

"Although... I wasn't aware they had a humanoid form."

"They don't," Doc said. "It's some kind of magic. Thaddeus tried explaining it to me. Or at least the theory of it."

"And I'm sure you pretended not to understand a word of what he said," Jury grumbled.

"Me?" Doc responded innocently. "You know how I feel about magic."

Jury snorted and said, "Just call me when you're done."

"It might be a minute."

"I'll take a nap."

Doc nodded and turned back to Markus. "Now where were we?"

19

By midnight, Doc was covered in blue goo, Markus was wheezing, and Doc had very little information he hadn't had before he'd started.

He cleaned his knife on Markus's pant leg and sat down on the edge of the desk with a sigh. "I don't understand why you're being so difficult. Mitcham is dead; you're dead. It's over."

"Then why do you care?" Markus sneered.

Doc refused to concede the point.

"Would you just kill him already?" Jury muttered from the corner.

"Goddamn!" Doc snapped. "For once I have the chance to know exactly what is going on, but no! Do you know how annoying that is?!"

"Who cares?" Jury said. "The thing is whatever their plan is, you're going to stop it. You always do. So knowing what it is doesn't actually change anything."

"Fine!" Doc growled, tossing a knife at one of Markus's feet. The knife tore through both his shoe and his foot before sinking into the wooden floor beneath, and Markus howled in pain.

It was the perfect time to ask him more questions, while he was writhing in pain and wishing it would stop; but Doc had wearied of the game a few hours ago, so without a word, he thrust another knife into Markus's other foot.

Markus's cry of pain turned into a whimper, and his eyes locked onto Doc's. "You can't stop it," he whispered, bloody mouth curving upward. "You can't stop it." Then his head slumped forward, and his chest ceased its movement.

"What a waste of time," Doc growled, pulling the silver wrist cuff from Markus's wrist. Markus's body shifted, and suddenly he was a Zeniu.

"How did you do that?" Jury demanded.

"It's this bracelet," Doc explained. "I've seen it before."

"Can I see it?" Jury asked excitedly.

Doc tossed it to him, and Jury put it on. Nothing happened.

"Thaddeus implied that it's connected to the species it was made for," Doc said.

"Interesting," Jury said distractedly. "I wonder if I can figure out how it works."

"Knock yourself out," Doc said. "I'm going to finish off this bottle of whiskey and wash the Zeniu off me."

"Yeah, yeah," Jury said, sitting behind Mitcham's desk and probing at the bracelet with a hair-thin finger of magic.

When Doc was clean and dressed in a fresh suit, he went downstairs and sat in the cold, stiff parlor. He leaned his head against the back of the rigid settee and contemplated his day.

Even after Doc had removed them, Markus had been very tight lipped. The only things Doc had been able to glean was that their plan to rile the Hidden was supposed to take place after the summit and that William Grakstone, Attikus, and Ella Glass were all involved. Markus refused to answer a single question about Alex, either because he didn't know Alex or because Alex was somehow integral to their plan. All in all, it wasn't much; certainly not enough to justify torturing Markus for eight hours straight.

Mitcham had essentially told Doc his entire plan, but Doc wasn't sure that knowing it would really help him stop it. He didn't know who Mitcham's agents were or where they were stationed. He didn't know how Mitcham contacted them. He didn't know anything.

Doc yawned and let sleep overtake him.

"Death is on you," Meli whispered, running her cold hands over his shoulders.

"Is it?" Doc asked, stepping carefully away from her.

"And violence," she purred. "I can almost taste it."

Maybe he should scrub his scent. If he did, maybe Meli wouldn't be able to find him. Then again, maybe she would.

"What time do you live in?" she asked silkily.

"The regular time," he replied. "What about you?"

"I do not know. I am dead. What does time matter to me?"

"So you don't know how long you've been dead?" he asked.

"No. Do you?"

"Why would I?" Doc replied, in what he hoped was a casual tone. She might be dead, but her essence still packed a punch. Just being near her was making him antsy. He hadn't felt this way... in a very long time.

"I think," she said thoughtfully, "that I might not be as dead as someone might have hoped."

"Interesting," Doc said.

"Perhaps I can live again," she said, black eyes pinning him in place. "I would like that," she said, stepping closer and laying her hands on his chest. "I would like that very much."

Doc woke with a start. He wasn't alone.

"The spirit in your dream is... evil," Thulan said.

"I'm aware," Doc said sharply, annoyed Thulan had managed to get so close without Doc waking. Andrew would be so ashamed.

"Then you know not to listen to her," Thulan added, empty eye sockets focusing so intently on Doc that he was certain Thulan could see him.

"Obviously."

"You did well with the ears," Thulan said. "You almost tricked me."

"That was Jury's handiwork," Doc said. "It was his first time."

"Very impressive for such a young witch."

"He's pretty incredible," Doc agreed.

"I met him once before," Thulan said. "He was quite young, but seemed to possess a quick and clever mind."

"If you knew the ears were fake how did you know what we wanted you to say?" Doc asked.

"I could see what you wanted me to see," Thulan said softly. "I could see the truth and the lie."

"I suppose I owe you a thank you then," Doc said. "You bought us some much needed time."

"And you put that time to good use," Thulan replied "I can think of no one else with the ingenuity to do what you did."

"You mean kill Mitcham?" Doc asked.

"Yes," Thulan agreed.

"I'm very good at killing people," Doc said with a shrug.

"You're nervous," Thulan said. "But not about Mitcham's

plan or the Hidden; you're nervous about the spirit in your dream."

"Yes," Doc replied tensely, wondering how a man with no eyes could see that. Doc generally needed to see people to know what they were thinking. "But right now I'm dealing with Mitcham's mess," Doc said. "The spirit comes later."

"I see."

"Can you tell me how Mitcham always knew what people were saying about him?"

"He didn't," Thulan said calmly.

"Come again?"

"Kings, emperors, dictators, tetrarchs, presidents, all rulers use a classic set of techniques to control their subjects," Thulan explained, sitting next to Doc. "One of the most powerful is mythology."

"I'm not sure I'm following you," Doc said. "Like Zeus and Odin?"

"No," Thulan chuckled. "The mythology of the ruler, the mythos. Very important. Mitcham used two basic myths to keep control of the Hidden. One, that he was invincible and could not die. A myth you proved to be false. The other was that he had eyes and ears everywhere."

"But he didn't?"

"Of course not. How could he?" Thulan replied.

"Magic?" Doc suggested.

"Whose magic would be powerful enough? And who would he trust enough? Even Bosch, one of his closest comrades, turned against him."

"Rumor had it Bosch thought Mitcham was going to kill him," Doc said.

"Of course he was. There can only be one ruler, after all."

"So how did he do it?" Doc asked.

"Simple. To begin with he found some people who quite openly disagreed with his policies. They disappeared. He continued to remove anyone who was open in their dissatisfaction, and eventually people grew wise and became less open. This is the point at which the mythos began to grow," Thulan said. "Mitcham sent out spies, people pretending to hate him to ferret out those who really did; and sometimes, Mitcham removed random people who'd done nothing, then spread rumors that they had spoken out against him. As more and more people disappeared, the remaining populace became even more cautious."

Thulan paused for a moment, and when he went on, his voice was solemn. "He removed the competition, removed members of the council who voted against him, and ferreted out more holdouts. Meanwhile, his agents spread the rumors that Mitcham knew everything, had eyes everywhere, heard even the slightest mention of his name. He didn't, but the people had become too frightened to speak. Occasionally, a lone voice would rise; but one person is easy to suppress, especially when everyone else is too scared to join him."

Thulan gestured vaguely and added, "Mitcham's talent for persuasion made the task of convincing every one of his mythos even simpler than usual."

"People keep telling me how persuasive the Zeniu are, but I hated everything Mitcham had to say," Doc pointed out.

"Your mind is firm, not easily moved. Most minds are pliable, like water, and the Zeniu can push it where they want it to go."

The more Doc contemplated what Thulan had said, the more he was a little annoyed he hadn't thought of it himself. "The simplest solution," he muttered.

"Very clever in its simplicity," Thulan said. "All rulers have a mythos. They must. What will yours be?"

"What? No," Doc laughed. "I'm only doing this until I clear out the summit."

"You are a good man, John Holliday," Thulan said thoughtfully. "Not too many men can say that."

Doc chuckled lightly. "I think you've probably got that wrong. At best, I'm neutral."

Thulan smiled. "As you say." He stood, then said almost as if an afterthought, "The spirit is attached to you now. It will not leave."

"I was afraid of that," Doc sighed. He watched Thulan walk steadily towards the staircase and, as Thulan began to climb the stairs, grinned. Mitcham may have taken Thulan's eyes, but he hadn't taken his sight.

Once Thulan was gone, Doc stared moodily at the ceiling. No sleep. No Jury. No women. And another day until he could kill anyone. That only left whiskey. Whiskey and one of the terribly gruesome looking books in Mitcham's office.

The next day passed in much the same way. Doc had meetings with Ella Glass, Grakstone, and Attikus, and he felt his way carefully through the meetings, mentally marking each of them for death. He knew it was impossible to remove every single person involved in Mitcham's plan, but he could at least remove the first and second row of pawns.

Towards evening, Simon arrived. "Tetrarch Mitcham," he said smoothly as he sat across from Doc.

"We aren't really doing that, are we?" Doc sighed. "I'm getting tired of pretending to be a villainous psychopath."

Simon grinned sharply. "But I hear you are doing such a fine job."

"Shut the door, Birdwell," Doc ordered.

Jury rolled his eyes, but shut the door and, glamour fading, sat beside Simon.

"All the members of the summit have arrived," Simon said.

"Excellent," Doc replied. "I'm looking forward to meeting them."

"I'm sure you are," Simon replied.

"Will the council be there as well?"

"Yes."

"How many members of the council truly support Mitcham?" Doc asked.

"Truly support? Only Attikus."

"You're certain?"

"Yes."

"How many men can you provide tomorrow?" Doc asked.

"Twenty-four."

"We'll need more than that," Doc mused. "We'll have to neutralize the Magistratus, as well as, any guards belonging to Mitcham's supporters. I'll see how many men Jervis can spare and call Ana and Ina."

"Ana and Ina?" Simon asked.

"Some friends of mine," Doc said easily. "Vampires."

Simon arched an eyebrow. "The Zaitsev sisters?"

"You know them?"

"Only by reputation," Simon said.

"Were you aware that Markus was a Zeniu?"

"Was? And no."

"He was unfortunate enough to be about the same height as Jury."

"I see," Simon said.

Doc grinned and went on. "I think he and Mitcham might

have been brothers. Markus was rather reticent when I questioned him."

Jury snorted, but didn't look up from his sandwich.

"In any case, I don't yet know how to fix the damage Markus caused within the Hidden. I don't know if he has a network of people riling up the other cities around the country, and I don't know what their plan was to push the cryptids into attacking the norms." Doc sighed. "Basically, I don't know a lot. I'm hoping that by derailing the summit and announcing to the Hidden at large that Mitcham is dead and his plan will not be carried out, most of it will take care of itself."

Doc drummed his fingers on the desktop. "It's not a great plan," he said thoughtfully.

"It's more than anyone else has," Jury said.

"That's probably true," Doc said wearily. He opened the desk drawer and pulled out a fresh bottle of whiskey and three glasses. He filled them all to the brim, then pushed two across the desk towards the others. "This isn't really important, but there's something I'd like to know," he said. "How did the summit members get here?"

"What?" Simon asked.

"How did they get here? I can't imagine every single cryptid is walking around with a token that can make them look human. It can't be that simple because Jury still hasn't figured out how Markus's bracelet was made. So how did they get here?"

"Mitcham built a private airfield out on the plains about twenty years ago," Simon said. "Then he went on to build an airfield on each of the other continents. Really simplifies things, I suppose."

"Interesting."

"Before that, cryptids like myself would have had to travel crate method. Not the most comfortable way to fly, or so I've heard."

"I'm beginning to understand where Mitcham was coming from," Doc brooded. "You're clearly a superior species, and yet you have to hide to escape detection. Cryptids, with all their skills and attributes, are reduced to skulking around in the shadows, while norms run around making a mess of things. It's almost... nonsensical."

Simon and Jury both stared at him, faces blank.

"What?" Doc asked. "Don't you see it?"

"I think every cryptid sees it," Jury said.

"So how did we get here?" Doc questioned.

"I think it was something of a surprise," Simon said softly.

"A surprise?"

"Most cryptids rely on their instincts and their natural abilities to survive. At least they used to, but for some reason that's never been enough for mankind. I cannot speak for the other continents, but when the Westerners arrived on our shores with their weapons and their greed, we simply did not recognize or understand it, and by the time we did... it was too late."

"I see," Doc said.

"We could overthrow them now," Simon went on, "trample them under our feet and enslave their children, but to do so would make us no better than them. So most of us do our best to live in the shadows. However, if light should ever reach those shadows, revealing us, we would not make the same mistake twice."

Simon's solemn words filled the dark room, then faded into tomblike silence.

After a moment, Doc nodded and said cheerfully, "I'm

glad you have a plan. The other day you mentioned Mitcham's second in command?"

"Yes."

"Where is he?"

"New York."

"Of course," Doc said. "Will he be at the summit?"

"No."

Doc growled. It could never be simple. He just wanted to wrap it up with a nice little bow on top, kill everyone involved, and be done with it. He absolutely despised loose ends.

"Then how do we handle him?" Doc demanded.

"The council will have to put out a kill order for all of Mitcham's associates," Simon explained.

"Ugh," Doc complained. "I hate politics."

"I think you're doing rather well," Simon praised with a wide smile.

"You enjoy his slash and burn technique?" Jury chuckled.

"It gets the job done," Simon replied.

"What is the reason Mitcham gave the other leaders for the summit?" Doc asked.

"It's been planned for nearly two years," Simon replied. "A year before I was offered up as his personal honor guard."

"Still bitter about that?" Doc chuckled. "It was an honor."

"Perhaps," Simon said without inflection.

"So you don't know the reason he gave them?"

"Until Mitcham came to power, the Hiddens all stood on their own. Mitcham changed that by slowly insulating himself into as many Hiddens as possible and, more or less, taking over. Each Hidden still has its official leader, but Mitcham pulls the strings. And by pulling the strings, he's able to utilize cryptids from all over the world. To what final purpose... Only he could have told you."

"I'd rather you not point out things like that," Doc murmured.

"It drives him insane," Jury put in. "The not knowing."

Simon continued with a grin, "There's a rumor that Mitcham found a way to physically connect the Hiddens, somewhat like the library system or the doorways, and the idea is that he called the summit to lay his plan before the leaders. But you and I both know that can't be the real reason."

"Right," Doc said. "Because if Mitcham had a way to connect the Hiddens, he would have just done it."

"Exactly," Simon said.

"I'm so glad you stopped by," Doc drawled. "Really helped clear up things."

Simon laughed softly and stood. "May I take Min with me?" he asked. "Our building encircles a small wooded area. Just a bit of home."

"You know Min?" Doc asked in surprise.

"No. I only know of her. She was the head of the tree spirits before she disappeared; she was quite well known for her outspoken distaste of Mitcham. Her people will be overjoyed to hear she is alive."

"She can go with you," Doc said. "But only if you can move her without notice. We're so close; I'd hate to slip up now."

"Perhaps it is best to wait," Simon conceded. "I will at least give her my respects before I leave."

"Wait!" Doc said, stopping Simon. "Do you know who handled Mitcham's surveillance?"

"No."

"Do you have any guesses on who it could be?"

"No," Simon replied. "Mitcham kept everything very

compartmentalized so one hand didn't know what the other one was doing."

"Fantastic," Doc muttered. "Go on then."

The door closed behind Simon, and Jury said, "It's almost as if just sitting behind the desk conveys some sort of power."

"What?"

"Everyone who comes in here defers to your will, and it's not as if you've even asked them to."

"You think it's the desk?" Doc said. "You should try it." He got up, taking his whiskey bottle with him, and sat in Simon's vacated chair. "Go on," he urged.

Jury laughed and sat behind the desk. He winked at Doc, then straightened his shoulders and squinted angrily. "I'm channeling my father," he whispered.

"I can tell," Doc drawled.

"Fill the buckets with oil," Jury snarled. "Man the catapults. Lock up the women and children."

Doc struggled not to grin, but he couldn't help it. "Up the accent," he suggested.

"Tonight we roast our enemies over the fires of hell!" Jury exclaimed, British accent rolling easily off his tongue.

"I actually believe your father has said that as least once," Doc chuckled.

"Hearts on a pike!" Jury shouted. "Fill the gibbet cages!"

Doc burst out laughing. "I think maybe your policies are a couple hundred years out of date," he gasped.

"Never!" Jury yelled. "Never! Tonight we drink from the skulls of our enemies, and we pick our teeth with their bones!" Then he began to laugh so violently that he couldn't speak anymore.

After their laughter had died down, Jury said, "I don't think it's the desk. It must just be you."

20

"You're looking a bit... worn," Jury commented after they had toasted Phillip Jury and his archaic ways. "When was the last time you slept?"

"Yeah," Doc said. "And anyway, I'm not even sure I need to sleep."

"I hate it when you say 'yeah' like that," Jury sighed. "Why aren't you sleeping?"

"I've slept," Doc replied evasively.

"Fine, don't tell me," Jury muttered. "It's not like I'm your best friend or anything."

"Now you're starting to sound like Thaddeus."

"I'm beginning to wonder if he only started sounding like that after he came to live with you."

"I doubt it," Doc snorted.

"Why aren't you sleeping?" Jury asked seriously.

"The Black Shaman latched onto me."

"What does that mean?"

"It means that every time I close my eyes, a psychotic, ultrapowerful, mostly crazy, god-like being is there, putting her ice-cold hands on me and piercing me with her... her... her piercing stare."

"Sounds fun," Jury commented.

"Not really."

"You do have a tendency to attract crazy women," Jury teased.

"It's not funny."

"Remember that one who followed you to Italy?"

Doc shuddered.

"And then to get rid of her, you somehow convinced her to join a nunnery," Jury reminisced. "I'm still not sure how you did that. I've always said just being available is not a good enough guideline."

"It works," Doc argued. "Ninety-seven percent of the time."

"So if you sleep with a hundred women a year, at least three of them are crazy? Does that sound about right?"

Doc frowned. "There's no way I sleep with a hundred women a year."

"How many have you slept with in the last week?" Jury asked.

"Just Ana."

"Going through a dry spell, huh?" Jury snickered.

"When the hell have I had the time?" Doc demanded. "I'm trying to save the goddamn world here!"

"That's drumming it up a little."

"Alright, I'm trying to save at least this little corner of the world."

"Better. So before Ana, you slept with my wife—"

"She's not your goddamn wife!"

"Let's not get hung up on the details," Jury tsked. "Anyone else?"

"Sagena, and none of them are crazy."

"That's not the point. I'm doing math here. Did you say Sagena? Isn't that Simon's sister?"

Doc shrugged.

"Are you insane? If he finds out he'll probably kill you."

"He already knows."

"How can you be sure?"

"Just trust me," Doc sighed.

"Whatever," Jury muttered. "Risky, that's all I'm saying. Now, that's three women in a three week span, so that puts you at fifty two women a year. So at least one and a half of them will be crazy."

Doc stared incredulously at Jury over the desktop. "One and a half?" he demanded.

"Yes."

"Which half?"

"Does it matter?" Jury replied.

They started to laugh again, and after a while Doc said, "Do you think maybe this house is driving us crazy?"

"It's possible," Jury said, casting a glance up at the mural. "So what're you going to do about the shaman?"

"Not sleep?" Doc shrugged.

"I've heard better plans."

"What do you suggest?"

"What was that thing Andrew had?" Jury asked.

"A dreamcatcher," Doc replied irritably.

"Well?"

"Well," Doc snapped. "Charlie made it for him."

"Oh." A small ball of light appeared in Jury's hand, and he tossed it into the air, then caught it. "You could ask that Ahanu guy."

"Absolutely not," Doc said with a cringe. "He'd consider

that a favor, and then I'd owe him, and I don't want to owe him ever again."

"We're taking on the entire summit tomorrow," Jury stated. "Over seventy-five leaders will be there, and they'll all be cryptids so killing them may not do you any favors. My suggestion is to run out and get a midnight snack if you're not going to sleep and eat like a normal human being."

Doc gave Jury an irritated look. "Just because you're still behind the desk doesn't mean I'm going to listen to you."

"No," Jury said, "you're going to listen to me because I'm right."

Doc sighed. He was feeling worn out, but it wasn't physical. It was mental. He hated sitting behind Mitcham's deranged desk all day, making overt threats to keep people in line, and plotting the demise of the norm world.

"How do politicians do it?" he asked. "It's exhausting."

"I'm beginning to think they're so drunk on the power of it, they don't even realize how tiring it is," Jury replied.

"They can have it," Doc muttered. He pulled out his phone and texted Jervis. "I need a meal, multi-course if possible."

"Give me a minute, sir."

"Also, I need some men at the summit tomorrow. Use the private security firm's uniforms."

"Obviously."

"Sorry," Doc texted. "I've been lining out people all day."

"I understand."

"Also, see if Ana and Ina can come. We're going to need all the people we can get."

"I'll take care of it, sir."

Jury was bouncing his ball of magic off the ceiling now, and Doc hurled a knife, pinning the ball to the grotesque mural that covered the entire ceiling.

"You could have just asked me to stop," Jury chuckled as the magic ball dissipated.

"What I want to know is what sort of self-respecting artist creates artwork like that?" Doc said, staring at the spot where his knife had pierced. He tilted his head sideways. "It's eating that woman's leg, and she's not even dead yet."

"It's better than his desk," Jury said. "Did you see this portion of the carving over here?"

Doc shuddered. "I don't want to talk about that portion. It... It makes me queasy."

Jury tore his eyes from the desk and made another ball of light. "So you watched the video on light orbs, huh?"

"I watched all the videos," Doc said.

"Really?"

"Really."

"When the hell did you have the time?"

Doc shrugged. "I enjoyed the one on dead stuff, like plastics."

"Thanks."

"Although I did wonder if perhaps you're the one who gave Bosch the idea in the first place."

"That's ridiculous!" Jury exclaimed. "Like you said, I only have a hundred and two followers."

"Yes, and one of them was Sofia."

The blue ball fell to the floor, bounced once, then rolled under the desk. Jury gaped at Doc for a second before saying, "Nah, you don't really think?"

"I did think," Doc drawled.

"Well fuck. I mean, I never really thought about... Goddamn."

Doc's phone beeped, and he read Jervis's text. "Lily Buffmack and her suitor Joe Bishop were charged with abusing her elderly mother, but the charges were dropped. The mother died three days later, and Lily inherited over 3.5 million, not including the property. I've no way to confirm they killed her; I leave that up to you." Jervis had gone on to include Lily's address.

"Got something?" Jury asked.

"Yes," Doc said. "We're going to have fun with this one."

"We?"

"Alright, I'm going to have fun, but you have to come with me. I need a disguise."

"I liked your grunge look," Jury chuckled.

"It was too obvious," Doc said, pulling open the office door. "We're going out," he told Nick as they passed the Takaheni guard. "But we won't be long. No one comes in or leaves."

"Yes, sir."

"Definitely not the desk," Jury muttered as they slipped outside.

As soon as the air hit Doc's face, he paused and took a deep breath.

"I hadn't realized how stifling it is in there," Jury murmured. "No wonder I've been so hungry."

"When we're done with this, we're burning down his house and building a park," Doc said firmly.

"I think they'll like that," Jury said thoughtfully.

"They're probably not even there," Doc replied, walking quickly towards the exit into the norm world. "But if they are..." He hoped they weren't. He wouldn't care if Mitcham's soul was trapped in a stinky dungeon for all eternity, but he hoped the several hundred dead prisoners were free, wandering the earth or the Underworld or sleeping happily in the mother's womb. He didn't care where they were, as long as they weren't here.

They left the Hidden and hailed a taxi.

"You think two's enough?" Jury asked as they rode across town.

"It better be," Doc replied. "I'm not just going to wander around town looking for people who'd be better off dead."

"You did that one time we were stuck in Nairobi."

"Slightly different," Doc drawled. "I didn't have people there."

"We were at it all night."

"You try getting gored by a rhinoceros!" Doc snapped.

"I'd rather not," Jury laughed.

"I don't know why you're in such a good mood," Doc grumbled.

"I don't know," Jury said. "I think I'm just beginning to realize that I'm free."

"Just now?"

"It's not as if we've had a lot of down time since... Well, you know."

"Since I saved you from being eaten alive by Marie Baudelaire?"

"Yeah, since that. Then Mitcham had us tied up, but now he's dead too. I could go anywhere," Jury said thoughtfully. "Do anything, marry anyone. I could dye my hair purple, start talking in slang, and no one could say a thing. I'm not a Jury anymore. I'm just Jury."

Doc swallowed a laugh. Jury had always been Jury; he just hadn't realized it. "So where will you go?" Doc asked.

"Nowhere," Jury laughed. "Or everywhere. Who knows? Right now, I'm here, with you, about to rock the Hidden on its ass. Can you imagine the look on my father's face when he finds out? He'll probably send me a stern lecture about honoring the Jury name and title, and I won't even read it.

Because I'm a free man." Jury rolled down the window, stuck out his head, and yelled, "I'm a free man!"

Doc watched him with a grin.

"It's good to be me," Jury said as he sat back onto the seat. "Just don't fuck it up by getting us both killed tomorrow."

"The thought never even crossed my mind," Doc promised cheerfully.

The taxi cruised to a halt, and they exited it, paid the driver, and approached Lily's house. "I'll wait out here," Jury said. "It's not like you need a glamour for this."

Doc knocked on the door and adopted his most serious expression.

A middle-aged woman answered the door, a frilly apron tied around her waist and her mass of blond hair loosely twisted into a bun. "Can I help you?" she asked.

"Lily Buffmack?"

"Yes."

"My name is Tom Mackey. I'm with the IRS, and I need to speak with you about your inheritance tax."

Her brow wrinkled with confusion. "But we sent everything in months ago. Our accountant said everything was fine."

"I'm afraid there's been an error," Doc said gravely. "May I come in?"

"Yes, I'm so sorry." She held the door open wider, and Doc walked past her into a comfortable living room. He found it somewhat amusing that it never even occurred to her to ask why he would be there after eight o'clock at night. When people started to panic, they simply stopped thinking.

"Joe!" Lily called out. "Would you please come here?"

A stout man entered the room, eyes narrowing when he saw Doc. "Is something wrong?" he asked.

"This is Mr. Mackey, from the IRS," Lily said softly. "He says there's a problem with the taxes."

"Nothing that can't be fixed," Doc said. "I just need to ask you a few questions."

"Shoot," Joe said, sitting on the couch and wrapping his arm around Lily's shoulders. They both looked at Doc expectantly, and he pinched his lips in disapproval.

"How long was your mother sick?" he asked.

"Oh, she wasn't sick," Lily said.

"Then what was the cause of her death?"

"The examiner said her heart gave out."

"What does this have to do with the taxes?" Joe demanded.

"I'm getting there," Doc said loftily. "Were you here the night she died?"

"Yes," Lily replied.

"Did she suffer?"

"What?!"

"It's a simple question. Did she suffer?"

"I don't... I mean..." Her face paled. "You're not really with the IRS, are you?"

Doc shrugged and asked, "How did you kill her?"

"I didn't!" she protested, but she was lying because her eyes slid to the side and she started blinking anxiously.

"How did you and Joe kill her?"

"You need to leave," Joe said, lurching to his feet. "I don't know who you are, but we haven't done anything wrong."

"Did you bribe the examiner?" Doc asked.

"How—" Lily started to exclaim before her eyes grew wide and she stopped herself.

"So you did."

Joe grabbed Doc's shoulders and started trying to shove

him towards the door, but Doc grasped one of Joe's hands and spun him around, then locked his arm around Joe's neck.

"Tell me how you killed her," Doc told Lily, "or I'll kill him."

"Please don't hurt him," she begged. "It wasn't like that, I swear. I didn't have a choice. She was going to kick us out, and we didn't have anything! We would've been homeless. Surely you can understand that?"

"How did you kill her?" Doc demanded.

"I had to do it," she sobbed. "I had to. I would have had to whore myself out on street corners. Don't you understand?!"

"I don't suppose it ever occurred to you to just get a job," Doc said flatly. "How did you kill her?"

"I put water hemlock in her tea," she sobbed.

"Water hemlock?" he muttered. "God, you're cruel. How long did it take her to die?" he demanded, tightening his hold on Joe to keep him from struggling.

"Don't hurt him. You promised."

"How long?"

"Hours," she whispered.

"Hours?! You couldn't just have done the decent thing and choked her out?" Doc snarled.

"I didn't... I wasn't..."

"Shut up, and call the police," Joe rasped.

"Let me show you how painless and quick it could have been," Doc said, tightening his hold on Joe's neck even more.

"No!" Lily shrieked. "You said you wouldn't hurt him!" She tore at Doc's arm, trying to loosen his grip, but her attack was pathetic and weak.

"Run," Joe gasped just before he blacked out.

"Stop it!" she screamed. "You're killing him!"

She grabbed a vase and threw it at Doc's head, but it streaked past and shattered against the wall.

"He's not in any pain," Doc said evenly. "He's not vomiting or chewing off his tongue. He's just going to sleep."

"You're a monster!" she shouted, throwing a plate at him. The plate grazed his temple, then hit the wall behind him.

"I didn't kill my own mother," Doc said. "I wished I could have, to end her pain and suffering, but I didn't. You on the other hand, wanted your mother to suffer. And why? So you could have her money? Who's the real monster here?"

Lily's cheeks were streaked with tears, and she screamed angrily as she picked up a pillow and hurled it at his head.

"A pillow?" he laughed.

His tattoo was beginning to warm, and he could feel the tendrils of power running through him so he dropped Joe's body and stepped towards Lily.

"Shall I poison you?" he asked. "Like you did her?"

Her nostrils flared with fear, and her eyes darted around the room. Suddenly she turned and fled. He ran after her, tossing a knife towards her hand when she reached for the back door. The knife tore completely through her hand and stuck to the door frame, and Lily stared at the gaping, bloody hole, shrieking hysterically.

Doc clamped his hand around her mouth and whispered, "Shhh... Wouldn't want you to wake the neighbors."

He studied the kitchen chairs and briefly considered tying her to one and dragging it out a bit, but there was nothing to be gained from it. He could, however, make her feel it.

He drew another knife and placed the tip on her chest, just outside her heart. "This is going to hurt," he said softly and began to push the knife point slowly through her ribs. She bucked and screamed, but his hand muffled the sound.

He pushed firmly, and the knife blade crunched through

her bones and began to enter the flesh of her heart. Her screams turned panicked, and she clawed at his hand.

"This is how your mother felt," he said. "And you just sat there and watched her."

He gave the knife one last push, burying it deeply inside her heart. She tore at his arm desperately, then her body went limp, and his tattoo flared with heat.

21

"I just had a realization," Doc hissed to Jury as they walked towards the building where the summit meeting was being held.

"What's that?"

"Mitcham's probably met all these people."

"So?"

"So?! I don't have the slightest idea who they are."

"It's called a bluff, Doc," Jury said. "You've got this."

"I'm not sure I like this new you," Doc muttered. "You're too goddamn cheerful."

"Better get used to it," Jury laughed. "'Cause I'm feeling good."

"How's my face?" Doc asked, pausing in front of the doors.

"You look like you've swallowed a hot poker," Jury responded. "Classic Mitcham."

"Fantastic."

"This is a stupid question," Jury said, "but do you actually have a plan?"

"Flush out the norm-haters, kill them, hand over the keys to the kingdom, and go take a shower."

Jury nodded thoughtfully. "More details than I expected actually."

"Was that sarcastic?" Doc demanded.

"Not in the least."

Doc rolled his eyes, and greeted Simon as he approached them. "Mr. Redgrove. Would you lead the way?"

Simon nodded and headed into the large building. Doc immediately knew Mitcham had built the building; there was just a feeling to it, a coldness and an overall oppressive feel, a suspicion that you might never see the sunlight again. Doc hated it and made a mental note to have it torn down as well.

The entryway was crawling with Magistratus, and Doc raised one eyebrow when Grakstone looked his way. Grakstone dropped his gaze immediately, and Doc grinned. Mitcham's mythos had become so powerful that even his advisors believed it.

Simon pushed open an arched wooden door, and they entered a large semi-circular room with chairs surrounding an upraised dais.

"Is the dais my spot?" Doc asked in a low tone.

"Yes, tetrarch," Simon replied softly.

Remembering what Jury had said, Doc just nodded tersely to people as he walked down the aisle towards the steps. It's not as if Mitcham was the type to have friends. Just associates, followers, victims, and enemies.

As Doc walked up the short staircase, his mind raced, trying to figure out the best approach, but there really wasn't a best approach. He'd just have to wing it.

"Fellow leaders!" he called out when he'd reached the top of the dais. "I cannot say how pleased I am to see you here today! This moment is the culmination of years and years of planning and labor."

The assembled leaders clapped enthusiastically.

"I know you've traveled a long way to be here," Doc said. "And I promise you it will be worth your while."

He paced the dais for a moment, studying the faces in the audience. "I see quite a few of you brought guards along with you, but there's no need for that here," Doc said sternly. "Furthermore, what I have to say needs to stay between leaders until we work out all the details. Mr. Redgrove will lead your men out into the foyer where he's arranged for some delectable Lutin pastries and coffee."

There were a few unhappy murmurs, but the assembled leaders began to send their guards away, which only reinforced Doc's suspicion that Mitcham, somehow, had an iron grip on all of them.

Jury had sat in the front row, and when Doc caught his eyes, he mouthed furiously, "I can't do it from that far away!"

Doc gestured towards Jury and said, "While we're waiting, I'd like to introduce my close associate, Markus Johanns. He's been working on this project with me, and he'll stay so he can offer his insight."

Another round of murmurs, but Doc just smiled in that peculiar way Mitcham had, the one that suggested you were irritating him greatly, and said, "Does anyone have an objection to that?"

No one did.

"Excellent," Doc said.

He waited until the doors closed behind the last of the guards, and then he gazed out into the audience thoughtfully. There were many different types of cryptids assembled. The five Zeniu were sitting together, but he was pleased to see that none of the others had segregated with their own kind. The United States council was present, including Mr. Birch and a few others Doc recognized, and he laughed mentally when he saw the old Jury witch in the audience, the one who had wanted to kill him at Jury's wedding. The Baudelaires were probably out there somewhere, but he couldn't say for sure having never met them.

It was truly an insane play. The kind of play only desperate men made, but that's what was so brilliant about it. He was about to kill half of the Hiddens' rulers, and when he was done, the Hiddens would thank him. Now he just needed to figure out which half.

"After today," Doc said enthusiastically, "the Hidden, no, the world, will be a very different place."

The Zenius grinned, and Doc marked them for death.

"What I have planned will change the balance of things, putting us, the cryptids, back on top, where we belong!"

Several of the leaders nodded emphatically, and Doc memorized their faces.

"I have agents in place all over the world, and with your support, we are going to launch a war; a war that will bring the norm world to its knees!"

More than half of the leaders stood and clapped eagerly. The others stayed seated, looking rather glum and a little bit scared.

"I see some of you haven't yet come fully around to my point of view," Doc said in that tone Mitcham used to convey deep disappointment. "That is, of course, why I called you here today. To convince you that this is the right plan, the right path. Indeed, the only path."

Doc's eyebrows raised as the old Jury witch stood to speak. "I was under the impression that you called us here to discuss a means of interconnecting the Hiddens," the old man said.

"I apologize for the deception," Doc replied. "It was necessary. I need to know I have your absolute support."

"To wage a war against the norms?" the witch snorted. "Why would we do that?"

"Because the balance is skewed," Doc said flatly. "We are the predators; they are the prey."

There was a loud round of applause.

"The humans have never been our prey," the Jury argued loudly. "That goes for many of the cryptid species who are here today. The Takaheni, the tree spirits, the Worms—"

"You cannot say the Worms do not prey on humans," Doc interrupted.

"Not in the way you're suggesting," the old man said irritably. "The Worms are like the fungi in the forest; they take the bodies and return them to the earth. They serve a function."

"And so do we!" Doc shouted. "In our rightful place we keep the norms from overrunning the earth! Why should we hide in our ten percent while they destroy the places we used to call home? Why should we twist our bodies to fit their hideous forms just so we can walk free on their streets?"

"What the fuck are you doing?" Jury mouthed.

"Trust me," Doc tried to say with his eyes.

Attikus stood, mumbling the same words Thypon had said, and transformed into his cyclops' form. "It is easy for the witches to come and speak of peace," he rumbled. "They are basically norms. They walk among the norms, take norms as their lovers, breed bastard norm children. They are not confined within weak bodies and forced to masquerade as less than they are!" Attikus threw back his shoulders and roared, "I support Tetrarch Mitcham! It is time we take back the earth!"

"To what end?" a serpent woman retorted. "Shall we cage them, like they would cage us, and eat them at our leisure?"

"YES!" several leaders cried out.

"I will not!" she declared firmly. "I do not prey on weakness, and I will not support this plan."

"Your voice has been heard," Doc said silkily. "Let us be clear on what lies before us. I propose we go to war against the norms and take back what is ours. All those with me say 'aye'!"

A chorus of 'ayes' filled the room, and Doc grinned.

"As I expected, there are some of you here who resist change," Doc said casually. "I want the opportunity to speak with each of you, to hear your concerns regarding my plan, and see if I can't convince you to accept the inevitable." Doc paused and stared at them. This was the moment. The moment of truth. "All those who oppose my plan," Doc said, "move to the east side of the room. All those who support me, move to the west."

In the audience, Jury rolled his eyes.

Fear filled some of the faces, but they bravely stood and moved to the east; the serpent woman, the old Jury, and Mr. Birch were among them. Triumph filled the other faces as they moved towards the west.

"Let me be absolutely clear," Doc said when everyone had settled. "We cannot be divided on this. The Hidden must stand as one. So if you have any concerns at all, I want you to voice them now. If you have chosen the wrong side, now is the time to change. I promise that I will root out anyone who is not firm in their support, and it will not go well for them."

The tension was palatable because everyone in the room

knew what he was really doing. He was dividing them, and some of them were going to die. He was Mitcham. He was a god. No one stood in his way and lived to tell about it. No one opposed him. But these few, these very few, could not stomach what he was asking of them, could not join him or support him, and so they were willing to die if need be.

The whole thing made him furious. The easiest solution was for those who opposed Mitcham to rise up and kill him, but none of them believed that they could. And so they would stand firmly on their honor, hold tightly to the vestiges of their belief in good, and die knowing they had not given in. As opposed to living and actually taking steps to protect the Hidden from evil. It would serve them right if he killed them all.

The Mitcham supporters were talking amongst themselves, and while they talked three of their number stood very slowly and moved to the east. Doc studied the remaining supporters. Most of them were practically vibrating with excitement. Those of them who weren't, he studied long and hard; and a few of them moved to the other side, including all the members of the United States council, except Attikus.

"Excellent," Doc said slowly. "It pleases me to see that the vote is weighted in my favor." He turned to the east. "Believe me when I say that you should rest easy in the knowledge that your decision here today saved your lives."

He turned and grinned at the more than fifty leaders who had sided with Mitcham. "Reverse that for you."

The leaders hadn't even begun to process his meaning by the time several of Doc's knives tore through the stale air and ripped through several throats. A few people managed to scream before Doc's second round of knives cleaved through another group of throats. He'd aimed for the humanoid looking ones first, trying to eliminate all the witches. If the Baudelaires were out there, he wanted them dead.

"It's not Mitcham!" Attikus yelled suddenly. "Kill him!"

The other leaders milled in confusion and panic. They weren't used to being told to kill someone, and they weren't used to someone trying to kill them. They were politicians not fighters, and they generally had people for moments like this.

While they wrestled with the idea of getting their hands dirty, Doc leapt from the dais and headed towards them, Jury at his side. Doc discarded his suit coat as he walked, noticing that Jury had dropped both glamours.

"Nice speech," Jury said as he pulled his gun. "Even I almost sided with you there at the end."

"I was a Zeniu," Doc said with a wide grin. "I had to be persuasive."

He pitched another knife and sighed with disappointment when it hit a wall of solid air and rebounded past him. He'd missed a goddamn witch.

"We should have brought the plastic stuff," he told Jury.

"This'll be more fun," Jury responded as his signature blue magic ripped a chair from the floor and hurled it towards the invisible barrier.

"If you say so," Doc grumbled.

Somehow in the few seconds it had taken Doc to approach them, Attikus had managed to organize the remaining leaders. He'd formed them into ranks according to strength, but the two witches Doc had missed were at the back, guarded by the Zenius.

Jury heaved an entire row of chairs at the wall of air, and the border wavered slightly, allowing one of the chairs to break through and crash into the leaders.

"Allow me," a cultured voice said from behind Doc.

Doc glanced over his shoulder. "Nice to see you again," he drawled.

The old Jury gave him a withering look. "Don't flatter yourself, Holliday."

Jury took a step back and said, "Doc, meet my grandfather, Drustan Jury."

"Ah," Doc said. "You'd be one of Cynric's brothers then."

"Don't speak that name to me, gutter trash. I expect a full accounting when this is finished, Thomas," Drustan growled. "You're a Jury. You shouldn't be masquerading and using deceit. Absolutely disgraceful."

Doc caught Jury's gaze and rolled his eyes. Jury grinned.

"I hate to be a bother," Doc said, "but if you both could hurry it along." Attikus was speaking furiously to his fellow leaders, and Doc didn't want to give them enough time to formulate a workable plan.

"Can't you see I'm working?" the old man snapped.

Doc couldn't, but Jury gestured towards the ceiling, and Doc glanced up. His jaw dropped in surprise. He could not believe that this man had just been going to let Mitcham kill him. What a goddamn waste.

There was no glow around Drustan, no indication whatsoever that he was using magic. He hadn't muttered any Latin words; he hadn't used a spell. Apparently, he didn't need to. Strips of the wooden ceiling were peeling away and coming together in the air above him. Piece after piece until the hovering object resembled a gigantic spear tip.

"Be ready, whelps," Drustan ordered. "It won't keep the barrier down for long."

"Why didn't you do that?" Doc hissed as he and Jury readied themselves.

"Didn't think of it," Jury shrugged.

"I thought you were basically a god."

"Basically. But remember, I did say I was the most powerful witch in North America."

"Your point?"

"Grandfather's from Europe."

"Goddamn," Doc muttered. "And I was going to smash open his head like a melon."

"Aren't you glad you didn't?" Jury laughed.

"We'll see," Doc replied.

Attikus and his fellows were backing slowly towards the door, and Doc frowned. If the angle was just right... He turned, to check, but it was too late; Drustan had already flung the spearhead towards the magic barrier.

"Block the door!" Doc shouted as the spearhead sailed effortlessly through the space where the barrier had been and cruised directly towards the locked and barred door.

"Shit!" Jury hissed. "I can't—"

He never finished his statement because at that moment the spear crashed through the huge doors, breaking them to pieces; and the rogue leaders scrambled for the exit.

"Block it!" Doc ordered, leaping forward, knives singing from his fingertips.

"I'm trying!" Jury snapped.

Doc glanced back at Drustan, but apparently he'd used all his strength because he was sitting in one of the chairs, head in his hands.

"Goddamn it!" Doc growled. He hated it when a plan fell apart.

Jury had already managed to block the door, and his barrier was holding. The leaders were hammering at it frantically, but it wouldn't take them long to realize all they needed to do was turn around and attack Jury. Doc would just have to kill them all before that happened.

"You and I have a score to settle," Attikus said, easily blocking Doc's way forward.

Doc glanced up at him, sighing inwardly. Why did cyclopes have to be so damn humongous?

"I don't have time for scores right now," Doc muttered, dodging Attikus's wide punch and scrambling between his legs, slicing through both of the giant's Achilles tendons as he did.

"I'll squash you!" Attikus roared, stumbling slightly, but managing to keep his feet.

"I think your son said that very same thing," Doc mocked as he threw several knives towards Attikus's eye.

Attikus's huge hand quickly blocked Doc's attack, and he glared furiously at Doc as he knocked the embedded knives from his hand.

"I'm going to grind your bones into powder," he growled.

"Yes, I know," Doc sighed. "And make it into bread. Blah, blah, blah; can we get on with this?"

"You goddamn worm!" Attikus roared, swinging both his hands towards Doc at once.

Doc held himself steady, then jumped, grabbing the back of Attikus's hand and sawing at his wrist with all his strength. Blood spurted everywhere, coating Doc and loosening his grip so that when Attikus flung his arm to the side, Doc tumbled through the air, landing with a crash in the middle of the corrupt leaders.

Doc quickly regained his feet, stabbing through hearts and heads as he did. The leaders were still trying to break through the magic barrier, which just went to show that politicians weren't really that smart.

Several of them turned to confront Doc, and a weak punch managed to land on his chin. A cold blade slid neatly between two of Doc's ribs from behind, and Doc turned, striking downward with his palm and breaking the arm attached to the offending knife in half.

Teeth suddenly tore through the back of Doc's thigh as a shapeshifter in wolf form grabbed hold of him and jerked him towards the floor. Attikus was stumbling towards them, face black with rage; and Doc knew he needed to break free before Attikus grabbed him with one of his huge, meaty hands.

He threw a couple of knives towards Attikus's eye and jerked his right leg forward, tearing the muscle from the bone. He spun around, swallowing a gasp of pain, and severed the wolf's spine. The wolf dropped dead, releasing Doc's leg; and Doc leapt forward, barely escaping Attikus's grasp.

Before Doc could attack, a heavy weight slammed into his back, knocking him to the floor. Doc tried to roll, but a second wolf sank his sharp teeth into the back of Doc's neck, holding him still.

"If Dublin were here," Doc muttered through the pain. "He'd kick your ass."

Doc wrapped his left hand around the wolf's neck, holding him in place, then stabbed blindly through the shapeshifter's head with his other hand. He flinched as the knife tore through the skull and into his own skin, but the wolf's jaws fell open, and Doc was able to roll free.

And not a moment too soon because Attikus's foot slammed down where Doc had just been, completely obliterating the wolf's corpse. Doc jumped to his feet, threw a knife straight for Attikus's groin and bolted past him, tackling the vampire who had almost reached Jury.

The vampire hissed and tried to turn towards Doc, but Doc twisted his hand into her hair and held her tightly, keeping her fangs far away from him. Then he pulled a knife and started sawing at her neck.

"Behind you!" Jury shouted.

Doc rolled to the side, taking the vampire with him, barely escaping Attikus's grasp once more. He kept rolling, sawing as quickly as he could, but no matter how fast he sawed, the vampire's neck refused to sever. Even as Doc cut, the vampire's flesh healed.

"Goddamn," he hissed, rolling to his feet and dragging the woman upright. He cast a glance at Attikus, then pushed the woman away, slicing through her neck in a single flawless arc. He caught her head as it dropped and flung it across the room towards the dais.

Then he ducked once more, slicing through the fingers on one of Attikus's hands as he did, but not moving fast enough to avoid the blow from the other. Doc flew through the air, only stopping when the ridge of the dais broke his fall. And his spine.

He dropped to the floor with a groan. For a second he'd been in intense pain, but nothing hurt now. Not a thing. He tried to crawl to his knees, but his knees felt like they were a mile away and they weren't interested in moving.

"Well hell," he hissed as Attikus's feet moved into his line of sight.

"I've got you now, you shit worm," Attikus menaced. "Can't run away, can't fight. I'm gonna eat your fingers while you watch."

Doc closed his eyes and focused on his body. He could feel it healing. His vertebrae were slowly moving back into place and fusing together. A torn nerve regrew, and a burst of pain radiated through his body, causing him to hiss, but he still couldn't move.

This wasn't how it ended. It couldn't be. He couldn't die today because Andrew needed him. And Jury needed him. And goddamn it, when he did finally die, it wasn't going to be like this. Come on, he thought. Just another second.

He felt Attikus's sweaty palm touch his hand, and he grinned inwardly. Because he'd FELT Attikus's sweaty palm touch his hand.

He left his body limp, but cracked open his eyes and waited. He watched as Attikus raised his hand towards his snarling teeth. He watched as Attikus opened his mouth and prepared to bite. He felt the rush of warm breath on his fingers.

Then just as Attikus pulled Doc's hand closer, Doc punched forward using the full weight of his body. His wrist ripped from Attikus's grip, and his palm struck Attikus's front teeth with such force they shattered like glass. Before Attikus could recover from the pain and shock, Doc had already driven two knives through Attikus's eye and deep into his brain.

The giant's face went slack, and Doc ripped his arms free and jumped to the side, just barely avoiding being crushed by the cyclops' dead weight.

22

Doc swept his gaze around the room, taking stock of the situation. He'd already managed to kill a good third of Mitcham's followers, and the remaining ones had split into two groups. The group still trying to hammer through Jury's wall of air, and the group trying to hammer through Jury.

Fortunately, a few of the honorable leaders, such as Mr. Birch and the serpent woman, had finally come to their senses and were fighting to protect Jury. Not that Doc trusted them to do the job.

It made him absolutely furious to see the remaining leaders huddled in the far corner of the room, frightened faces blank with terror. They looked so pathetic that he briefly wondered how they had ever managed to accomplish anything, but he'd deal with them later.

He strode forward, past Jury and the others, wrapped his arm around a cryptid he couldn't name and broke the man's neck. The cryptid dropped to the floor, and Doc moved on, shoving two knives through a vampire's heart before ripping off the vampire's head with his bare hands. The body didn't drop immediately, instead the hands grasped the air frantically, and Doc made sure to hurl the head behind him before kicking the body to the side.

The Zenius were still in the fight, and they were working as a cohesive unit, sweeping across the floor with deadly purpose. They managed to drag the serpent woman to the floor before Doc could reach them, but Doc leaped forward, ripping the Zenius from the woman.

They turned towards him, mouths and razor-sharp teeth coated in blood. "You're next," they chorused.

"I don't think so," Doc snapped as he began to hurl knives towards their feet. Several knives hit the mark, but the Zenius were remarkably quick, and before Doc realized it, the remaining three had pulled him to the ground. Their teeth tore at his flesh, and he lashed out with his elbow, knocking one off of him.

He hadn't been overly impressed by a creature whose heart was in its foot, but it turned out the Zenius were extremely difficult to kill. They howled when he stabbed them, but it didn't stop them or even slow them down.

Doc growled in frustration as a set of teeth ripped through his side. He wrapped his hands around the offending Zeniu's head and ripped, tearing off the head completely. Blue goo spurted all over Doc, nearly blinding him, but he pushed the other Zenius to the side and scrambled over the headless one, stabbing it brutally through its hearts.

He leapt to his feet and faced off against the final two. They rushed toward him, eyes full of rage. He dropped to the floor and rolled into their legs, knocking them over, and before they could recover, he had already pinned their four respective feet to the floor.

Doc stood, wiping the goo from his eyes and turned,

sighing wearily when he saw a Worm heading towards him, huge mouth open and so large that Doc could have easily walked inside it. Doc took a full step back; he'd never killed a Worm before. He'd killed a worm, as a boy, and it had taken a considerable amount of effort. He'd eventually squished it flat with a rock, but this Worm was a little too big for that tactic.

He retreated slowly from the huge, gaping mouth, tossing knife after knife as he did. The knives slid through the Worm's skin, into the flesh, and disappeared.

"Oh good," Doc sighed.

"They have hearts somewhere in there," Mr. Birch said from beside him.

"Where?"

"I couldn't say."

"Is there another way to kill them?" Doc demanded.

"A dry sidewalk," Mr. Birch said dryly.

Doc turned to glare at him. "I can't believe you're making jokes at a time like this. And that wasn't even funny."

Mr. Birch shrugged. "I suppose you had better find the heart then."

"It would be easier if I had a sword," Doc said pointedly.

"The Magistratus removed my sword at the door," Mr. Birch replied.

The Worm was so close now Doc could smell its fetid breath.

"Fine," Doc sighed. "I'll do it the hard way; I always have to do everything the hard way."

He took a deep breath and ran into the Worm's mouth, slashing with both knives as he did. The mouth closed over Doc, encasing him in slimy darkness, and Doc began to wonder if it wouldn't have been just as easy from the outside, but it was rather too late now.

He stabbed his knives high above his head and ripped them down to the floor, slicing the Worm in half. The sides of the Worm flopped open, and the entire creature collapsed onto Doc, coating him in slimy Worm guts.

Doc held his breath and tore at the slippery flesh with his hands, trying to find a way out. Relief filled him when a furry hand caught hold of his arm and dragged him free of the oozing corpse.

"A dry sidewalk would have been less messy," Mr. Birch said.

Doc began to laugh. "It was a long setup," he chuckled as he stabbed a knife through a humanoid cryptid's head. "But funny in the end."

"Doc!" Jury yelled. "The door!"

Doc quickly turned and saw that a huge troll was crashing into Jury's barrier over and over. Sweat poured down Jury's temples as he struggled to hold it, but Doc could see he wouldn't last long.

"Protect Jury," Doc ordered Mr. Birch before he ran through the small group of Mitcham supporters, slicing necks as he went. He threw a knife through a cheetah shapeshifter, killing the cheetah instantly. He jumped forward and slammed into the troll just as the troll was charging towards the barrier once more.

The troll stumbled slightly as Doc crashed into him but didn't fall. Doc, however, dropped to the ground in front of him, feeling like he'd just run into a stone wall. He barely managed to duck a heavy punch; and while he was crouched, he rushed forward and wrapped his arms around the troll's waist. At least if he was close, the troll would have trouble hitting him. Or not.

A hand pummeled Doc's head like a falling boulder, and

Doc shuffled under the troll's arm and around to his back. Doc kept hold with one arm, and with the other drew a knife and stabbed it in between two scales. The troll howled angrily and jerked from side to side trying to dislodge Doc, but Doc tightened his hold and shoved another knife in with the first one.

The troll dropped, trapping Doc's legs, and rocked his head back and forth, trying to hit Doc's head. Doc quickly rammed a third and fourth knife between the scales. The troll moaned and started to fall backward, so Doc twisted his body to the side trying to avoid getting completely crushed. And since there was no way to make sure the troll was really dead, Doc pounded a knife through his ear, just in case.

Doc tried to wiggle his legs free; but when he found that he couldn't, he slammed a knife into the wooden floor and used it to pull himself out from under the troll's heavy body.

Doc crawled to his knees, sighing deeply when he saw he still had a few people left to kill. Mr. Birch and the others had nearly finished off the group attacking Jury, but there were still about seven cryptids bashing against Jury's barrier.

Doc stood, flinching as his broken legs crunched and the bones pushed sharply against his flesh. He hated fighting trolls. They were always breaking things.

He wiped a smear of blood from a cut on his arm with a frown. It didn't usually take him so long to heal. He'd killed at least a few witches, and he should have absorbed their considerable life force. He tried to remember if his tattoo had grown warm at all during the fight, but he was fairly certain it hadn't. So either something was keeping his tattoo from working, or he hadn't finished the job. In the meantime, it looked as if he'd have to keep going with broken legs.

He looked past the doorway and suddenly grinned. Simon

and his men must have already cleaned house in the foyer, because Simon was waiting, sword drawn, a phalanx of men behind him.

"Drop the barrier!" Doc shouted.

It dropped, and Mitcham's supporters rushed forward, too frantic to realize that death was waiting for them on the other side. In mere moments, Simon and his men cut down every single fleeing leader; and, just like that, it was over.

Simon and Doc regarded each other across the expanse of bodies.

"You're looking a little worse for wear, my friend," Simon said solemnly.

"Nothing a very, very, very thorough shower wouldn't fix," Doc said with a shrug. "The Magistratus has been neutralized?"

"Indeed. Mr. Grakstone died at the end of my sword, and many of his men joined him. However, quite a few made the wise decision and surrendered."

"Excellent. What about the leaders' guards?"

"That was a somewhat trickier matter since I didn't know which ones would ultimately support Mitcham," Simon stated. "They are currently detained."

"Perfect," Doc said, swallowing a gasp of pain as one of his leg bones snapped back into place. "It looks as if you have this under control."

Simon shook his head slowly. "No."

"Mr. Holliday," a stern voice said.

Doc controlled his sigh and turned to face Mr. Birch. "Yes?"

"Am I to understand that Tetrarch Mitcham is dead?" Mr. Birch demanded.

"Yes."

"And you killed him?"

"Yes."

"But you continued forward with the summit as a way to root out his supporters and eliminate them for the good of both the Hidden and the norm worlds?"

Doc wasn't sure he liked the way this was sounding. "Technically accurate," he said warily.

"In that case, the United States council calls an emergency meeting," Mr. Birch pronounced.

"You don't need my permission," Doc replied.

Mr. Birch gave him a stiff nod. Then he and several other cryptids gathered together in a corner and began to whisper furtively.

Doc shrugged and turned back to Simon. "How is the head of the Magistratus usually designated?" he asked.

"The tetrarch."

"Naturally," Doc muttered. Killing was always the easy part. Clean-up was the worst. He cast a glance at Jury.

"I've got a thing," Jury mouthed, slowly inching away from Doc.

"You don't have a thing!" Doc mouthed back.

"I do. I met this girl named Michelle. Her legs are... Well, let's just say we could do it anywhere."

"Classless," Doc mouthed. "You can't leave me."

"I think I can. If I stick around Grandfather will yell at me for underhanded tactics," Jury mouthed with a shrug.

"No."

"Yes."

"No!"

"Yes." Jury grinned and began to walk towards the broken door.

"You walk through that door, and I will... Cut your hair!" Doc yelled.

"I'll grow it back. Then give you a reverse mohawk, but refuse to fix it," Jury retorted.

"I hate you," Doc said through gritted teeth.

Jury winked and disappeared behind Simon's men.

"I'm going to kill him," Doc muttered. Later though. Right now he had to deal with this. "Did we lose many men?" he asked Simon.

"Eleven," Simon replied gravely. "Eight of them to Grakstone."

"I'm sorry," Doc said softly.

"Nine of them were yours."

Doc felt a surge of grief. He was glad more of Simon's men hadn't been killed. There were too few of them already, but it saddened him greatly to know that his own people had fallen. He had asked, they had come, and they had died.

"It is difficult being a leader," Simon said quietly. "Knowing that each of their deaths rests on your head."

"But how many more deaths would be on our heads if we had done nothing?" Doc responded.

"Too many. I lost my brother today." Simon's words were soft and thick with grief.

"I am sorry," Doc said softly. "I once lost a brother. It is not an easy thing."

"No." Simon was quiet for a moment, then he said, "There will be time later to mourn. Right now, we must handle this."

"I suppose we have to at least say something to the remaining leaders," Doc sighed.

"That's a good place to start," Simon agreed. "Meanwhile, I will sort out the guards."

"You can't leave me in here with all these politicians," Doc argued.

"I'm afraid that my position as honor guard requires me to secure the premises," Simon said, lips twitching faintly.

"You're the business man," Doc countered. "You probably deal with politicians every day."

"But today, I am a warrior," Simon said.

"Fine; go on," Doc sighed. "Abandon me too. It's not like I need you; I can deal with these vipers on my own."

"That's the spirit," Simon chuckled.

Doc faced what was left of the leaders. If it were up to him, he'd lock them in Mitcham's dungeon for a month or two. For no particular reason other than for being a bunch of cowards.

"So you are the ones your people have chosen to lead and protect them," he said acidly. "If only they could have seen you today."

"I don't even know who you are," one of them snapped. "What right do you have to rebuke us?"

They thought they were on firmer ground now that the killing was done. Words they could handle. Or so they thought.

Doc grinned sharply. "I'm the man who saved your lives. If I hadn't intervened, you'd be dead right now. Food for the Worms. And your people, the people you promised to protect, would be left defenseless against Mitcham's plan. You're lucky I don't kill you where you stand."

"Dare you threaten us?" another of the leaders exclaimed.

To keep his rising anger from exploding, Doc took a slow deep breath. Anger was not useful here; cleverness was what was needed.

He'd handled the immediate threat. He had protected his Hidden, and he had probably put a stop to Mitcham's plan. As far as he was concerned, his work here was done.

"Obviously you have this under control," Doc said easily. "I'll just see myself out."

Confusion crossed their faces. And terror. Because they didn't have anything under control. They were used to Mitcham telling them what to do, and now that he was gone, they were at a loss.

"If I may interrupt, Tetrarch Holliday," Mr. Birch said.

"Oh no, no, no," Doc protested. In his mind he watched the tides of luck roll firmly out to sea. To stay.

"Quite so," Mr. Birch stated.

"No."

"Yes. The council has agreed."

"That's ridiculous!" Doc argued. "Even I know the tetrarch is elected, not appointed."

"Elections take time, Tetrarch. A year at least, and in the meantime, the Hidden needs a ruler."

"Pick someone else," Doc ground out.

"I'm afraid that's not possible. There's a precedence."

"What?!" Doc snapped, horror filling him. "I don't... Are you serious right now?"

"Quite serious," Mr. Birch said. "One of the original laws states that within a tetrarch's term of rule another member of the Hidden can challenge his rule, and the champion then becomes tetrarch. You challenged Mitcham, defeated him, and so are now the tetrarch."

Doc blinked. Opened his mouth. Gestured with a finger and started to say... Anything that would get him out of this. But he couldn't think of anything. Not a damn thing. The council had neatly maneuvered him into place. Checkmate. Goddamn, he hated politicians.

He tried one last time. "Surely the old law meant challenge through discourse or a re-election? Not by battle to the death."

"It wasn't specific in any way," Mr. Birch said with a shrug. "You know how vague these old laws can be. Very open to interpretation."

"You're extremely lucky that I hold you in high regard," Doc snarled. "Otherwise I would be tempted to kill you."

"Killing the messenger doesn't change the message," Mr. Birch said solemnly.

"It should," Doc muttered. He closed his eyes for a moment and allowed his mind to process this unwanted development. Would he rather be sipping whiskey on the beach with a willing woman beside him? Certainly. But the retreating tide had carried that ship with it.

Doc opened his eyes. "Tell me this, I understand why the Zeniu leaders supported Mitcham, and even some of the others, but what did he have on these leaders? How did he manage to gain so much control over the other Hiddens?"

"Money," Mr. Birch said. "He's bailed each of them out at least once. Without him, they would have floundered. In addition to that, if their norm governments asked for a certain type of cryptid, Mitcham would usually provide the cryptid so they didn't have to, which kept their people happy."

"And allowed Mitcham to get his men into place all over the world," Doc said softly.

"Exactly."

"As Mitcham's replacement, are his contracts now mine?" Doc asked.

"Our Hidden is set up much like the norm world," Mr. Birch stated. "Usually when someone dies, their assets would pass to the next of kin."

"Yes," Doc said, knowing it was coming. "But?"

"But," Mr. Birch said, "in the case of Mitcham, the council has determined that his actions were treasonous, and so the council has seized his assets. A vote was taken, and the council has decided that his assets, contracts, and properties will be given to the new tetrarch to use for the purpose of the Hidden, and that would be you."

Doc grinned widely. "I didn't realize politicians could work so fast. In fact, I would have bet that it took the council three years just to decide on which flavor coffee to serve during meetings."

"Hazelnut," Mr. Birch said with no inflection whatsoever. "With a variety of creams. And it only took us an hour to decide."

Doc didn't believe that for a moment.

"First order of business," Doc said briskly, "call the Worms and get this place cleaned up. Second order, I want this meeting moved to one of the private rooms at the Banshee. Third order, I'm going home to take a shower. I will be there in two hours. I want everyone there, ready and waiting when I arrive. Is that clear?"

"As ice," Mr. Birch replied.

Doc glared at him. "Clear ice, I hope?"

"Perfectly clear."

"Good. I'll alert Simon to the change in venue."

"Yes, Tetrarch," Mr. Birch said.

Doc shuddered and walked towards the ruined doorway.

"Where are you going?" Drustan demanded. "You owe us an explanation for this mess."

"I owe you nothing," Doc snarled, taking a step towards Drustan and feeling a great amount of satisfaction when the elder witch retreated. Doc surveyed the leaders and said flatly and firmly, "If you are wise, you will obey my orders. Mr. Birch is in charge in my absence."

Thankfully, no one else challenged him, and Doc turned

to leave once more. "I just had to get involved," he muttered as he stepped over a body. "I couldn't just travel the world for a decade or two. No. Not me."

He entered the foyer and stalked to Simon's side.

"Yes?" Simon said.

"You shouldn't have left me like that," Doc said irritably. "I regret it, and you're about to regret it too."

Simon's eyebrow rose in question.

"You are now speaking to the tetrarch," Doc ground out.

Simon's normally impassive face twitched as he worked out Doc's words, and then he began to grin. His grin grew wider and wider until he was suddenly laughing.

"I'm glad you think this is funny," Doc snarled. "Head of my honor guard."

That just made Simon laugh more robustly.

"Escort everyone to the Banshee," Doc ordered over Simon's laughter. "I want the council and all the leaders there. Arrest the guards who need it; release the others. I also want you to text me a list of the remaining leaders, their names and physical descriptions, and what countries they represent. I'll be at the Banshee in two hours. Don't keep me waiting."

Doc spun on his heel and stalked towards the exit.

"Yes, sir, Tetrarch Holliday!" Simon called out, voice full of laughter.

23

Doc entered his suite and went straight to the kitchen to get a bottle of whiskey. As he walked morosely through the sitting room, Thaddeus said, "How did it go? I assume by the level of gore about your person that it went quite well."

"I'm not in the mood to talk, old boy," Doc said. "I just... You'll..." He sighed. "Sorry."

"So not good then," Thaddeus muttered.

"No, not good at all," Doc said as he closed his bedroom door.

He threw Mitcham's clothes into the trash can and took the bottle of whiskey into the shower with him. He'd once been seconds away from death, minutes at most, and he'd felt more cheerful, more hopeful than he did right now. He felt as if... There was absolutely no way to describe it.

He drank the entire bottle as the searing water washed the slime and blood from his skin. He didn't have to stay. He could run. He had once been exceptionally good at running. It was easy. You just turned your back on the place you didn't want be anymore and walked forward.

He wanted to run. He really did. But he couldn't. Because even though he really didn't want to, he cared. He cared about the Baker children. He cared about Aine and Bree. He cared about the LaRoches and Dublin's pack.

"Dublin," he muttered. "Now that's an idea."

Doc finished his shower, quickly dressed, and called Jervis. "Is Dublin here at the hotel?"

"I'm very glad you're still alive, sir. Thank you for informing me."

Doc rolled his eyes. "Somehow I think if I died, you'd know before me."

"Probably true, sir. Yes, Mr. O'Connell is here."

"Excellent. Have him meet me in the parking garage."

"Is everything alright, sir?"

"No," Doc said flatly. "It's absolutely dreadful.

"Dreadful? Losing an arm would be dreadful. Being crowned tetrarch is more along the lines of irritating."

"How did you even know?" Doc demanded.

"It's my job to know," Jervis stated haughtily.

"I wish you had warned me. If I had known I would have opted for the beach."

"I don't believe that."

"I don't want to be tetrarch," Doc sighed.

"But you will."

"I suppose. It will make for an interesting line on my resume," Doc said, trying to see the humor in the situation.

"I'll be sure to type it in," Jervis said.

Doc snorted. "Don't forget about Dublin," he said, then he disconnected and headed for the parking garage. Within a minute, Dublin arrived.

"Get in," Doc ordered, gesturing towards the passenger side.

"Not even gonna buy me a drink first?" Dublin questioned with a laugh.

"No, but you can have a drink of mine," Doc said, handing him the nearly empty bottle. "It's my second bottle anyway."

"Isn't there some kind of norm law about drinking and driving?" Dublin laughed.

"How would you know?" Doc snorted. "You've never even driven a car."

"Did you wake up with a shark in your bed this morning?" Dublin replied casually.

Doc stopped himself from growling and exhaled slowly. He wasn't mad at Dublin. He wasn't mad at Simon. He wasn't mad at anyone really. Just the situation and the fact that he couldn't do anything to change it. Well, he could. He could change it, but he couldn't.

"So where are we headed?" Dublin asked.

"The Banshee."

"Is it open this early?"

"I don't even know what time it is," Doc muttered. "But it doesn't matter. It'll be open when we get there."

"What is going on?" Dublin demanded. "You're acting even stranger than usual."

"That's because... I'm now the... the... the goddamn tetrarch," Doc managed to say.

"You're what?!" Dublin exclaimed.

"You heard me."

"But you're kidding, right?"

"No."

"Great Manannán," Dublin hissed. "You're not... You're serious right now?"

"Yes."

Predictably, Dublin started to laugh. "Sir Tetrarch

Holliday!" he roared. "That is the funniest damn thing I've ever heard. Can I have your autograph?"

"Keep laughing, Commander O'Connell," Doc drawled.

"Wait, what?"

"I need a new head of the Magistratus, and you are he."

"What?! No!"

"Yes."

"Why?!" Dublin demanded.

"Because you know how to fight, you know about weapons, you know how to lead men, and you run a very tight ship."

"But you can't just... Shouldn't you at least ask first?" Dublin complained.

"No one asked me," Doc shot back. "However, if you find you don't care for the job, as long as you find a suitable replacement, you may leave anytime."

"I don't see why you have to drag me down with you," Dublin said irritably.

"I knew Jury wouldn't do it, I need Jervis where he is, I already have plans for Simon, and you're the only other man I trust."

Dublin flopped back against his seat and said, "Well, when you put it like that..."

"Thank you," Doc said as he parked his car. "Now let's go change the world, shall we?"

"I'd rather not," Dublin muttered.

They entered the Banshee and were met immediately by Aine. Her eyes were solemn as she studied Doc.

"Are you certain you want to do this?" she asked.

"Absolutely not," Doc replied. "But what choice do I have?"

"Someone once told me there's always a choice."

Doc shrugged. "Just not always a choice you can make."

"In that case..." She smiled brightly. "Knock 'em dead."

"Already did that," Doc grinned. "These are the ones I kept alive."

"Tactical error," Dublin snorted.

"And that's why you're here," Doc said cheerfully.

Doc studied the doors in front of him, and in his mind he heard Francisco's voice. "If you want people to listen to you," Francisco had once said, "you don't just walk in like you own the room." Francisco had grinned sharply and looked Doc straight in the eyes. "No. You walk in like you own the room, the table they're sitting at, the chairs they're sitting on, and the goddamn clothes they're wearing. You walk in like that, and before long, you'll own them too."

"I can do that," Doc murmured.

Simon approached him, and Doc said, "Simon, meet the new head of the Magistratus, Dublin O'Connell. Dublin, this is Simon Redgrove, my personal assistant and head of my security."

Simon didn't even blink at his change in title, just shook Dublin's hand and greeted him politely.

"Simon, Dublin," Doc said as he pushed open the doors and walked forward. "With me."

They didn't argue. How could they? He was the goddamn tetrarch.

When Doc stepped into the room, the council stood. He acknowledged them with a short nod, then raised his eyebrow as he studied the other world leaders. They dropped their gazes and stood as well. Doc hid his grin and sat at the head of the table, Simon and Dublin flanking him.

"Sit," Doc ordered. Everyone sat. So far, so good. "According to my council," Doc said, "the United States Hidden has been financially supporting several other nations for some time now, which is a situation that needs to be rectified."

Drustan Jury spoke up. "What does this have to do with Mitcham's plan?"

"Nothing at all," Doc said evenly. "I'm aware that Mitcham has agents in place all over the world, and he was able to do this because other leaders, such as yourselves, allowed him to do so."

He paused there to give his meaning time to soak in, and several of the leaders shifted uncomfortably in their seats.

"I said we would have change, and so we shall," Doc said after letting them sweat for a moment. "It's not to the benefit of our respective Hiddens for one man to have so much control. Mitcham could not have possibly been well-versed enough in Ethiopian politics or day-to-day living as to have had the Ethiopian cryptids' well-being in mind," Doc said pointedly, staring directly at the Ethiopian leader, who was, according to Simon, an impundulu or a lightning bird.

She held his gaze thoughtfully then nodded. "What do you suggest then, Tetrarch Holliday?"

Doc allowed himself a faint smile. "Excellent question, Chief Zewdu. Allow me to tell you how we are going to proceed. To begin with, the Bureau of Cryptid Affairs is dissolved from this point forward. I will send someone out to each Bureau location to make sure it is shut down properly and to preserve the information they've collected over the years. With any luck, that information can be put to good use.

"Secondly," Doc went on, "within the next two years, all the Hiddens will be required to hold elections and none of the currently elected officials will be allowed to run."

"That's outrageous!" Drustan exclaimed. "And you've no right to set that in place!"

"I've every right," Doc said evenly. "I own you, all of you. What was owed to Mitcham is now owed to me." His tone allowed for no argument, and as he worked his way around the table with his gaze, none of the leaders could hold his eyes for long.

"Once the terms I've laid down have been met," Doc went on, "I will forgive any debt that is owed, and from that point forward, each Hidden will stand or fall on its own."

"You would do that?" Chief Zewdu demanded.

"I would."

"What are the remaining terms?" she asked, a glimmer of hope lighting her face.

Doc leaned back in his chair, making sure to use a pose of power not one of retreat, and quickly ordered his thoughts. He hadn't walked in with a specific plan; and since he didn't keep a close eye on politics, or any sort of eye at all, he wasn't particularly in the know.

He motioned to Simon, and Simon leaned down beside him. "Do we have any other terms?" Doc asked softly.

"The heads of the respective police forces should also be removed," Simon replied. "And the leaders need to make it clear that anyone who attacks norms or puts a Hidden in danger will be charged with treason."

"Is that all?"

"There needs to be an allowance made for norms within the Hidden. I'll work something up in the coming months, but you should get their agreement today to abide by it."

"And?" Doc prodded.

"That is all," Simon said.

"In addition to the two terms I've already laid out," Doc said loudly, "the leaders of your police forces must be replaced with new leaders by a vote of your people. Also, a law must be put in place making it clear that any cryptid who attacks or hurt norms with the intention of revealing the Hidden or starting a war will be charged with treason. And finally, my assistant, Mr. Redgrove, will work up a plan that makes allowances for norms within the Hidden proper, and you must agree that your Hiddens will abide by this plan and put it into effect."

There was a moment of silence while each of the leaders considered Doc's words, but then the Ethiopian leader spoke. "That is more reasonable than we deserve; I accept your terms."

"As do I," another leader said.

This went around the table until only Drustan remained.

"Well, Mr. Jury?" Doc said, raising his eyebrow.

"I don't like you," Drustan growled.

"I didn't ask you to like me," Doc shrugged. "In fact, I doubt if you liked Mitcham either. I have, however, saved your life; and I am willing to forgive your debt, with very little work on your part." Doc paused, then added thoughtfully, "There was a moment there when I considered killing all of you, just to wipe the slate clean. I did not, but I'm still on the fence about it, so I suggest you at least try to curry my favor." He grinned, but in that way that said he was neither happy nor pleased.

Drustan's face turned red, and Doc knew Drustan's pride was getting in his way.

"Just a note of warning," Doc said easily. "I don't like it when people try to use magic on me. It rather irritates me. And you've seen firsthand what happens to people who irritate me."

Behind him, Doc heard Dublin growl and Simon's sword slide in its sheath.

"I accept your terms," Drustan grumbled.

"I'm sorry," Doc said, tilting his head. "I didn't quite hear you."

"I accept your terms."

"Was he speaking to me?" Doc asked Simon.

"I can't be sure," Simon replied, moving his sword out of its sheath another inch.

"I accept your terms, Tetrarch Holliday," Drustan said clearly, face red with anger and embarrassment.

"Excellent!" Doc praised. "I'm so glad to hear it. Once each of you signs the contract Mr. Redgrove writes up, you may return to your homes."

Doc sighed and said, "Just one final order of business." He stood and stared firmly at Liechtenstein's leader. "I cannot think what possessed you to move to the east," he said menacingly. "I can only assume you somehow knew all along I wasn't Mitcham, but couldn't risk alerting the others."

"I don't know what you mean," Liechtenstein's leader stuttered.

"You and Mitcham have been playing this game for a while," Doc said. "Deceiving your fellow cryptids, masquerading as someone else."

"Masquerading?" the woman repeated.

"Yes, Elder Ducote, masquerading. Tell me, what species of cryptid are you?"

"Species? Why? What does that have to do with anything?" Ducote replied, eyes darting from side to side.

"It doesn't really," Doc said. "But I don't know why you wouldn't just answer."

All the other leaders were staring curiously at Ducote now.

"I'm a Lougreselli," Ducote said stiffly.

"Interesting," Doc said. "That's exactly what species

Markus Johanns claimed to be. For those of you who don't know, not Ducote of course, Johanns was the local leader of the anti-norm movement. And he was very persuasive," Doc said pointedly.

Ducote was sweating, but she tried one last time to bluff her way out. "I have no idea what you're talking about, Tetrarch Holliday. I've never heard of this Johanns until today."

"I see." Doc gestured towards Ducote's wrist. "Would you mind removing your bracelet for me?"

"That's ridiculous!" Ducote exclaimed. "Why would I do such a thing?"

"Why wouldn't you?" Doc said evenly. "It's just a bracelet."

"It's my bracelet, on my person!" Ducote snarled. "I refuse to bow to yet another tyrant."

"As if you even have a choice," Doc drawled. "Remove the bracelet, or I will remove it from your corpse."

One of the leaders gasped and exclaimed, "Surely such threats aren't needed, are they?"

Doc ignored that statement, refusing to break his eye contact with Ducote. Ducote finally dropped her gaze and wearily removed the silver cuff she wore. Her form immediately shifted into that of a Zeniu.

"What?" Drustan exclaimed. "Zenius aren't shapeshifters!"

Doc ignored that as well and asked Ducote, "How did you know I wasn't Mitcham?"

"I didn't at first," Ducote replied resentfully. "But Ambrose never would have said he apologized."

"Ah," Doc nodded. "Simon, would you please have your men take Ducote into custody? I'll have a private word with her later on."

At Doc's words, all the leaders cringed noticeably, and Doc grinned. Apparently he was already building his mythos.

Once Ducote was gone, Doc turned to Simon. "I'll let you take over now. Let me know how it goes."

"It will be done, Tetrarch."

"I hate that," Doc hissed.

"I'm aware of that, Tetrarch," Simon said with a grin.

"Let's go," Doc told Dublin. "We've one more stop to make."

"Where're we going?" Dublin asked as they left the room.

"To Mitcham's house."

They walked together in silence for a moment, then Doc said, "I'll leave it up to you and Simon to sort out the Magistratus. If you don't trust someone, get rid of them."

"Get rid of?" Dublin asked pointedly.

"Yes," Doc said. "If needed. I trust you to know the difference. I would strongly suggest you hire Ana and Ina though; you're going to need them."

"The Zaitsev sisters?" Dublin groaned. "They hate me."

"But at least you know where you stand with them," Doc chuckled as they passed through a doorway into the upper Hidden.

He was glad he didn't have to pretend to be Mitcham anymore, and he was glad he was done with Mitcham's house. If he'd had to spend another day in there with those murals he would have needed a whole case of whiskey.

He pushed open Mitcham's front door and gestured for Dublin to go first. "We're going to search the premises until we find the records of Mitcham's government agents," Doc said.

"And then?" Dublin asked.

"You're going to hunt them all down and kill them."

24

It most likely would have taken Doc and Dublin hours to find Mitcham's hidden records room if Thulan hadn't intervened.

"It's behind his wife's wardrobe," Thulan said as Doc banged on yet another wooden panel.

Doc turned slowly to look at Thulan and said, "What is?"

"What you are looking for."

"Which is?"

"Mitcham's records, isn't that right?"

"I don't suppose you could have told me this sooner," Doc growled.

"You weren't looking sooner," Thulan stated.

"You can't kill him," Dublin said as Doc stepped forward menacingly. "Not now that you're the tetrarch. I can arrest him though."

"What do you mean I can't kill him now that I'm the tetrarch?!" Doc demanded. "That's my goddamn thing. I kill people!"

"Bad publicity," Dublin replied.

"I don't care," Doc ground out. "I do not want to be tetrarch; I do not need good publicity."

"Still," Dublin cautioned.

Thulan chuckled softly. "Already making your mark, I see."

"Get out of here!" Doc ordered. "I have wardrobes to tear open."

"There's a latch," Thulan offered.

Doc sighed. It was just one of those days. From someone else's perspective maybe it was quite a lucky day. There were probably dozens of people who dreamed of being tetrarch, but he was not one of them.

"Show me," he said, voice like steel.

Thulan laughed and led the way up the stairs. He walked easily into Mrs. Mitcham's room and found the latch to open the secret panel with no trouble at all.

"I don't think he's very blind," Dublin whispered.

"You don't say," Doc replied scathingly.

Doc studied the secret room in dismay. In addition to a large desk in the center of the room, there were filing cabinets lining the walls and papers stacked in piles on the floor.

"You can't be serious," Dublin exclaimed. "I hate paperwork."

"That's why you're getting paid the big bucks," Doc said, backing towards the exit.

"I'm getting paid?" Dublin asked.

"Sure," Doc said. "The big bucks. Have fun."

"Doc!" Dublin yelled as Doc closed the door and ran down the hallway. "Get back here!"

Doc laughed as he hurried down the stairs. If he was quick...

"Tetrarch," Simon said from the entryway. "There you are."

Doc sighed. "What is it?"

"The leaders are on their way home."

"Good riddance," Doc muttered.

"There are a few matters we should discuss though."

"Of course there are. Here's one, when we're in private, call me Doc. That's an order. If you don't, I'll shave off bits of your fur."

"That's a terrible insult," Simon said, eyebrow raised.

"Good," Doc growled.

"Shall we go into the office, Doc?" Simon said, grinning faintly.

"Why not? As soon as all the prisoners are settled though, I want this house burned down."

"I'll make a note."

"And the summit building too. Build parks in both places," Doc ordered.

"Alright."

"Now what did you have?"

"Ella Glass was not at the summit today," Simon said.

"Of course she wasn't. Have Dublin issue a warrant for her arrest," Doc said. "What about the Baudelaires?"

"There was one Baudelaire among the dead," Simon said thoughtfully. "But there should have been three."

This day was never going to end. Doc glanced up at Nick who was standing just inside the doorway. "Could you run upstairs and ask Dublin to come down, please? He's in Mrs. Mitcham's closet."

Nick's eyebrows rose, but he obeyed Doc without question.

While he waited, Doc opened the desk drawer and pulled

out a half empty bottle of whiskey. "It's not enough," he mumbled, taking a swig.

"I thought I was doing paperwork," Dublin complained as he sat down beside Simon.

"It's not as if it's going anywhere," Doc pointed out. "I need you to issue an arrest warrant for Ella Glass. She was one of Mitcham's close associates. Dead or alive, but be aware she's an anaconda shapeshifter."

"Really?" Dublin grinned. "I like the sound of that."

"You would," Doc snorted.

"You need the council's approval for a kill order," Simon interjected.

Doc rolled his eyes and said, "Dublin, bring in Ella Glass by whatever means necessary."

"Yes, sir," Dublin grinned.

"I also need you to build a team to hunt down the remaining Baudelaire witches and..." Doc glanced at Simon, then carefully said, "remove them."

"That's stepping outside of our Hidden," Simon cautioned.

"As it stands right now," Doc drawled, "I pretty much own the Hiddens, so if I want to kill off a few psychotic witches, I'll damn well do so."

Doc tapped his fingers on the desktop. He wanted to crush all of Mitcham's supporters as quickly as possible. "I assume we have a way of contacting the other sections of the United States Hidden?" he asked Simon.

"Yes."

"Well, do it then, and find out what the state of affairs is. Send trusted men to each city to check things out, remove Magistratus officers who need removed, and so on. I want all talk of war or exposure to norms quelled," Doc said fiercely.

"You're scary good at this," Dublin chuckled.

"It's just the desk," Doc said. "Simon, do you know who Alex is? Mitcham met with him frequently."

"No."

"Fantastic. Let's keep an eye and ear out for him. I don't have any description of him whatsoever. I have a suspicion that he's the one who handled Mitcham's surveillance. We could still be under observation, so keep an eye out."

"Yes, Tetrarch," Simon said.

"Doc," Doc growled.

"Doc," Simon agreed.

"Is that all?" Doc asked. "Can I go home now and pretend to be normal?"

"Normal?" Dublin laughed. "What's normal?"

Doc glared at him.

"Sorry," Dublin said, not sounding the least bit sorry. "I'll handle my end of things. Simon, will you please escort me to the Magistratus headquarters? I need to do some housecleaning and assign some duties."

"It would be my pleasure," Simon said. "I will see you in the morning, Tet... Doc."

Doc sighed heavily as he watched them leave. He was not pleased with this turn of events.

"I absolutely despise this," he said offhandedly.

"Sorry, sir," Nick replied.

"I'll have my manager send over some Dulcis employees to get the prisoners settled," Doc said. "Until Dublin gets back, I need you to guard the secret room."

"Yes, sir."

"It's very important, and maybe no one knows about it or maybe Alex knows about it. Just close it, and don't let anyone near it."

Doc tapped his fingers rapidly. The information in that

room was important. He could feel it. Hypothetically, if Nick guarded it, it would be safe. But... It was possible Doc wasn't the only person who employed shadow phantoms, and it was nearly impossible to keep a shadow from coming and going.

"We'll just have to move it," Doc muttered.

"Move it?"

"Yes, the contents of the room. Unless..." Doc trailed off, mind racing.

He called Jervis.

"Sir?"

"Send a team to Mitcham's to transport the prisoners home, and I need to speak to Enoshi."

"Certainly. I will inform him."

Doc waited impatiently. When he could stand it no more, he ordered Nick to sit down. "Do you play poker?" Doc asked.

"Yes, sir."

"Good."

Doc shuffled and began to deal. "Five card stud," he said as he laid out the first two cards.

"What are we betting?" Nick asked.

"Nothing."

"What's the point then?"

Doc grinned. "The point is to win."

"Then I may as well not play," Nick said. "Simon says you always win."

"Humor me," Doc pleaded.

Nick nodded, and they played several hands before a tall shadow drifted into the room behind Nick. It had taken Doc years to learn to tell them apart, but he knew instantly the shadow phantom in front of him was Enoshi, something about the way his head tilted slightly to the left.

"Holliday," Enoshi said.

Nick jumped and whirled around in his chair.

"It's just Enoshi," Doc said. "I have a job for you, if you'll take it."

"Yes."

Suddenly Doc felt very paranoid. What if someone was listening, watching, writing down every word they said? Someone besides Emily, of course.

"How do people live like this?" he exclaimed.

"Like what, sir?" Nick questioned.

"Like... Like... Oh, never mind. Nick, watch the front door. Enoshi, with me."

Enoshi followed Doc silently upstairs and into the secret room. Once there, Doc wrote on a scrap of paper, "I need the entire contents of this room moved to the transfer point."

Enoshi nodded.

"Quickly."

Enoshi nodded again.

"Thank you," Doc said aloud.

"You've no need to thank us," Enoshi said softly. "We are still thanking you."

"There is no debt owed," Doc replied. "There never was."

"Perhaps," Enoshi said. "It will be done."

By the time Doc arrived home, it was nearly two in the morning. He'd only been the tetrarch for half a day, and he was already sick of it.

He was ready for a drink. And a snack. Another shower to get the pandering politician stink off his hands. A woman to distract his mind. And a nap. In any order. But he'd settle for a drink.

He pushed open his door with a sigh. He may not have

a woman, but at least he'd finally have some peace and quiet.

"ALL HAIL THE TETRARCH!!!!" several voices shouted at once.

He was going to kill them. All of them. Jury, Jervis, Aine, Bree, the Baker children, Frankie, Boudica, and especially Thaddeus.

"Goddamn you, Jury," Doc hissed as magical firecrackers suddenly exploded, casting blue sparks all over the sitting room. "I thought we were friends."

"We are," Jury laughed. "And this is the happiest moment of my entire life; I had to share it with you!"

"We made the banner!" Johnny and Jules interrupted excitedly. "Do you like it?"

"I can't believe you're the tetrarch now," Jules added. "Do you realize you're the first ever norm tetrarch?"

Doc's head began to ache, but he smiled at them and said, "I love the banner, but shouldn't you be in bed?"

"Mr. Jury insisted we come," Frankie said apologetically.

"Of course he did," Doc muttered.

"I couldn't throw you a party without all your friends," Jury said happily. "After all, you have so few."

"You know what I'm going to do?" Doc muttered.

"What's that?"

"I'm going to use that artifact to raise Marie Baudelaire from the dead so you have to marry her."

"Don't be such a spoilsport," Jury chuckled. "Have some whiskey."

Doc took the whiskey, and then he sat on the couch and listened to everyone, except Jervis, laugh and be merry. On another day, he might have managed to join them, but not today. He was too tired. And not because of what he'd done, but because of what he was going to do. He felt as if he'd just sat down to play poker, but instead he was playing Pişti, and he didn't even know the rules.

"That was an expected turn of events, wasn't it?" Jervis said softly as he sat beside Doc.

"Maybe," Doc stated.

"Maybe?"

"I have a suspicion Simon set me up," Doc said. He emptied the bottle, and Jervis handed him another one. "What are the chances that Mr. Birch, who if you will recall is Simon's cousin, just happened to remember an antiquated law that could be interpreted vaguely enough to allow them to vote me in as tetrarch?"

"Fairly slim," Jervis replied.

"Not only that, but when I asked Simon's advice, he specifically told me the council would support me only if I killed Mitcham."

"Rather damning evidence," Jervis agreed. "Would you like me to make your irritation clear?"

"Oh no," Doc replied, grinning sharply. "I have plans for Simon."

"Glad to hear it. Shall I remove these miscreants from your suite?" Jervis offered.

Doc studied the laughing faces. These were the people he'd done it for. The ones he wanted to protect. And right now they were happy.

"No," he said softly. "Let them stay."

"As you wish, sir, but I do believe there's an emergency in the kitchen."

"There's always an emergency in the kitchen," Doc laughed.

"You know how melodramatic Pierre can be," Jervis said

flatly. "Just yesterday the wrong cheese was delivered, and he threw a pan of soup at the delivery driver."

"Just go," Doc said, rolling his eyes.

"As you wish, sir."

Jervis left, and Jury sat in his empty spot. "Tetrarch, huh?" Jury chuckled.

"Please tell me you didn't know that was going to happen," Doc said.

"Know? Of course I didn't know!" Jury replied. "If I had known, I would've stayed just to see the look on your face."

"You want to trade?"

"I don't think that's a thing," Jury said. "And I wouldn't be the right man for the job anyway."

"As if I am?" Doc declared.

Jury shrugged. "The thing about you is that you'll do what no one else will. And you'll do it in a way no one else can. You're always just slicing right through the Gordian knot while the rest of us are still trying to figure out exactly what the problem is. You may not like it; but, honestly, if I had to pick someone to be tetrarch..." Jury grinned. "It'd be you."

"That was... surprisingly nice," Doc said.

"We are friends," Jury shrugged. "I usually try to say something nice every twenty-five years or so."

"In that case," Doc drawled, "I really like your shirt."

"Me too," Jury said, plucking at his sweater sleeve. "Fashions keep getting stranger and stranger, but the classics stay... well, classic."

"Like us," Doc chuckled.

"Exactly," Jury replied. "No matter what happens, we'll always be in style."

Hours later, everyone was finally gone and it was just Doc and Thaddeus; but Doc had poured enough whiskey into Thaddeus's pot to put him under for a week because he didn't want to talk about it anymore. He just wanted to be alone with his thoughts.

He stretched out on his couch and stared at the ceiling. "Tetrarch Holliday," he said softly. It didn't sound any better than it had when he first heard it. He'd make the best of it though. He'd pass a law against—

He never finished his thought because he suddenly couldn't keep his eyes open, not if he wanted to, which he did. He fought the wave of darkness trying to pull him under, but he couldn't. He couldn't fight it, and then he was asleep, and she was there.

"You fed me today," Meli purred, her claws scraping his cheek hard enough to draw a line of blood. "You fed me, and I felt my heart beat."

Terror flooded Doc as he suddenly realized why his tattoo hadn't given him the life force of any of the witches he'd killed. It couldn't because she was somehow feeding through him, stealing his kills.

"John does not fit you," the Black Shaman whispered. "From now on, you will be my champion, my warrior." She wrapped her cold hand around his throat and pulled him closer, black eyes boring into his, and stated with a terrible finality, "You are mine."

Read Next:
The Immortal Doc Holliday Book 6

Visit Amazon to order ***Empire*** today.
Just search for **M.M. Crumley** or ***The Immortal Doc Holliday Book 6***.

Don't Miss Out on a Single **M.M. Crumley** New Release...

Visit **www.mmcrumley.com** and sign up for the VIP newsletter to receive your **FREE eBook *Regnum*** and always be the first to know when a new M.M. Crumley book releases! Also follow M.M. Crumley on Amazon to receive Amazon notifications of new releases! And while you're there...

Don't Forget to Check Out
The House of Graves Series

"*You HAVE to read this book. My warning... Do not drink your coffee while reading; drink it before. Ms. Crumley has a gift of sneaking hysterically funny parts in. My eReader got a coffee bath!*" 5-star review

New from the world of the *Immortal Doc Holliday*, follow three generations of Graves women as they work to untangle the secrets of their past. Just search for *The House of Graves* or **M.M. Crumley**.

The Legend of Andrew Rufus Series

If you're willing to follow a boy down the bloody road to manhood, fighting shoulder to shoulder with legends, then start reading Andrew Rufus today. You won't regret it. The entire seven-book series is available on Amazon; just search for **M.M. Crumley** OR *The Legend of Andrew Rufus*.

M.M. Crumley grew up in the woods of Colorado. She spent most of her time outside weaving stories in her mind while she explored.

About her writing, she has this to say:

"My characters are real to me, and on the page they become three dimensional. They are not stagnant. They change; they screw up; they conquer their fears. Sometimes they're unlikable. Sometimes they're broken. Sometimes they're on top of it all. Sometimes trouble finds them, sometimes they go looking for it, and sometimes that trouble defies explanation."

She also writes psychological thrillers under the name M.M. Boulder.

Sign up for M.M. Crumley's VIP newsletter at www.mmcrumley.com to receive notifications of new releases and other fun stuff!

To connect on **Facebook**, just search for **M.M. Crumley**

Manufactured by Amazon.ca
Bolton, ON